SHADOWS OF THE PAST

SUGAR SPRINGS
BOOK 1

ALEXA ASTON

 Created with Vellum

PROLOGUE

SUGAR SPRINGS, TEXAS—TWENTY YEARS AGO . . .

P aige Laramie knew she had aced the spelling test. Nana had practiced the entire list of words with her last night. Not that Paige needed her to do so. Nana just liked helping Paige with her homework while Mama pulled a double shift at the diner.

She was the smartest girl in her class. Danny Henderson was the smartest boy. They always competed against one another. Danny had the edge in science, while Paige was better with math. They were pretty much the same in everything else—writing, grammar, social studies. Danny thought he was better, though, because he was rich. He always had the newest tennis shoes and the latest cell phone. His dad was president of the local bank, and his mom didn't have to work.

Her mom worked all the time. Her dad? Not so much. At least he hadn't before The Divorce. Paige didn't know where Daddy worked now or what he did or where he lived. When her parents had been married, Daddy sometimes worked as a mechanic at the local body shop. Or he drove a truck, making a run from Dallas to Houston and back a few times a week. After The Divorce last year, Mama got full custody of

Paige. Daddy was supposed to pay money for her food and clothes, but he hadn't done so yet. She had only seen him once, on Christmas Day, and that was only for an hour. He'd showed up two hours late and had driven her to the local park. They sat on a picnic bench and she watched him drink a six-pack.

When he drank, three things happened. After the first two beers, he became funny and charming. After two more, he grew loud and belligerent. That was when she had to be careful around him. One wrong word would set him off—and when he was mean, he would yell and sometimes hit her. Another two beers in him, and Daddy grew sappy and sleepy. He'd cry a little and then say he was sorry. Then he'd fall asleep.

On Christmas, he'd actually asked her a few questions about school at first. She'd told him about winning the school spelling bee and how she'd done more push-ups and sit-ups in the fitness challenge than any other girl in her entire elementary school. He'd listened in that distracted way and then apologized, saying he didn't have a present for her because things had been tight. When he finished the third beer, she put some distance between them, going to sit on the swings and staying there even as he yelled at her and told her she was just as worthless as her mother. By the time he opened the last beer in the six-pack, he was blubbering and telling her how sorry he was.

Paige doubted things would ever change.

She waited until he put his head down on his forearms before she left the swings and came closer. His loud snores let her know it was time to leave. Mama had told her even before The Divorce never to get in the car with Daddy when he was drunk. She walked the two miles home, thankful it was just cold and not windy. Cold, she could take. Cold and windy, and she was miserable. When she grew up, she was going to be a famous writer and travel the world. She would have a house on the beach and another one in the mountains, two places she'd never seen in person, but she liked the looks of them on TV.

Mama had taken one look at Paige when she got home and wrapped her arms about her daughter. They might not have much, but they had each other. And Nana. After The Divorce, they had moved from their trailer into Nana's small house, a few blocks off the Sugar Springs town square. Paige and Mama shared a bed and room, but it was so peaceful at her grandmother's house. No one yelled. No one hit. The house was just full of love—and the good smells from Nana's baking.

The teacher asked Paige to collect the spelling tests and she did so, each student passing them to the front of the row so she could come by and gather them. Miss Biggs then told everyone to take out their books for thirty minutes of free reading time. The class went once a week to the library and checked out a book for free read. Paige always finished hers by the next day. Because of that, she got to help Miss Biggs while the other students in the class read. Not even Danny Henderson got to be a helper like Paige because Miss Biggs had told Danny he was fast but careless, and accuracy was important.

Handing Miss Biggs the stack of papers, the teacher said, "Would you like to grade these for me, Paige?"

"Yes, ma'am," she said with enthusiasm.

"Let's pull yours out first and see how you did."

Miss Biggs located it and skimmed a finger along the twenty-five words. Smiling, she said, "Perfect, as always." She marked *100* on the top of the page. "You may use yours as the key, Paige. Remember, no half-offs. Each word must be legible and the entire word spelled correctly to receive full credit."

"Yes, ma'am."

She'd done this before, many times. Miss Biggs didn't even need to give her a points chart. Paige just did the math in her head and took four points off for each misspelled word, placing the score at the top of the paper. If someone had a perfect score, she would draw smiley faces inside the two zeroes of the *100*.

Glancing up after she finished grading the stack of spelling tests, she saw Danny Henderson glaring at her. She narrowed her eyes and glared right back. He rolled his eyes and mouthed a dirty word and went back to his book. She didn't tattle on him. Mama had told her not to, saying Danny was a bully and that Paige should ignore him.

She brought the papers to Miss Biggs, who gave her a note to take to the office. Paige loved being in the halls when no one else was in them. It was as if the entire school belonged to her. She loved school. Mama said that was a good thing because if Paige wanted to go to college, she would need to do well in school and earn a scholarship. Mama had gone a year to community college and said she always regretted not having more education. But Daddy had come along and charmed her into marriage.

She wondered what Daddy had been like before the drinking. She had looked at pictures of her parents in those early years. They looked so young and happy. Mama was thirty now, but Paige thought she looked much older than that. And Daddy had looked terrible on Christmas, with his bloodshot eyes and uncombed hair and stubble on his face. Paige swore she would never get married and if she did, her husband would never drink and he would shave every day.

After she returned from her trip to the office and reading time ended, they broke into groups for a half-hour to work on a Social Studies project, then it was time for lunch and then recess. She had her usual peanut butter and grape jelly sandwich, along with a banana. It was the lunch she had started making for herself so that Mama didn't have to. Paige had learned to do lots of things for herself when she was young. Mama had worked in a restaurant before The Divorce and she always said customers at night tipped better. Daddy was supposed to stay with Paige when Mama waited tables nights, but he rarely did. She had learned to take a bath and brush her teeth and hair and put herself to bed, even saying her prayers, while Daddy was out doing whatever he did with whomever he did it.

It was okay. They were okay. The Divorce had been good for them. It let her and Mama live with Nana and she didn't have to worry about Daddy yelling at her or slapping her or punching Mama. Paige didn't realize how tense everything at home was until after The Divorce and they moved to Nana's. Nana baked banana bread, cakes, and pies, and she cooked a heavenly goulash. She hummed when she did her housework and let Paige watch TV. She and Paige worked in the vegetable garden together. Life was blissful, one of this week's spelling words.

At recess, her stomach dropped to her knees when she saw Daddy standing at the far end of the school-yard. He was on the other side of the fence and beckoned her—another spelling word last week—to come over. She did so. Reluctantly.

"Hi, baby girl," he said.

She ran her eyes up and down him. He was dressed decently, his clothes clean, a flannel shirt and a pair of jeans. His eyes were clear. He smiled, all his attention on her, and suddenly Paige could see how Mama might have fallen in love with a younger version of him.

"Hey, Daddy," she said cautiously. "Why're you here? I haven't seen you in four months. Not since Christmas."

"I wanted to apologize about Christmas," he began. "I was in a bad place back then. I want to make it up to you. What about after school I take you to get some ice cream?"

Her belly did a flip-flop, her guard still up. Daddy had never taken her for ice cream, not once in her life. Her body tingled in a funny way, and she knew she shouldn't trust him.

"I've got newspaper club today," she told him, hoping he would understand. "We're turning in our stories and deciding what'll be in the newspaper we put out next week. It's our April edition. It'll be published before Easter."

"I'll bet you have a great story for them," he praised.

"I do. Two, in fact."

He looked pleadingly at her. "Could you turn your stories in and then go for ice cream with me? Please?"

Against her better judgment, Paige heard herself say, "Okay. But just for a little while. And you'll need to drop me off a block from home."

Anger suddenly sparked in his eyes. "Why? Does that old woman still talk bad about me?"

"Nana never talks bad about you," she said, defending her grandmother. "She never talks about you at all."

"Hmm."

Glancing over her shoulder, Paige said, "I need to go. Recess is over."

"All right, baby girl."

"I'm not a baby anymore, Daddy. I'm in fourth grade. I'm nine—almost ten."

He grinned. "Whatever you say. See you soon."

Paige ran and fell in at the back of the line of students entering the building. She focused on the math worksheet waiting on her desk, not wanting to think about Daddy or The Divorce or what Mama might say about her skipping newspaper club to go eat a treat with Daddy.

When the bell rang, Miss Biggs dismissed them, reminding them newspaper club would start in ten minutes.

She let the class file out before she approached Miss Biggs, her two stories in hand.

"Miss Biggs? I can't stay today—but here are my stories. One is on the Sugar Springs farmers' market starting back up. The other is the interview I did with the fire chief."

Her teacher accepted them. "Oh, I'll bet they are wonderful, Paige. You are such a strong writer. It is a delight to read your work."

"I want to be a writer when I grow up."

Miss Biggs smiled approvingly. "I think you'll make for a terrific writer. I'm sorry you can't stay today."

She thought Miss Biggs would have asked her why she couldn't stay after school, but she didn't. Paige said goodbye and returned to her desk, collecting her backpack and heading out the front door of the school. She glanced up and down the street, not seeing Daddy. A tiny part of her felt disappointed.

He'd probably already forgotten he promised to take her for ice cream. It sure would've tasted good, now that spring had arrived.

Dejected, she turned east and began walking home, not in the mood to go back to newspaper club. She hadn't gone two blocks when a horn honked beside her. Turning, she saw a black pickup truck, Daddy behind the wheel.

"Get in," he called cheerfully.

She did so, asking, "When did you get a new truck?"

"Oh, I borrowed it from a friend. I did a few favors for him, and he's letting me use it for a while."

"Oh."

She buckled her seatbelt and locked her door, always conscious about safety, especially with her father behind the wheel. But she hadn't smelled any beer on his breath. His eyes still looked bright and clear. Relaxing, she began answering his questions about school.

Then Paige realized they were leaving town. Panic filled her.

"Where are we going?"

"Oh, just the next town over from Sugar Springs. They've got a new ice cream place. I think you'll like it."

Uneasiness filled her. She tamped it down, wanting to trust him, wanting desperately for him to be a dad like all the other dads.

He pointed to the cup holder. "Hey, I got you a drink. You still like lemonade, right?"

"Yes. Thank you."

Paige was thirsty and drank the cold, refreshing lemonade quickly. Lemonade was a treat she didn't get very often.

They were on the highway now. She sighed, feeling sleepy. Her eyelids grew heavy and she leaned her head against the window.

When she woke up, it was dark.

And they were still driving.

"Daddy? Where are we? Where are we going?" she demanded, keeping her tone even though panic swelled within her, causing her heart to race.

He turned, his face no longer affable—a spelling word from two weeks ago.

"We're going away for a bit," he informed her, his voice harder now.

"Where? Why?"

"Because I need to punish that bitch," he spat out.

She sensed the waves of anger rolling off him and wanted to make herself small. Then she noticed the open beer can in the cup holder next to him.

And three others crushed and in the floorboard beneath her feet.

"She ruined everything," he railed. "She couldn't like me for who I am. She was always complaining. She said I couldn't see you."

"That was the court, Daddy. And they did say you could—"

"Shut your trap!" he roared, slamming his fist into her belly.

Pain filled her, followed by terror when she couldn't breathe. He hadn't hit her in a long time. She was out of practice. The air would come. It just took a minute. Her brain told her not to worry, that her insides were paralyzed, but they would unfreeze.

When they did, she gasped air into her lungs, breathing quick and hard. She realized now he had drugged her. The dashboard clock said eight forty-eight. She had no idea where they were or how far away from Sugar Springs they'd gone. Mama would be getting home soon. Nana would be worried. They would call the police. They would look for her. They had to. Please, God, let them find her.

Daddy continuing cursing and badmouthing Mama. What Paige got out of his rant—a last year spelling word that fit Daddy's words to perfection---was that he didn't really want her. He just didn't want Mama and Nana to have her. She worried he might kill her and dump her body somewhere. She had to pretend to like him. Pretend to like what he was doing.

It just might save her life.

"Thank you, Daddy."

His head whipped toward her. "For what?" he asked, suspicion in his eyes.

"For coming for me. I always liked you better than Mama. I'm glad we can live together. I know you said you don't want me, but I can be good, Daddy. I can help you. I'll clean and cook for you. I'll take care of you. You'll be so happy you came and got me."

"Huh."

They drove on into the night.

"You'll need a new name. We both will."

Smiling brightly, hoping he bought into her act, Paige asked, "Can I pick it, Daddy? My new name?"

"Sure," he said agreeably, surprising her.

"I think I'll be Nancy," she said. "After Nancy Drew. She's a girl detective. Nana bought me some of the books at a garage sale, three for a quarter, and I—"

"Don't talk about her again," Daddy warned.

Paige played dumb. "Nancy Drew?"

"No, that woman. Or your mama."

"Oh, okay." Her mind raced, knowing she walked a tightrope. "But I can still be Nancy, right?"

"Sure. Be whoever the hell you want to be. Doesn't matter to me."

That worried Paige. It still sounded as if he were going to do something to her.

Well, she would do something first. She would get away. She would be smart like Nancy Drew always was.

And when she got back to Sugar Springs, she would never leave it. Ever again.

~

TANNER HADDOCK WASHED down his burger and fries with a Coke, enjoying the burn in his throat from the soft drink. Summertime was meant for drinking a cold Coke over crushed ice, and on this hot, late summer evening, the soft drink had hit the spot.

"Ready for dessert?" his mom asked.

"Really?"

"Whatever you want," his dad added. "Pie. Ice cream. Call it an early birthday celebration."

Annie, who owned the diner, came over. "Any dessert tonight, folks?"

He grinned. "I'd like a chocolate soda. Vanilla ice cream with chocolate syrup. About half the glass filled with the soda water."

Annie smiled. "Three scoops good enough, Tanner?"

"Yes, ma'am!"

"Pie for Helen and me," Dad said. "Apple for both of us, Annie. Hold the ice cream."

"You got it." Annie jotted their orders onto her notepad and moved toward the counter.

"Thanks again, Dad," Tanner said.

"You pitched a good game today, son. I thought a little treat would be nice."

His parents started talking about a cow whose milk had dried up. Bored, he stared out the window, watching a truck pull into the parking lot. A man got out and motioned. A girl climbed out from the driver's side. Tanner thought that odd, wondering why she didn't get out on her side of the truck. Maybe the door was broken. But the truck looked pretty new.

As they moved across the parking lot, the man placed his hand on the girl's neck. She winced, keeping her head down.

Something didn't seem right.

His dad had always told him to pay attention to details. Not that Tanner wanted to go into police work, a job where you had to really look at the nitty-gritty. He wanted to either be a famous baseball player or an actor. Maybe both. Either way, he knew he wanted to leave Owens, Oklahoma. Living in a small town, everyone knew who he was, especially with Dad being the chief of police. He wanted to go somewhere that had a million people or more, not the two thousand plus in Owens. He wanted to see the world. Make money. Discover new things about himself.

The door to the diner opened and the man moved the girl through the opening. They had to be father and daughter. At least he thought they must be. Then he decided that he shouldn't assume anything.

"Sit anywhere you'd like," Annie called from behind the counter.

His family were the only customers in the diner since it was almost nine and closing time. Most people had eaten dinner long ago. They'd come from a baseball tournament two towns over, and Mom had suggested grabbing a quick dinner after his dad had stopped and changed a flat tire for the Baptist preacher's wife on their way home. His little sister, Alana, was spending the night with a friend, so they didn't have to worry about getting home to relieve a babysitter.

Now, he watched the man pick a table in the corner, his eyes searching the place. The girl sat, her head still bowed.

Tanner got a bad feeling. He continued watching them as Annie delivered dessert to the Haddocks, his father digging into the pie with gusto, his mother taking dainty bites. Tanner sipped some of the soda and then spooned ice cream into his mouth.

Annie took the newcomers' orders and then the girl said something to the man. He nodded and they both stood up, Again, he put his hand on her neck, guiding her past their table.

Tanner's gaze connected with the girl's for a brief moment, and then they passed. He glanced down and saw she held her left hand out, palm facing him.

Help.

That was the word dug into her palm.

Cold fear puddled in his belly. Quickly, he swung his head around and watched them continue toward the restrooms. He turned and looked at his dad, who was talking and laughing.

"Gotta go to the restroom. Be right back," he said, sliding from the booth and following the pair through the door.

The girl went into the ladies' restroom. The man stayed in the tight space that led to both restrooms.

"Uh, excuse me," Tanner said, brushing past the man and entering the men's restroom.

Inside, his brain was spinning in fast-forward. The man lingering outside the door, waiting for the girl, was weird enough. She had to be at least nine or ten and should've been able to go to the restroom herself. But the fact that she'd carved *HELP* into her hand told him she was in trouble. Big trouble.

He washed his hands and left, the man still hovering outside, waiting for the girl. Squeezing past the man again, he looked up. What he saw in the guy's eyes frightened him.

Tanner hurried back to the table and interrupted his mother's story. "Dad."

Mom frowned. "Tanner, you know not to—"

"There's a girl in trouble in the restroom," he hissed. "I watched her and maybe a guy who's her dad come in. He keeps his hand on her neck. He guided her into the diner and then to the restroom. He didn't even go himself. He's just waiting for her."

"Well, some fathers are a little overprotective," Dad said, frowning slightly.

"No," he insisted. "I saw her hand. She held it out to me when she passed our booth." He swallowed. "Dad, it said *HELP*."

Immediately, his father's demeanor changed. "You saw that word?"

"Yes," he said, nodding vigorously. "Like she'd carved it there. She needs us, Dad."

His father's eyes glanced to the back and then returned to Tanner. "They're coming," he said quietly, taking a bite of pie.

As the two moved passed their table, Tanner noticed the girl kept her hands by her side this time. The hand with her cry for help was on the far side and couldn't be easily seen anyway. She was smart not to try again a second time.

Once the pair returned to their table, Dad said, "Stay right here. I'll be back. Don't look at them. He might spook."

Dad scooted from the booth and called to Annie, "Left my wallet in the car. Be right back."

Keeping his eyes on Mom, Tanner asked, "Is Dad calling for back-up?"

Mom had her back to the man and girl. She nodded. "He will. He'll also run the plates. See if the vehicle is stolen and who it's registered to." She reached out a hand and he gave her his. "That was very brave of you, Tanner. And very observant. Let's just hope this girl isn't in trouble. That it's all a misunderstanding."

"She is, Mom," he said earnestly. "I can tell. She doesn't look up. She's not talking. Girls are always talking, all the time."

He remembered the look in her green eyes in that brief moment when their gazes had connected. Something told him he would always remember those eyes.

Dad reentered the diner and slid into the booth. "Let's get the two of you out of here now," he said quietly. "Helen, take Tanner. Go to the car and lock the doors."

Tanner had barely touched his chocolate soda but it didn't matter. He couldn't eat it. Not when that girl was in trouble.

"Check, Annie," Dad said, standing to let Mom out of the booth.

"Right away, Chief. Let me get this order out." She scooped up two baskets from where the cook had pushed them through the pass-through window and headed across the diner.

As he pushed out of the booth, Tanner watched the man react to hearing Annie call her dad that. His eyes narrowed. He frowned. Tanner looked away and could sense the stranger's gaze boring into his family.

"Changed my mind. We need these to go," he told Annie as she set the food on their table.

"Okay. Give me a minute to box them up for you, sir." Annie took out her pad from her apron's pocket and tore off the ticket, placing it on the table. "Here's your check."

She turned to leave, baskets in hand again. Tanner's heart raced as he glanced up. His gaze met that of the girl's once more. In it, he saw both sadness and fear.

The stranger jerked her to her feet and moved them toward the door.

"Dad, he's leaving with her. Stop him," he begged.

Dad slipped his gun from its holster. "You two get under the table. Now," he urged, and Mom slipped into the booth again, both of them immediately sliding beneath the table.

His dad raised his gun. "Stop right there!" he said, his voice calm and firm and full of authority.

Tanner could still see from his vantage point and watched the man whirl, his left hand tightening on the girl's neck as his right jerked a pistol free, swinging it up, pointing it at Tanner's dad.

Annie screamed. He heard two shots fired almost simultaneously, the noise deafening. His father grunted and fell back two steps, giving Tanner a good view of the blood that stained his dad's shoulder.

"Dad!" he cried, scrambling out.

"I'm okay, son."

"You're shot!" Mom cried, bursting from the floor.

Tanner did the same, except he looked to the other side of the diner. The stranger had collapsed on the floor, his body still. Blood pooled around his head. Tanner knew the man was dead.

He was drawn, though, to the girl. She stood stock-still, gazing down at the body. Her own started trembling as she looked up. Tanner moved to her and stopped in front of her.

"Thank you," she said, tears welling in her eyes and then spilling down her cheeks. "You saw my message."

He reached for her hand and lifted it, her palm facing up. The four letters were etched into the smooth skin, an angry red in contrast to the white of her skin. He searched her face.

"I did it and didn't know if anyone would ever see it. I tried showing it a few times."

Tanner said, "You are very brave."

"Thank you," she whispered, tears pooling in her emerald eyes.

Sirens sounded in the distance, and he supposed Annie or someone had called for help.

"Come meet my dad."

He took her wrist, afraid to hold her hand because it might hurt her, and led her toward his parents. Mom had called for clean dish towels and had wrapped them around Dad's shoulder.

"Dad? This is—"

He stopped because he hadn't even asked the girl her name.

"I'm Paige," she said, her head held high, her voice strong. "And I want to go home."

Dad smiled. "We'll get you home, Paige. I promise you that."

"Thank you," she said softly. "He . . . He was my daddy. But he was a bad man. Can I call Mama and Nana now? I know they're worried about me."

Mom produced her cell phone and stepped to the girl, wrapping a protective arm about her. "You can use mine, honey. Let's go outside and sit in the car."

"Good idea," Dad said.

As Mom led Paige away, she turned over her shoulder and mouthed, "Thank you," to Tanner.

He smiled and gave a wave.

With his good arm, Dad drew Tanner into a bear hug. "You did something wonderful tonight, son. You saved that girl's life."

Tanner knew he would never forget this night.

Or Paige.

1

MALIBU, CALIFORNIA—MARCH

Tanner Haddock wrapped the bath sheet around his waist and secured it, taking his time to shave the heavy beard which he'd had for several months during the filming of his latest movie. As America's most recognized—and bankable—movie star, he would have preferred keeping the beard and hoping for a little anonymity during his hiatus. But his mom liked Tanner clean-shaven. Since he would see her later today, he wanted to keep her happy.

Besides, he wouldn't see many people in Owens, Oklahoma, his hometown of two thousand, if you counted the chickens and pigs within the city limits. On his trips home, people left him alone for the most part. Hardly anyone new ever moved to Owens. Those living there had known him since he was in diapers. They had seen him grow up. Pitch baseball games and act in school plays. Truth be told, Helen Haddock was the star of the family in this corner of the state. His mom's horses were some of the most in-demand in the racing industry. She had even bred two Kentucky Derby winners, making her royalty in a state that valued cattle and horses.

The beard now gone, Tanner studied his image in the mirror and found himself again after being Drake Billings for the last several months. Each time he took on a role, he disappeared into it as much as possible. For *Caught*, he'd played a CIA operative on a dangerous mission behind enemy lines, one who had been abandoned by his special ops team in a country which loathed Americans. The shoot had been grueling and yet satisfying, his sixth film with George Madison, a director he admired, and a man whose friendship he treasured.

It was George and his wife, Hailey, who had advised Tanner to book something beyond his usual action-adventure film after the third time Tanner had worked with the director. The couple had him over for dinner and encouraged Tanner to push his limits and try something new so that he wouldn't become typecast. He'd followed their advice, signing on to do a romantic comedy, and had garnered rave reviews for stepping out of his usual action/adventure mode. After that, he alternated doing a film with George and then another director. Several had been indie flicks which didn't pay much, but he made more than enough off his popcorn movies. Tanner carefully studied his directors—their methods and direction. How they drew certain emotions from their actors. How they worked with the camera crew and lighting people and extras. Their relationship with the producer on set.

When they were two-thirds through shooting *Caught*, Tanner had told George and Hailey that he was finally ready to direct a picture of his own. George had quizzed him for over two hours after that announcement. At the end of filming, the director had agreed that it was time for Tanner to branch out and give directing a try. He urged nothing large-scale, similar to what the two of them worked on together, but rather something more intimate.

Tanner had decided that a piece set in a small town was the answer.

He'd grown up in Owens, Oklahoma, about ten miles northeast of Broken Bow. It was where he retreated for a week or two after he completed each film. He stayed on his parents' ranch. Rode with Mom. Fished and hunted with Dad. Visited with his sister and her husband, who helped train the horses on the ranch. Owens grounded him. Calmed him. Helped him remember who he was.

As for Hailey, she had been poring through scripts from her clients the last two months after Tanner declared his intention to direct. She knew he wanted something that revolved around a small town. Those were his roots. He knew those places. He believed he could bring out the best in himself and the material if it involved a small town. So far, Hailey hadn't found the right property yet among her clients. Tanner had Jeanine Young, his agent, also working on it. Quietly. Very quietly. He wanted to keep his ambition of moving in a new direction as much on the down-low as possible. Yes, word would eventually leak out, but he wanted to maintain anonymity as long as he could.

Hopefully, either Jeanine or Hailey would find a property that might interest him soon. As of now, he wasn't committed to a role in any future projects, which was unusual for him. Tanner Haddock usually filmed one movie, had another either being cut or in the can awaiting release, and a third playing at the local cineplex. He also automatically signed on for one or two other films before he finished filming his current project. Something had told him to hold back —so he had. When he found the right property, he wanted to devote his all to it and not worry what was down the road. He didn't want to be rushed in prepping, filming, or editing. It was important to him to get his first directorial effort right, so that there would be other opportunities down the line. Acting was still in his blood. He wouldn't give that up in the foreseeable future.

But his interests lay in directing. Adding that to his wheelhouse. Eventually, when his body gave out or his looks faded, he might be able to turn to directing full-time.

Dressing casually in a T-shirt and jeans, he placed his shaving kit inside his duffel bag. He had only packed a few things since he left a sizeable amount of clothing, boots, and shoes at his parents' ranch.

The ding for a text message sounded and he pulled his cell from his pocket. It was from Ron Jackson, his stunt double and close friend.

Out front. Whenever you're ready.

TANNER SENT a thumbs up and slipped the duffel's strap on his shoulder, stopping to grab a bottled water from the fridge as he left the house. He opened the rear door and tossed the duffel bag inside the vehicle and then climbed into the passenger seat of Ron's Jeep.

His friend stroked the beard he still had. "Guess I couldn't pass as your double right now," he teased, turning the car and heading down the driveway toward PCH-1.

"Mom likes to see her baby boy's face," he said, laughing.

"Should I keep the beard? You haven't mentioned what the next film is."

"That's because I don't know."

Ron whipped his head toward Tanner. "Seriously?" He looked back out the front windshield. "I've never known you not to have something lined up."

"I'm taking a little break."

"Hmm. Guess that means we're taking a break."

Ron had exclusively worked as Tanner's double since his second film, which was over a decade ago.

"I guess I should've given you a heads up," Tanner apologized. "So you could line up another gig."

Ron laughed. "Are you kidding me? I would love a break, buddy. With you, it's go, go, go. I have plenty of money in the bank. Hell, I can even take a vacation now that I know we've got some time off."

"You know you're always welcome at the ranch. Mom loves you, and Dad can't get enough of your stories."

"Pass this time, bro. If I truly have a stretch of time off, I'd like to go backpacking in Scandinavia."

"Scandinavia?"

"Yes. I fell in love with Norway and Finland when you did that spy thriller, what, six or seven years ago. The people are friendly."

"You mean the girls are hot."

Ron grinned. "Well, yes, that. But the countryside is beautiful. And everyone seems to speak decent English. It would be easy to move around."

"Do it," Tanner urged. "I won't be taking on another role for at least a year. Maybe more."

Ron pulled up to a stop sign and placed the back

of his hand on Tanner's brow. "Just checking for a fever. You don't seem sick. Are you worn out, buddy?"

"A little," he admitted. "But I have a goal in mind." He paused. "I want to direct."

"Hell, yes!" his friend said enthusiastically. "You'd be a natural. You're always dogging the director on every movie we make. Asking a million questions. Talking to cameramen about angles. Quizzing the screenwriter. I can see you doing it. Do you have a script yet?"

"No. That's the holdup. I can't find anything I want. Jeanine and Hailey are scouring everywhere for me."

"It'll come," Ron said. "And when it does, you'll know it in your gut."

"It won't be a huge movie," Tanner explained. "I doubt any producer would give me, an untested director, a big budget. So, no car chases or explosions. Probably no stunt work at all for you."

Ron shrugged. "If you need me in any capacity, I'll make myself available. If you just want me to come hang out with the crew and watch your back, I can do that, too."

He smiled, appreciating the friendship Ron and he had built over the years. "That would be great."

They arrived at Hollywood Burbank Airport. It was a few miles farther from Malibu than LAX, but Tanner kept his private jet there. Ron would serve as his pilot today. Tanner, who also had his pilot's license, sometimes acted as the co-pilot. Today, though, he'd hired someone else to do the chore, wanting to relax after the long, grueling shoot he'd just come off.

Ron went through the pre-flight check as Tanner boarded the small aircraft, settling into his passenger seat. His cell rang, which was unusual. He rarely took calls, relying on texts a majority of the time.

"Have you left?" Hailey asked. "Tell me you haven't."

"Still here. Ron's walking the plane with his checklist. What's up?"

"I'm on my way to you," she said. "I have a script, Tanner. It may be the one you've been looking for."

"That would be awesome, Hailey. I'll be sure we wait for you."

"I'm about ten minutes out. See you soon."

Rising, Tanner went to the front. Ron was settling into the pilot's seat, along with the co-pilot.

"We need to wait. Hailey's a few minutes away and has a script she wants me to read ASAP."

"Not a problem, bro."

Leaving the plane, Tanner waited in the hanger. Soon, Hailey came into sight, driving her baby blue Camaro convertible. She pulled in next to him, handing him a thick envelope.

"My gut tells me this is it, Tanner."

He accepted the package. "I hope so. Has George read it?"

She nodded. "He has. We both think you could do something with this."

"Is it written by one of your clients?"

"Yes. Laramie Fisher."

He thought a moment. "I've heard the name. From where?"

"Laramie wrote a rom-com that came out two years ago."

"Oh, the one with Knox Monroe," he said, nodding his head. "I remember that. Crisp writing. I enjoyed it."

"I've also sold another screenplay Laramie's written. It's in pre-production now. I think it could be his breakout script."

He glanced at the envelope he held. "What's this one about?"

"It's set in a small town. And not a rom-com. It's a suspense. Two people who dated in high school then parted ways after graduation. Years down the road, the guy comes back to their small town. He's a serial killer and stalks his former girlfriend while striking in the nearby, surrounding towns, keeping his skills, shall we say, up-to-date."

Tanner's wheels were turning already. Shooting in a small town would help the budget. He could even rent a few houses which could serve as the main characters' homes and shoot a bulk of scenes inside them, as well as using parts of them as the locations for the serial killer's murders. Hell, the houses could even double as places for him and the leads to bunk.

"You've never been associated with anything like this," Hailey continued. "It would be hard, but George and I think you should cast yourself as the killer."

"Really?" He was intrigued. "I've always been the hero. Playing against type would certainly be unexpected. Okay. Let me read it on the plane and I'll get back to you."

"Sounds good," Hailey said. "You know you can talk it over with George. He's such a fan of yours. He thinks you can do anything."

"And you?" Tanner pressed.

Hailey met his gaze. "You've really grown as an actor, Tanner. You listen well. You take direction even better. You've learned a lot on sets during the past decade. I think you could make something of this. If you decide to pass, though, I already know where I'll shop the screenplay next."

He laughed. "Hey, don't take it away from me just

yet. I'll call you when I land and hopefully, I'll have an answer for you by then."

Tanner bent and kissed Hailey's cheek. "Tell George hello."

"Enjoy Owens. Recharge and reload. Bye."

He watched her back out of the hangar and drive off, waving her hand in the air as she sped away. Once again, Tanner mounted the steps and boarded the plane.

"We can go anytime, Ron."

"Roger that."

Returning to his seat, he buckled his seatbelt and removed the script from the envelope, setting his phone in airplane mode.

MIDNIGHT in the Shadows by Laramie Fisher

TANNER SETTLED BACK, script in hand, and began to read.

Two hours later, he read the final page, chills rushing up his spine. He let out a long breath which he hadn't realized he'd been holding.

Laramie Fisher's script wasn't just good.

It was incredible.

The pacing was taut. His descriptions setting up each scene gave him a clear vision of where he would want to take the material. It had one of the bravest heroines he'd ever read, along with one of the most cunning, diabolical serial killers that would ever be brought to screen. Move over, Hannibal Lecter. Harmless-looking Peter Willoughby, with his beguiling smile and non-descript brown hair and eyes was the most vicious monster Tanner could imagine.

And Tanner wanted to play Peter, as well as direct.

"Hey, we'll be landing in a few," Ron called out.

He watched out the window as Cox Field came into view. Paris, Texas, was the closest airport with refueling capabilities. Ron would gas up the jet and return to California after a short break. Tanner had already arranged for Billy Stewart, his best friend from high school, to meet him and ferry him to Owens. Billy had remained in their hometown and worked as a plumber, alongside his father.

They descended and touched down. As they taxied along the runway, Tanner took his cell out of airplane mode and called Hailey.

Her first words were, "What did you think?"

"I think you need to tell me where Laramie Fisher lives—because I want to meet him and convince him I'm the only one who can do justice to this screenplay."

Hailey laughed. "I knew you'd be hooked. I'll email Laramie and see if he's willing to meet with you."

"Can't you call him? Or text? I want to jump on this, Hailey. I need to do this story."

She sighed. "You might as well enjoy your weekend, Tanner. Laramie Fisher has made it clear that he doesn't respond to emails on the weekends. That's when he does his writing. I assume he has a day job that keeps him pretty busy during the week. And I don't have a cell number for him. He refuses to talk on the phone. All our transactions occur via email."

"That's crazy."

"From what I can tell, my client is a very private, guarded person. You go do your thing. I'll email Laramie now. Hopefully, he'll get back to me sometime on Monday, and then I'll be in touch with you."

"Do whatever it takes, Hailey. I mean it. I want to direct this film. Work your magic—but get me a meeting. In person. As soon as possible. I'll pay whatever this guy wants."

"Will do, Tanner. In the meantime, relax. Enjoy your time with your family. There's nothing you can do this weekend to speed up the process."

He sighed. "Just keep me posted, Hailey. Talk soon."

Tanner hung up. The plane had already come to a halt, so he unbuckled his seatbelt and claimed his duffel bag, slipping the script inside it. Descending the stairs, he saw Ron and the co-pilot stretching their legs.

"I'll get us refueled, and we'll be back in the air within the hour," his friend said. "We're going to go for coffee and grab some lunch if you want to eat with us."

He wanted to tell Ron to wait, thinking he might need the plane to get to Laramie Fisher on Monday. But he didn't want Ron to have to hang around the entire weekend and beyond, especially if the reclusive screenwriter didn't bother to respond to Hailey's email for several days. Besides, he could always fly commercial to wherever Laramie Fisher lived.

He was wired, though, and tried to tamp down his excitement. Talking about the script might jinx things. Though Tanner wasn't superstitious, he wanted to keep this news to himself.

"Sounds good. I'll text Billy and see where he is."

He stopped to do so, and his friend said he was about ten minutes outside Paris.

"Billy'll be here soon. Go enjoy lunch—and Scandinavia." Tanner wrapped Ron in a bear hug. "Enjoy your vacay. Send me pictures."

"Of all the blondes? Or the glaciers?" Ron teased.

"Both," he said, laughing. "Stay in touch, buddy."

Tanner moved toward the terminal, deciding to wait outside in front of it for Billy. Every nerve he had was firing inside him.

He couldn't wait to meet Laramie Fisher and convince him that Tanner Haddock was the man meant to direct this film.

2

———————

*L**aramie Fisher had an email.*

Paige Laramie checked the Laramie Fisher account once a day. She wanted to do so more often but told herself that the movie business was iffy. That Laramie might not hear anything about the screenplay submitted to Hailey Madison for days. Even weeks. After all, she had just sent it to Hailey late Thursday night, and it was only Saturday afternoon now. Her agent had many other clients. She had thought it would take Hailey a good two weeks to even get to the script, much less begin to try and market it.

Then she reminded herself that she hadn't received an email from Hailey yesterday acknowledging receipt. That must be what this email was, one saying that the agent had gotten the screenplay. Hailey was good about telling Laramie Fisher where he was in her queue, as well as the studios and producers which Hailey would pitch to after she'd read the property and thought about the best avenues to pursue.

Sighing, she decided not to even open the email.

At least she had an agent. That was more than many writers could say, whether they wrote fiction, non-fiction, or for the stage or screen. Paige had spent a good six months after completing her first screenplay studying agents and the market. She had narrowed her choices down to three agents. One, she had never heard back from. Not even a "Hey, I got it, but no thanks." Just silence. Another was more encouraging. Said the screenplay had potential but small-town romances were on their way out. The agent had even provided a name and email address of someone at Hallmark for Laramie to contact regarding the script, saying it was more suited for a TV movie than the big screen.

But Paige had put that decision on hold, hoping to hear from Hailey Madison. Hailey, the wife of director George Madison, was her first choice for representation. Everything she had read about the agent made Paige want to wait to hear from Hailey before she acted. She decided to give it six months and if she hadn't received a response to her query by then, she would get in touch with the Hallmark exec. In the meantime, she did what countless other writers did.

Started her next project, her second screenplay.

Fortunately, Hailey had replied to the query four weeks after receiving it. She said Laramie had talent. A unique eye and a knack for natural, crisp dialogue. She'd given Laramie a few pointers and asked for some rewrites based upon them. Paige had taken a rare sick day from school on a Friday and did a marathon, three-day writing session, updating the screenplay with the tips from Hailey. She went back and read straight through it, tweaking a few things in the revised screenplay. Then she waited two days and re-read the entire thing again, finding only a single typo and nothing she wanted to change, content-wise.

She'd emailed it back to Hailey—and heard a week later that the agent loved the rewrites and wanted to sign Laramie Fisher immediately. Hailey asked for a cell number so she could get in touch.

But Paige didn't want that. She didn't want anyone in Sugar Springs to know she'd written a screenplay. That's why she'd taken a pen name and filed for a DBA—doing business as—legal document, which was good for ten years in Texas.

So, she'd emailed Hailey, explaining that she was the stereotypical writer—shy and reclusive—and preferred all contact to be via email. Hailey had responded quickly, agreeing to conduct all their business via email. The agent had sent a contract, which Paige had carefully perused. Nervous that she might miss something, though, she finally broke down and made an appointment with Campbell Cox, a local attorney, and had him go over the contract with her. Mr. Cox had assured Paige that attorney/client privilege would keep him from revealing she was Laramie Fisher, and he would keep quiet about her turn of good fortune as long as she wished him to do so. He'd even agreed to continue to be the attorney of record for Laramie Fisher if she so desired. While she could have searched for an entertainment lawyer, she'd known Campbell Cox her entire life and thought him intelligent and professional. She'd agreed to keep him as her representative in all Laramie Fisher-related matters.

Confident that she was making the right decision, Paige emailed the contract back to Hailey, along with her lawyer's contact information.

Her new agent found a buyer for the script, and it became an indie hit two years ago, with Laramie even receiving a nomination for Best First Screenplay from the Film Independent Spirit Awards, which were always held the day before the Academy Awards. While she had chosen not to go to California for the ceremony to guard her identity—and had lost—the actress playing the lead in the film won, thrilling Paige beyond words.

With her secret safe, Paige had completed another screenplay last summer and sent it to Hailey. This second script received more attention than the first had, thanks to the nomination her first effort had received. Hailey had sold it to a major studio. Unlike the small amount she'd received for her first-purchased script, this second effort had rewarded her handsomely, so much that she had paid off the small house she lived in and even bought Nana a new TV and both of them new iPads. Production would be starting soon in Vancouver, where a bulk of the filming would occur.

In the meantime, Paige had kept her head down and her mouth shut, only telling Nana that teachers had received a bonus at the end of the last school year and that was why she was able to purchase both of them new iPads. When not baking or watching her cherished cop shows on TV, Nana was glued to her iPad. Paige had introduced her grandmother to TikTok and Instagram, and Nana spent time on both sites each day, constantly telling Paige about what she was learning.

The third screenplay she'd submitted to Hailey was markedly different from the first two, which were both light and breezy and ending with happily ever afters for the lead characters. Her third script was based upon the darkness that had lurked within her for years. Some of it involved the lingering aftereffects of what had happened to her years ago, during the time after The Divorce, when her father had kidnapped her. She used elements of that experience to craft a suspenseful, wild ride of a story set in a small town. She was curious about how Hailey would react to something so different from her. Maybe she should open the email acknowledging that the agent had received the script. Paige hadn't placed any disclaimer in her email to the agent, merely telling Hailey that she could find the latest work attached to the email.

Her cell chirped with an incoming text and she picked up the phone from the armrest, seeing it was Vivi. She hadn't spoken to her best friend in over a week, merely trading a few texts each day, their preferred method for staying in touch. Vivi was a sous chef at a Dallas steakhouse, while her brother Dante was the executive chef at a competing restaurant three blocks away.

Between lunch & dinner shifts. You
have time to talk?

QUICKLY, Paige typed her reply and waited for her cell to ring. Moments later, it did.

"Hey, what's up?" she asked. "I can hear street noises in the background."

"It's two now. The Saturday lunch crowd has dried up to a dribble," Vivi said. "I said I was taking a smoke break and left."

"But . . .you don't smoke," she pointed out.

"True. I needed privacy, though. I wanted to talk to you about Dante. And my parents."

"Dante first," Paige said. "He's easy to discuss because he's always limited to his latest woman or something with his job."

Vivi laughed. "The latest flame flamed out. She thought he was a masterful cook—and lover—according to my brother."

"Well, Dante has never been shy about anything."

"Nope. But the latest lover is done and gone. She said she couldn't live with the hours of an executive chef."

"Do you blame her?" Paige asked. "It's not just a lunch and dinner shift. It's being first at the market in the morning and buying a bunch of fresh food for that day. It's creating new dishes, testing them out, and then planning menus. Then cooking for hours and hours, getting home late. I'm surprised any chef can claim a personal life, unless they're Gordon Ramsay or Bobby Flay. They leave their restaurants in capable hands and do their reality TV series and travel the globe."

"Wow, you have learned a lot about the restaurant business, listening to me. Unfortunately, Dante doesn't have any TV series lined up. He's just married to his job, which his latest *amante* finally got tired of. But that's not it. Dante is wanting to open his own restaurant. Italian, of course."

"That's terrific. In Dallas, I suppose?"

"Yes, he loves the big city lights. And he wants me to come work with him. I'd be his sous chef. What do you think?"

"Hmm. You're both pretty strong-willed people, Vivi. I can see some clashes, for sure. And it wouldn't be a step up. You'd be doing the same job you have now. You've always told me a lateral move is a wasted one in your business."

"But it would be Italian food," Vivi pointed out. "Not steaks. That would be a plus. But you're right. Dante and I are like oil and water most of the time.

We're both temperamental when it comes to food and our vision of it. I'm not sure one kitchen would be big enough for the both of us, especially since it would be *his* kitchen."

"Then don't do it. Recommend his place to others. Don't sacrifice the good relationship you have by going into business together. Or actually, it would be Dante's business. It would be his way or the highway. You've never liked being told what to do, especially by your brother. I'd give that decision a hard look."

Resignation sounded in Viv's voice as she said, "That's what I thought. Much as I love my brother, he can be dictatorial in the kitchen. Working side-by-side, implementing his vision only, and not having any input? It would be tough. But I don't want him to fail. Most restaurants do. We know each other so well. I could really help streamline the cooking."

"He'll need to stand on his own, with or without you there. Just consider all the pros and cons, and then listen to your heart."

Vivi snorted. "My head was already telling me to steer clear. You just confirmed what I was thinking. That leads to the second part of this heart-to-heart."

"You mentioned your parents," Paige said. "What's going on with them? I was just in Romano's a few days ago, picking up a Wednesday special."

"Mamma said you were in. She thought you'd lost some weight."

She laughed. "Your mom always says that. I eat the same as always. Run, as usual."

Her friend sighed. "They're thinking about moving to Italy."

"Wait. Did you say *move* to Italy? When? Why?"

"Mamma has always missed the old country. You

know she came here as a teenager. She still has lots of family back in Tuscany."

"But your dad was born in the US. Is he onboard with this idea?"

"Actually, he is. Remember, he was born in New York City, not Texas. He grew up speaking Italian and didn't even learn English until he went to school."

"I know they've visited a couple of times over the years. After we finished fourth grade. Again, after our sophomore year of high school. I was so jealous of you getting to go to a foreign country."

"They went again about five years ago," Vivi reminded her. "Anyway, Mamma is tired of putting in twelve-to-fourteen-hour days, six days a week. She says they could live more cheaply in Italy and be around large, extended family. You know when Mamma makes up her mind, that's how it's going to be."

"So, will they just close the pizzeria? Or will they try to sell it off? I can't imagine anyone else but a Romano running Romano's."

"That's when we get to the part we need to talk about." A long pause sounded. "Papa wants me to buy them out."

"What? You'd be back in Sugar Springs? Oh, Vivi, that would be amazing!" Then Paige tamped down her soaring feelings, knowing how ambitious Viv was and that running a pizzeria in a small town close to nowhere hadn't been in her plans for the future. "How do you feel about that?"

"Well, I had my heart set on becoming an executive chef in Dallas or Houston. I've always wanted to run my own kitchen. If I bought Romano's, it would be more than running the kitchen. I would be responsible for the entire business. Ordering all the food and supplies. Hiring personnel. Keeping the books. Preparing a majority of the food. It's a little overwhelming, to be honest. Then there's the fact that I would have to go deeply into debt to buy them out. I wouldn't want to shaft them. They would need a great price because the money from the sale will be what they would live on the rest of their lives."

"I see." Paige picked at her cuticle. She caught herself doing it and stopped. "How much do they want? I know they already own the building."

Vivi named the price, and Paige could see why her friend hesitated. While Vivi earned a good salary as a top sous chef, Dallas was an expensive city to live in.

And then there was the whole thing with Beck and the financial disaster of that relationship. Vivi had been paying off her dead lover's debts for the past several years. Paige knew Vivi didn't have the money to buy her parents' restaurant.

But she did.

"I've saved a little in the last couple of months," Vivi said. "You know I started at nothing after . . .after Beck died. I don't even know if I could find a bank who would loan me the money I need to buy Romano's outright."

"I have savings, Vivi," she began. "You know I'm frugal. And I've started a side business which I haven't even mentioned to you."

"What kind of side business?"

"Well, it's just something I'm good at and has turned out to be lucrative. It may be more so in the future."

"Enough for you to stop teaching? I know you don't make a lot at that, Paige."

"It has the potential to pay better than being in the classroom." She took a deep breath. "Would you be willing to become partners in Romano's? I'd be the silent one, funneling you the cash. You'd make all the decisions because you know the business inside and out."

"I'll need to think about it, Paige. I called to pick your brain and talk about all the reasons why I should or shouldn't move back to Sugar Springs and take over the pizzeria. The money was the biggest con. There were a lot of pros, chief being we'd be in the same place and I'd finally get to hang out with you again. But I don't know about mixing our friendship with business."

She could hear the wistfulness in Vivi's voice and said, "I mean it. I would be a silent partner. No opinions whatsoever. You'd make all the decisions. Just think about it, Vivi. How long do you have to decide?"

"Papa has told me as much time as I need. Mamma will have some arbitrary deadline in her head. I know her. That's just how she is." Her friend blew out an audible breath. "Okay. You've given me lots to think about. Let me sleep on it and then we'll talk again, okay?"

"Okay. No pressure. If you decide to come home and can find financing on your own, do that. I don't have to be involved in this venture if you think it will hurt our friendship. We've been best friends since kindergarten. I'm not going to blow twenty-five years invested in us if you don't feel good about it."

"If I decide to stay in Dallas, will you come see me?"

Just the question caused Paige's pulse to race. Her mouth went dry. Her heart sped up.

"You know the answer to that, Vivi," she said quietly, hating that after all these years things hadn't changed.

"See? You not ever leaving Sugar Springs puts me in a bind. I have to come there if I want to see you."

"Hey, we FaceTime," she insisted. "And you do come home. Occasionally." But not really. Restaurant hours were cruel to its employees. She hadn't seen Vivi in person in almost two years.

"I miss you, Paige. I would love to be close by and see you all the time."

"Go think about things then. Love you."

"Love you more."

Paige set her cell on the coffee table in front of her.

Why couldn't she get over what had happened in her past?

It was why she'd never left Sugar Springs after she came home from those months where her father dragged her around from one place to the next. They'd been all over Texas. New Mexico. Oklahoma.

Thank goodness for the boy who had seen the message in her palm. Paige lifted her hand and studied it, the faint scars from the letters she'd carved into her skin with a straight pin faded after so many years.

At first, she just reveled in being home again and finally safe. Then it became her heaven—and hell—as she literally grew physically ill when leaving the Sugar Springs area. Oh, she'd been able to go to the nearby state park. Hike and wade in the water at Sugar Lake. But the thought of leaving Sugar Springs for any length of time left her in a cold sweat. She'd given up going on the senior trip to San Antonio in high school, pretending Nana was sick and she needed to stay home and care for her. She deliberately tanked her essay in ready writing for the state's UIL competition, not wanting to advance because it would mean leaving Sugar Springs for the state competition in Austin.

She'd even given up the college scholarship she'd won because the thought of trying to leave home made her nauseous. Instead, she'd attended the local community college and then done online courses at the University of Texas at Tyler, earning her teaching degree. There'd been no question that she'd stay in town and teach at the high school, which she'd done ever since graduating from college. She never left town, not even to visit Vivi in Dallas. Paige stayed put.

Where it was safe.

She never knew what happened to her father's body. She never even called him Daddy because of his betrayal. She could close her eyes and still see his arm swinging up, firing the shot at the nice policeman, whose name she couldn't recall.

What came back in waves was the blood. All the blood. Seeing blood still made her sick to her stomach, so sick she would throw up.

Paige pushed hard against those memories, locking them away again. They popped out every so often, but she had learned how to set them aside and concentrate on other things.

Like the email to Laramie Fisher.

"Might as well open it," she told herself, claiming the laptop and propping her feet on the coffee table as she clicked on Hailey's email.

LARAMIE –

I have incredible news. Yes, I received your screenplay and read it in one sitting. It is freaking amazing! So different from the other two properties I've represented you on—but I absolutely love it. So much that I sent it to a friend. Not a studio or a producer, but someone I know well and trust implicitly. He's interested. More than interested, Laramie.

He wants to buy it—and direct it!

Frankly, I think he'll wind up starring in it, as well. He's an actor with a desire to branch out. He's a sponge on sets, soaking up all aspects of the business. He's done several pictures with George, and we both are close with him. He's not just another hot guy who has no personality off-set. He's smart and kind and really funny.

The thing is, he wants to meet you. I told him you don't do meetings. That I don't even have your cell number. How we keep all business to emails. But he's persistent. He and George just wrapped their latest project together. I'm meeting George in Maui on Monday for some much-needed R&R. I'll be checking email, though, in case you do decide you would like to meet him in person. He's in Oklahoma now, with his family, his usual timeout after a long shoot. I can easily put the two of you in touch if you'll just say the word.

I haven't named him until now because I wanted you to hear about him first, without the name that dazzles audiences worldwide. I wanted you to understand he's a good man and a student of the business. He's paid his dues and constantly asks questions of everyone from the grip to the best boy to the prop master. He's more than ready to direct something on his own—and he is passionate about YOUR screenplay.

If you're willing to meet with him, email me back ASAP. I know you usually don't check your account on weekends, but I'm praying that you'll see this sooner rather than later. Or text or call me. I've given you my number before. I can tell you anything you want to know about him and reassure you in any way if you have any doubts. At least talk with him, Laramie, and that may lead to meeting in person. I hope you'll be open to that possibility because I know he wants to pick your brain and give you his vision of how he would bring your work to the screen.

Tanner Haddock.

That's our friend. George's protégé and frequent collaborator. A friend to us both and a man who may scream HOLLYWOOD—but he's the furthest thing from being Hollywood.

Hope to hear from you soon!

Hailey

P.S. If you call Monday, remember that I might be on a plane and my cell will be in airplane mode. I'll get in touch with you the minute I land, though, if you text or leave me a message.

Tᴀɴɴᴇʀ Hᴀᴅᴅᴏᴄᴋ.

Tanner Haddock.

Was there a bigger star on the planet? And he wanted to direct *her* screenplay?'

Paige felt dizzy. Lightheaded. She thought she might need to throw up but didn't trust getting to her feet. She reached for the glass of water sitting on the table. She left a glass of water everywhere, just like the little girl in the old Mel Gibson movie *Signs*.

Closing her eyes, she sipped on it, trying to calm herself.

Tanner Haddock wanted to direct his first movie. Her script.

And he wanted to meet her.

He was in Oklahoma. Not that far from her.

Would he be willing to come to Sugar Springs?

And if he did, would she be willing to talk to him in person? It would have to be here, at her house. They couldn't go anywhere in town—or the planet—where Tanner Haddock wouldn't be recognized.

If he bought her work and brought it to screen, she would hit the payday of a lifetime. She could simply give Vivi the money to buy out her parents' pizzeria. She would have enough to stop teaching and simply write for a living.

All it would take would be one meeting with Tanner Haddock. One, in-person meeting.

Opening her eyes, she gulped the rest of the water and rested the glass on a coaster. She cracked her knuckles and replied to Hailey's email.

HAILEY —

If you think Tanner Haddock is the one who could do my screenplay justice, sell it to him ASAP. I know you'll negotiate the best price. I appreciate all your hard work on my behalf. Hope you can get this done before you meet your husband for a much-needed vacation. I've never been to Maui, but I've heard it's beautiful.

I live in Sugar Springs, a small town in East Texas, if Mr. Haddock still wants to meet with me. I'm open to doing so, but once he buys the script, I know it's truly out of my hands and a meeting may no longer be necessary.

Texting you my number now if you want to talk.

Laramie

BEFORE SHE COULD CHANGE her mind, Paige hit send.

3

<hr>

Billy reached up and hit the remote, which opened the gate to the Haddock ranch.

"Thanks again for picking me up," Tanner said. "It's always good to catch up."

His friend chuckled. "You mean away from my loud brood. I know they're a pain in the ass, making noise in the background and interrupting every twelve seconds when we're trying to talk sports. Wait until you have kids, Tan."

Billy drove the car through the gate and headed toward the main house, asking, "When do you think you might make a brood of your own?"

He laughed. "I can't remember who TMZ has me dating this week. Whoever it is, I can tell you she's drop-dead gorgeous and shallow as hell—and that kids aren't on her radar."

Billy glanced over. "Are they on yours?"

Tanner sighed. "I'd like the whole package. Someday. A wife. Kids. Dog. Right now, though, I'm working so much, I don't have time to meet anyone, much less someone outside the business. I do not want to marry a fellow actor and then spend half the year away from her while I go off and film and then return to have her do the same. That's no way to create a solid marriage and totally unfair to any kids we might have."

He could see the main house coming up and began to relax, pushing aside thoughts of Laramie Fisher and directing and reinventing himself. For the weekend, at least, he would destress and simply enjoy being home.

"You have to be richer than Midas by now. How long do you think you'll keep acting?"

Shrugging, he said, "It varies. After a great shoot, I hope forever. After one which runs too long and has too many problems, I think I'm done. This last one with George was good, though." He paused. "I am thinking about directing in the near future."

He glanced at Billy, who nodded, seemingly liking the idea.

"I could see that. You've always been that life-long learner. I've heard you talking about aspects of the film business that most actors wouldn't have a clue about."

"I've been preparing for that day when I step from in front of the camera to behind it. I pump George like crazy for info, and I trail after everyone from lighting directors to associate producers to the screenwriter. When I find the right property, I'll be ready."

"Well, you always did your homework and were the most prepared person in school," Billy said. "Whether in the classroom or on the field. You'll be successful when you finally make that move, Tan."

"I hope so."

Billy pulled in behind a black Ford F-150, one which Tanner had bought for Billy a few years ago. He knew money could be tight with three kids to support, and he didn't mind sharing his good fortune with his best friend since kindergarten. Whenever Tanner flew in to see his family and Billy picked him up at the airport, he always asked that his friend leave his truck at the ranch and get Tanner in his own truck, just to save Billy the gas the ninety-minute trip took each way.

Swinging open his door, he retrieved his duffel bag from the back seat and met Billy in the gap between the two vehicles.

Wrapping his friend in a bear hug, Tanner said, "Thanks again for taking time out of your busy Saturday to play chauffeur for me."

"Enjoy whatever Miz Helen makes you for dinner," Billy said, grinning. "I know she likes to spoil you. Maybe you can come for dinner one night this week at our place. Margie and the kids would love to see you."

He doubted the two younger kids, girls ages two and four, really knew who he was, but Tanner thought Trey would like it if he dropped by. The two shared a love of baseball. While Tanner had enjoyed playing alongside Billy in high school, baseball had been his true love. Trey seemed to feel the same way.

"I'll text you and see what works for Margie," Billy added. "Later, man."

He watched Billy hop into his truck and drive away before heading to the front door of the house he'd grown up in. Since he'd hit it big in Hollywood, he'd helped his parents add on to the barn, as well as building two other houses on the eighty-acre property. His sister and husband lived in one of the houses, while Tanner infrequently occupied the other one. Still, he always stopped in to say hi and spend time with his mom and dad before he unpacked at his own place.

Tanner didn't bother knocking and knew the door was never locked. He entered the house and hollered, "I'm home!"

"In the kitchen, honey," Mom called.

Dropping his duffel bag at the door, he made his way to the bright, sunny kitchen which had always been the heart of their home. Before he arrived, Brownie met him. The five-year-old, chocolate-brown lab was an easygoing dog and his mom's constant companion.

"Hey, Brownie," he said, scratching the dog between its ears. "How are you, girl?"

The dog followed Tanner into the kitchen, where he spied his mom stirring a sauce at the stovetop. At fifty-eight, Helen Haddock was tall and reed-thin, with gray hair and crystal-blue eyes which she'd passed along to her son. Critics always compared Tanner's eyes to those of Paul Newman, which Tanner always took as a compliment. Newman had had a lengthy career as an actor and film director, as well as driving racecars and focusing on being an entrepreneur and philanthropist. The actor had won numerous awards for his career efforts and humanitarian work. Being compared to such a great man always humbled Tanner.

"Hey, Mom," he said, coming up behind her and slipping his arms about her waist, squeezing her affectionately. "Smells good."

"Meat sauce for the lasagna. I know how you love it. And your dad should be home soon. I told him to swing by the bakery after he left the station. He's bringing home your favorite cherry pie."

He took a seat at the table, Brownie curling up and resting her head on his feet. "I can see I'm going to need to keep up with my workouts while I'm here. You spoil me rotten, but all the food you feed me is insanely good."

She set down the wooden spoon. "Want some iced

tea?"

"Sure."

She prepared two glasses and then joined him at the table. "You look good, Tanner. Not as tired as you do after some shoots."

"This one went well. George Madison and I work like a finely-oiled machine. After so many collaborations, we can practically finish each other's sentences. We're like an old married couple."

"Well, I've been married to your father for thirty-five years, and I still don't know a thing that goes on in that man's head," she declared. "I actually like that he can still surprise me."

The back door opened, and his dad stepped inside, bakery box in hand. The years had been good to Jeff Haddock. A year shy of sixty, he still had a headful of dark hair and the same build his entire adult life. Looking at him, Tanner could see what he would look like down the line since he favored his father physically.

He rose and embraced the town's police chief. "Hey, Dad. Thanks for picking up the pie. Maybe we should have a slice now to celebrate me being home," he ventured.

"Agreed," his father said cheerfully. "I'll grab the knife and plates."

"I'll get you a glass of milk," Mom said, knowing how her husband liked milk with his pie and cakes.

They sat at the table and talked for over an hour, his mother getting up every now and then to stir the sauce, boil the lasagna noodles, and then layer the casserole and slide it into the oven. Tanner told them about his most recent film, while they caught him up with the gossip of Owens. He listened, glad to be home and happy that he had such a close relationship with his parents. Too many actors came from broken homes or had sad stories about their home life. Tanner knew to count his blessings.

"Alana and Karl will be at dinner," Mom said. "That'll be in about ninety minutes. Why don't you take your things over to your house and then head back here after you get settled in?"

"Good idea," Tanner responded. "I'll take Brownie with me."

He claimed his duffel bag and tossed it into his waiting truck, Brownie jumping in after it. The keys were still in the ignition. It took less than three minutes to reach his place. He took his bag inside and dumped it on the bed. His mom always had someone come in and air the place out, along with putting fresh sheets on the bed and stocking the fridge and pantry each time he came home for a visit. Though he usually ate most of his meals with his parents, he did enjoy some alone time. Tanner wasn't much of a cook. He had about three decent recipes in his repertoire and liked to test them out every time he came to Oklahoma.

As he unzipped the duffel, his cell rang. A rush of excitement poured through him when he saw it was Hailey Madison calling again.

"Tell me you've got good news," he answered, stroking the dog, which had jumped onto the bed.

"No hello?" she teased. "And the news is nothing short of spectacular, I'll say."

"Laramie Fisher will meet with me? In person?" Tanner asked eagerly. "Please tell me he said that."

"Laramie Fisher has agreed to sell you the screenplay, Tanner. *And* meet with you. That is, if you still want to get together. Get this—Laramie is a she. I just assumed Laramie was a man's name and never got corrected. But I talked to her a few minutes ago. We had an actual phone conversation."

"I'm stunned, Hailey," he admitted.

"Frankly, I'm still a little off-balance myself after our conversation. She said she's seen your work and likes it. I explained how you have a desire to direct and think her script is the one you'd like to make your directorial debut with. She'll sell it to you, but it won't be cheap."

Hailey named the price. While hefty, it wasn't outrageous. For a man who made the kind of salary Tanner did, along with percentage points of the profits from most of his films, it wouldn't be a problem, though.

"I'll agree to her price. Do I send it to you?"

His friend became all business. "I'll email you all the info, along with the contract and specifics, including my take. I can send the basics now and have my legal team draw up the contracts while I'm in Hawaii. George and I will be there for ten days. If you can be back in L.A.by the Wednesday after next, we can put a bow on the entire thing, and you can be ready to run with it."

"This is happening fast," he said. "My head is spinning a little, if I'm being honest."

"Do you still want to meet with Laramie? Once you buy it, the script is yours. You know you can do whatever you want with it."

"I do want to talk to her about it. I want to read through it again, but there are things I already know I'd like to pick her brain about. I know you said she's reclusive, but I would love to put her on salary and have her on-set while we shoot."

"I don't know about that, Tanner," Hailey said, doubt in her voice. "Yes, she agreed to meet if you thought it essential, but I sure don't see her being the type to hang around a film set. But if anyone could persuade her, it would be you."

"I have a thousand things to do and think about," he said, excitement rushing through him. "I'll probably drive George insane with all my questions. But yes, I want to meet this writer before I start anything. Storyboarding. Casting. Scouting locations. Just give me her number and I'll arrange to fly to wherever she is."

Hailey laughed. "You may be driving. I got out of her that she lives in a tiny blip on the map in East Texas. A place called Sugar Springs."

"Are you serious? I fly into Paris when I come to Owens. It's also in East Texas."

Quickly, he put Hailey on speaker and pulled up his map app, typing in Sugar Springs and using his location in Owens.

"Hell's bells," he said, laughing. "Laramie Fisher is a little over two hours from where I am right now. Text me her number, Hailey. I'll go see her before I head back to California."

"Don't scare her off," his friend warned. "She seems a little skittish to me, Tanner."

"I can be charming. I'll charm the socks off her."

"What if she doesn't wear socks?" Hailey countered. "Okay, hanging up now. Texting you her number, and I'll get my legal eagles to make everything official."

"Thank you, Hailey," Tanner said, taking her off speakerphone. "Thank you for thinking of me when you read this script. For sending it to me. For somehow getting Laramie Fisher to agree to not only sell her work to me but actually meet with me. You're a miracle worker."

"I can't wait to see what you do with your first film, Tanner. You've always had a great eye for details. I'll send you the specifics of what time we can meet and sign the paperwork once I know more."

"Enjoy Maui and all those little umbrella drinks you like," he said, laughing.

"Bye."

Tanner disconnected the call and stood still a moment, not believing his good fortune. He'd awakened this morning an actor. Now, he had a story to work with, a fantastic one. Ideas poured through him. He did a quick jig and shouted for joy. Brownie bounded to her feet and barked, joining in the celebration.

"I'm going to be a director, girl," he told the dog, grabbing the lab's face in his hands and kissing the dog's head.

He calmed, anxiety suddenly flooding him. "But I've got to call Laramie Fisher first."

What if she didn't like him?

What if, after talking to him, she changed her mind—and killed the deal?

No, that wasn't going to happen. He was going to tell the screenwriter his thoughts and get hers.

And he wanted to do so ASAP.

His phone chimed with a text, and Tanner saw Hailey had forwarded Laramie's number. Before he lost his nerve, he moved to the den and confidently added Laramie Fisher to his contacts—and then boldly added her to his favorites list.

Sitting on the sofa, Brownie bounded up next to him, placing her head in his lap. Absently, Tanner stroked the dog, taking a few calming breaths, and then called the number.

After three rings, he got a guarded, "Hello?" from a low, sultry voice.

"Hello, I'm looking to speak with Laramie Fisher. This is Tanner. Tanner Haddock."

A long pause caused his insides to turn to jelly. Then, "This is Laramie."

Pushing aside his crazy, sudden nerves, Tanner went into full acting mode, exuding a confidence which he didn't feel but could easily mimic.

"It's good to connect with you, Laramie," he said, his voice friendly and self-assured to his ears. "I want to tell you how much I enjoyed reading your script. I'm honored that you would choose me to direct it."

"You agreed to my terms?" she asked softly.

"Yes. Hailey is still headed to Maui to meet up with George, but she said she would have her people draw up the contracts. Consider your script off the market."

"Okay."

"I still would like to meet with you, though."

"It's yours. The screenplay. You can do with it what you want."

Boldly, he said, "What I want is to talk it over with you. Go over it, page by page. Pick your brain. Get your insight into the characters. Incorporate as much of your vision as possible into my own. I'll be honest and tell you that I read it on a flight this morning. I'll definitely read it again tonight and make notes. I plan to do several passes through it. But I'd like your input, Laramie."

"Why?"

She sounded puzzled.

"Because you're the writer."

A nervous laugh sounded. "I've sold two other scripts. Neither director wanted anything to do with me once they had my screenplay in their hands."

"I'm not any director. Yes, I am a first-time director. But I'll have my own way of doing things. A big part of that is collaborating with my screenwriter. Because of that, I'd like to meet with you tomorrow."

"Tomorrow?" she squeaked.

"Yes, tomorrow. I flew into Paris this morning. Paris, Texas. If I would've known I was in your back yard, I would've headed straight to your house. Instead, I came up to Owens. In Oklahoma. It's north of Broken Bow. Have you been there before?"

"I haven't been to Oklahoma since I was a child," she said quietly. "But I was in Owens. Once."

He laughed. "Well, that's more than most people can say. We can talk all about your trip to Owens when we—"

"No." The word came out fast and firm.

"Okay. Well, I'm not that far from you. My phone tells me a little over two hours or so. Can I stop by and see you tomorrow? Would that be convenient?"

"No. It won't be, Mr. Haddock. I've changed my mind. You can buy the script. It's yours. Do with it as you please. I'm out."

Shock poured through him. "Laramie, I'd just—"

She hung up on him.

No one had ever hung up on Tanner Haddock.

He touched her name again. Got her voice mail. What Tanner found interesting was that the message mentioned nothing about Laramie Fisher.

Instead, the recording said, "You've reached Paige Laramie. I can't take your call right now, so please leave me your name and number. I'll get back to you as soon as possible."

He assumed Laramie Fisher was a pen name for Paige Laramie. And Paige Laramie didn't want to talk to him. He hung up without leaving a message that he figured she would probably delete anyway.

First, he Googled Laramie Fisher and found very

little about her. Wikipedia assumed incorrectly that Laramie was male. The brief bio noted the rom-com for Fisher's first effort had been nominated for Best First Screenplay from the Film Independent Spirit Awards. Her second script was now in production. No personal information of any kind was available.

Then he searched for Paige Laramie.

Bingo.

The lone reference Tanner found was that she was on the faculty at Sugar Springs High School, teaching US and World History. That was it. Other than finding her staff picture in the school yearbook, Paige Laramie was like a ghost on the internet.

But a very pretty ghost.

She had honey-blond hair and emerald eyes which seemed to look from the screen into his soul.

"No!" he gasped.

It couldn't be. He stared at the image, long and hard.

He knew Paige Laramie.

Tanner had only heard her name once, just her first name, at that. A long time ago. Twenty years had passed, years in which he had moved on and locked away the memories of a horrifying night, deliberately never thinking of it again because his dad had been shot by a crazy son of a bitch and Tanner hadn't wanted to remember how close he'd come to losing the best man he'd known.

But he knew those eyes. Those incredible emerald eyes. He never forgot those eyes.

Or her.

Paige Laramie was the girl from the diner. Twenty years ago. The girl who had needed his help.

And now she'd come crashing back into his life.

4

P aige awoke early as she did every day. Before school each morning, she ran, usually starting at four and continuing at least for an hour. Sometimes ninety minutes.

It was Sunday, though, and her spring break was next week. She wished she could sleep in, but it just wasn't in her DNA. Nana was an early riser, as well, and her mom had been, too, often taking the breakfast shift at the local diner before heading to her regular job at the restaurant.

A lump formed in her throat. Mama had been gone fourteen years now. They'd had two happy years after Paige had been brought home to Sugar Springs. Then the breast cancer had struck like a thief in the night, ugly and vicious. Mama fought hard and beat it. At least for a while. It recurred as Paige started her sophomore year in high school.

The next July Fourth—Paige's birthday—it took Mama for good.

Paige never celebrated her birthday again.

She hibernated that day. While Sugar Springs held their annual parade and carnival and had a band playing and people setting off fireworks, Paige stayed in her house, in bed, mourning the woman who'd lost the fight for her life at only thirty-seven.

She sat up in bed, picking up her phone and finally turning it on. She'd shut it off immediately after hanging up on Tanner Haddock. He'd probably withdrawn his offer because of her rudeness. That would be a hard one to explain to her agent. But if someone such as Tanner Haddock thought the screenplay was good, then it was really good. Everything the man touched turned to gold, be it the summer movie of the year or a small indie effort. Everything he was involved with turned golden.

His acting work was stellar, and she believed he had the instincts to be a good director. For some reason, she'd always been drawn to his work. He had a quality about him which seemed familiar to her. She snorted. She and the entire female population of the free world had a thing for the rugged Hollywood superstar.

Paige only hoped that he wouldn't somehow blackball Laramie Fisher because she'd cut him off. She hadn't thought about that when she'd hung up. He'd sent her into a tailspin, talking about Owens. Just hearing the name of the town had caused her to have a panic attack. She couldn't talk about Owens. About what happened there. If he were from there, he probably knew what had happened to her anyway. Thank goodness cell phone cameras hadn't been prevalent then and that the diner had been almost empty. Truly, most of what had happened in the diner was a blur.

She remembered the feelings of hopelessness blanketing her, though, as her father had walked her into the diner. Rubbing her palm absently, she thought of how she had carved her one-word message when he handcuffed her to the bed's leg each night so she wouldn't run away. Paige had prayed someone would see it and help her. That it had been another kid hadn't surprised her. Adults rarely saw children. Oh, they saw them—but they truly didn't look at them. As a teacher, she tried to peer into her students' souls and made certain each one knew she did see and value them as individuals.

The boy must have told his father what he'd seen in her palm. Paige did remember the server calling the man *Chief*. How a chill had rushed through her, knowing he was a policeman. How her father had gotten her on her feet to hustle her out.

Then something was said. Her father's arm went up. A loud explosion occurred. And there was lots of blood. So much blood that it turned her stomach. But the blood meant her kidnapper was dead and she could finally go home. A lady had taken her out of the diner, and they'd sat in a car. Then a lot of flashing lights occurred. People showed up. It had started to rain. That had brought her relief, with the car's windows blurred by the rain. She hadn't wanted anyone to see her. She'd called Mama and even now, years later, could hear her mother's voice and the tears and relief from across the miles that separated them.

Paige had asked the woman where they were so she could tell Mama. The woman had said Owens, Oklahoma, and Paige had repeated it. After that, she put her head in the woman's lap and fell asleep, relaxing for the first time since she'd been taken on the road against her will. She couldn't recall how much time passed, only that Mama and Nana were there and they were hugging and crying. Some man said he was a doctor and wanted to examine her. She'd been terrified and pleaded for Mama to stay with her. The doctor looked her over and asked a few questions before he left the room. Then Mama's arms enveloped her.

That was all she recalled.

She couldn't say how they got back to Sugar Springs or even when they did. She just knew she wound up in Nana's house, in her own bed, holding her doll, a Nancy Drew book still under her pillow. She never cried after that day. Ever. To this day, Paige had never cried. Not at Mama's funeral. Not when she graduated and told her friends goodbye as they went their separate ways, most never returning to Sugar Springs.

Glancing down, she saw the message of one missed call. It was from the number that Tanner Haddock had called from. No voicemail. She supposed she'd have to wait to hear from Hailey to see if the actor might still be interested in her script or if he'd given it a hard pass after her boorish behavior.

Paige readied herself for her morning run. She would love to challenge herself and run a marathon, but that would mean leaving Silver Springs, something she never saw herself doing. She had researched, trying to attach a name to what was wrong with her. Agoraphobia was as close as she could come, an abnormal fear of helplessness that produced panic and anxiety. It was a condition that caused those who suffered from it to avoid open or public spaces, remaining chained to their homes, never venturing outside its doors. It didn't quite match her problem, but it was as close as she could come to self-diagnosing her situation. She could go out and do things in Sugar Springs and the immediate surrounding area. She just couldn't leave the town, else she'd suffer a panic attack.

No one had ever offered her counseling after her

ordeal. She was just loved on by Mama and Nana. The principal at the elementary school had assured them that she could move on to fifth grade, even though she hadn't completed the last couple of months of fourth grade. Miss Biggs had stopped by the house and brought her some books to read and offered to tutor her if she felt as if she were behind. It hadn't been necessary. She'd read all the books and then gone back to school a few weeks later, never missing a beat. She was still the best student in her class, especially since Danny Henderson's dad had gotten a job at a bank in Houston, and they had moved after the school year ended.

Once she'd finished dressing, she drank a couple of glasses of water to hydrate herself and then stretched for ten minutes before setting out. The sun wasn't up, but she was familiar with the streets of town after years of pounding the pavement. She ran several blocks to the town square and circled it before veering off north.

When she passed her grandmother's small cottage, she waved. Nana was sitting on the porch, newspaper in one hand and a cup of coffee in the other.

"See you for dinner tonight!" Paige called as she passed.

She ran for close to two hours, longer than usual, but she had nowhere to be today. No papers to grade since she'd taken care of all classroom housekeeping before she left school on Friday, spring break a welcomed relief. The academic year was three-quarters of the way done. She just had to keep the wandering attention of hormonal teenagers for one last grading period, and then school would be out. Her principal had asked if she would teach summer school, but she'd turned him down. She already had ideas for a new screenplay and thought she could outline and get most of the first draft done before school was out for the year. She'd spend her summer finishing up on it and then tweaking it to perfection before preparing for another year in the classroom.

When she returned to the center of town, she slowed and walked the square twice, gradually cooling down before she made a quick stop at Ida Lou's. The diner's owner and namesake placed a glass of water on the counter, and Paige gulped it down.

"Usual?" Ida Lou asked.

"I'm splurging. It's spring break. Make it a hot tea *and* a sausage roll."

"Ooh, living the high life, Paige," the owner teased as she poured hot water into a Styrofoam cup and dunked a teabag into it before placing a lid over it. Then she retrieved the roll.

"No bag needed," she said, grabbing a napkin from the dispenser on the counter. "I plan to eat this baby on my way home."

Ida Lou placed the yeasty roll on the napkin and handed over the tea. "I'll put it on your tab."

"Thanks."

Paige left the diner, sinking her teeth into the sausage roll, which had to be one of her favorite things on the planet. The roll was tasty and fluffy, the spiced sausage cooked to perfection. She finished it and dabbed her mouth with the paper napkin, wadding it up and slipping it into her pocket as she walked home, sipping on her tea every few houses.

Turning the corner, she saw an unfamiliar truck parked on the street in front of her house. A chill ran through her. The black truck looked nothing like the one her father had stolen in his mad dash from Sugar Springs, trying to exact revenge on an ex-wife by taking Paige away. Sometimes, she believed it was a miracle that he hadn't simply killed her outright in order to punish Mama. But she had never ridden in a truck since that day.

As she approached warily, she saw the silhouette of a man sitting in the truck, causing her alarm system to go straight to Defcon 5. She slowed, wondering if she should make a dash for her front door or simply turn and go around the block, coming in through the back yard instead.

Then he got out and turned, looking straight at her. There was no mistaking him for anyone else. The visitor was here for her. How he'd found out where she lived, much less in such a short amount of time, spoke to the power he wielded.

Paige approached him as he stepped from the street onto the sidewalk. With a bravado that she didn't feel, she smiled coolly.

"Hello, Mr. Haddock. I suppose you just happened to be in the neighborhood and thought to stop by for a chat."

TANNER ENTERED Sugar Springs around six-thirty Sunday morning. The sun wouldn't be up for almost another hour this time of year. He listened to the directions Siri gave, spoken in a British accent. Reg—Reginald Hyde-Smythe—had programmed his phone, making it as secure as possible. Reg, being a Brit, thought it great fun to have Siri speak as a Brit. Reg had headed up Tanner's security for several years, protecting the Malibu estate, all Tanner's electronic devices, and providing muscle for public appearances. Discreetly, of course.

When he decided he had to see Paige Laramie in person, he'd turned to Reg. Besides being a former special forces officer in the British army, working in intelligence, surveillance, and reconnaissance, Reg was a computer genius. He never had used the word hacker—and Tanner had never asked him to find anyone before—but he knew Reg had mad tech skills and would be able to track down Paige Laramie without breaking a sweat.

He'd called Reg, who was on holiday in Ireland, explaining that he needed the address for the screenwriter whose script he'd just bought, telling his security head that while he had her cell number and was supposed to meet with Paige the next day, he'd carelessly lost the address. He told Reg the writer was quirky and didn't usually take phone calls, preferring to do business over email, and was afraid she wouldn't see a message from him.

"What else you got on her, mate?"

Tanner provided the two names—real and pseudonym—the cell number, the name of Paige's town, and the high school where she taught. Half an hour later, Reg called back with a wealth of information. Not only did he have the address, but Reg had also found articles going back to Paige's years in high school.

And the incident in Owens.

Reg had met Jeff on a few occasions and mentioned he was sending Tanner all he'd found on the teacher turned screenwriter, saying that Chief Haddock was mentioned prominently in several of the articles about the little kidnapped girl who'd been rescued in Owens.

"I was there," Tanner had revealed, not elaborating

on the situation. "Just send what you have. And thanks, Reg. I know you're on holiday."

"Any time, mate. You pay me so bloody well as it is. This was child's play."

Deliberately, Tanner had left his phone at his house, heading for dinner with his family. It had been wonderful to see his sister, who had revealed she was ten weeks pregnant. His sister loved kids. He couldn't think of a better person to become a mom.

After their lasagna dinner, they'd talked another hour, then Tanner had yawned a few times and said he was ready to hit the sack. His dad asked whether he might want to go fishing the next day, but he said he simply wanted to sleep and loaf for a few days. His family knew how tired he was after a hard, long shoot. They would think nothing of it.

When he returned to his house, he combed through everything Reg had sent and knew he would drive to Sugar Springs, Texas, the next morning. After getting a few hours of sleep, he was up at four, making coffee and cooking eggs and bacon. He jumped into the shower and was on the road by a quarter till five.

"Turn left," British Siri instructed.

Tanner followed the directions and found Paige Laramie's street, parking in front of her house. No lights were on, though a few of her neighbors' houses had activity going on, with two claiming newspapers lying on their sidewalks and another pair leaving to walk a golden retriever.

Reg had been so thorough that he'd even sent the Sugar Springs High School academic calendar. Tanner had noted that the coming week was spring break for the district and worried that Paige might not even be in town. Or that he'd spooked her with his call and she'd taken off, not wanting to see him if he did show up.

He understood now why his mention of Owens had caused her to shut down. Hell, he had tried to push any memory of it away for years. He couldn't imagine being in her shoes. The articles Reg had attached about what had gone down in the diner had been eye-opening, written by a reporter who'd cobbled the account together talking to various sources. No one from the press had ever spoken to him. Tanner couldn't help but wonder about that and believed that his parents must have shielded him from being interviewed.

Reading the account of the incident as an adult, he had a greater understanding of the events. Still, he got why Paige Laramie didn't want to think about Owens, Oklahoma, and what had occurred there.

Did she know he'd been the one in the diner?

He hoped to find out soon.

Waiting for a light to come on the house, he studied the neighborhood. Every yard was neat. The houses all looked well maintained. No peeling paint or junky cars sitting in driveways. Just a quiet, manicured street in a small East Texas town.

Movement caught his eye, and he glanced in his rearview mirror. A woman was coming down the sidewalk with a cup in her hand, dressed in athletic gear. His gut told him it was Paige.

Tanner exited his truck and watched her approach. Her body language spoke of her wariness of a stranger parked in front of her house, yet somehow she still exuded confidence. She wore a long-sleeved shirt with a Dallas Cowboys logo on the front and tights that showed off shapely legs and running shoes. She wasn't tall, no more than a few inches over five feet, but her compact frame told him she did more than run.

She closed the distance between them. Her hair was swept into a high ponytail, and those emerald eyes jolted him back to a place he'd never thought to visit again.

"Hello, Mr. Haddock," she said, her voice low and slightly sarcastic in tone. "I suppose you just happened to be in the neighborhood and thought to stop by for a chat."

"Good morning, Miss Laramie," he said formally. "I was hoping you would have some time for me. Especially since you're on spring break."

"Hollywood did his homework, I see." Her tone had shifted to annoyed.

"You can call me Tanner," he said, his smile open and friendly, hoping to win her trust.

"And you can leave me the hell alone," she snapped, turning and crossing her lawn.

Tanner hadn't come this far to see her walk away. He strode after her, touching her shoulder.

And somehow found himself flat on his back, staring up at her, moments later. Her foot was on his throat, exuding moderate pressure.

"What the hell?" he rasped.

"Krav Maga," she said, retrieving the Styrofoam cup which had fallen to the ground in her sudden assault. "Be glad I stopped. Principles say I should strike my opponent until he is completely incapacitated." She smiled. "No one is here. No one saw anything. The great action star Tanner Haddock doesn't have to be embarrassed that he was taken down by a much shorter woman."

She removed her foot and took a step back. He sat

up and shook his head, then he realized she had already gone past him.

Quickly, he came to his feet and called, "Wait, Paige."

She stopped. Turned and faced him. "I did not want you to come to Sugar Springs, Mr. Haddock. You were not invited by me to come, and you are not welcomed," she said evenly. "If you still want to purchase my script, I am grateful. But I have nothing to say to you, about it or anything else. Goodbye."

Wheeling, she hurried to her front door. He had to stop her before she got in the house, or he knew he would have lost all chance of speaking with her.

"I'm the boy," he shouted in desperation. "The boy —from the diner. In Owens." He swallowed, praying she would react.

She did. She froze, her body so still that he held his breath, wondering if she had heard him. Then she turned gradually, as if she were in slow motion. Her jaw was slack. He saw tears brimming in her eyes.

Carefully, Tanner approached her, every step cautious and measured. She watched him, her lips moving silently, no words uttered aloud.

When he came to stand in front of her, she bit her lip, trying to keep from crying, but the tears already streamed down her cheeks. He reached out, his fingers brushing them away.

Her gaze intensified. It was as if Paige Laramie saw through to his soul.

"You *are* that boy," she said, wonder in her voice. "I never thought I would see you again."

Without warning, she threw herself at him, her arms locking tightly about him. Automatically, his arms came around her. He caught a faint scent of vanilla and the sweat from her run.

"Thank you," Paige whispered. "Thank you. For saving me. For helping me to come home again."

They remained in an embrace for a long moment, and then she pulled away, blinking back tears. She smiled, a genuine smile, one that caused a warmth to grow inside him.

"Would you like to come in, Tanner Haddock?" she asked shyly.

He returned her smile. "I believe I would, Paige Laramie."

5

Paige moved to her front door, numbly pulling the key from her pocket and sliding it into the lock. She opened the door and entered her house, quickly glancing about, seeing it through the eyes of Tanner Haddock. Silently, she berated herself for doing so.

Why should she care what some shallow superstar thought about her living room?

She turned and saw that Tanner had followed her inside. That he had paused at the mantle and picked up a picture, one of her with Mama and Nana. Fresh tears sprang to her eyes, the feeling odd after so many years of no tears at all.

He turned and looked at her. "This is your mom and grandmother. You were so eager to call them that night."

Blinking rapidly, Paige nodded. "Yes. I had missed them terribly. A lady took me outside and let me use her phone to call them." She paused. "I suppose that was your mother."

He nodded. "We were eating a late dinner in the diner that night when you came in. We'd been at a baseball tournament all day." His face softened, and he smiled wistfully. "I had pitched my first no-hitter. My birthday was also coming up, and Dad let me order a chocolate soda to celebrate it and the win."

Tanner placed the framed photo back on the mantle, and she asked, "Would you like to have a seat?"

"Sure."

He sat on her couch, and she perched on the edge of it, nerves running through her. Her knees began bouncing up and down from her legs trembling, and she pushed them down, flattening her palms and forcing her legs to stay still.

"I'll apologize for my earlier surliness," Paige began.

"You don't need to. You weren't expecting me. I took a chance in showing up." He smiled, the smile which caused women across America to sigh in darkened movie theaters. "I hoped if I came in person, you wouldn't turn me away."

"You mentioned that you landed in Paris yesterday."

"I fly into there when I come home to see my family. I would prefer landing at Callaham in Broken Bow, but they don't have pumps for planes to refuel there. Usually, my pilot, my friend Ron, heads back to California after dropping me off. He did so yesterday and is headed to Scandinavia now on vacation. He serves not only as my pilot and friend but my stunt double."

"Do you visit your family often?" she asked. "Your parents?"

Her thoughts took her back to that night. To the tall man who resembled the one now seated next to her. She could see his arm rise, gun in hand. Suddenly, Paige flinched, hearing the explosion again all these years later.

Tanner Haddock placed a hand over hers. "It's

okay," he assured her. "I know my presence is bringing back memories of that night."

She swallowed, more tears running down her face, and slipped her hand from his in order to brush them away.

"I haven't cried in forever. I'm sorry I'm like a sudden rainstorm, weeping like this."

"Cry all you want, Paige. I'm sure your memories are painful. Hell, they are for me, too."

She hadn't thought about that. He had been a boy, a few years older than she was, and seen his father shot in front of him.

"You must have been terrified by what happened," she said sympathetically.

He nodded. "My dad was—still is—the police chief in Owens. As you can imagine, it's a tiny place. Sugar Springs seems like a metropolis compared to Owens," he joked. "Intellectually, I knew police work could be dangerous, but it never seemed to be in a little place like Owens. That night, I was aware of Dad being shot. Of how close he came to dying."

Tanner shook his head. "No, I don't mean the bullet wound he suffered put him in any kind of grave danger. It hurt like hell and he did rehab on his shoulder, but it was obvious he was going to live even before the ambulance arrived. But I finally realized it could have been life-threatening. I'd always taken my folks for granted. After that, I suppose I learned to cherish them. Love them more deeply. That's why after every movie I shoot, I come home to them in Owens. To relax and recharge. And be with them."

He brightened. "My sister's there, too. She teaches kindergarten. She's pregnant. Ten weeks," he said proudly.

"You'll make a fantastic uncle," Paige told him.

"I hope so."

"Your parents are doing well?" she asked.

"Dad's great. Still loves police work. I have no idea if he has any plans to retire anytime soon. Mom trains horses, along with my brother-in-law. In Owens, Helen Haddock is the one who gets all the attention, not me. She's had two winning horses in the Kentucky Derby over the years and one each in the Belmont and Preakness. How about you? Do your mom and grandmother still live in Sugar Springs?"

Her eyes flicked to the picture on the mantle. She stood and retrieved it, sitting once again next to Tanner. Brushing her fingers along the photograph, she smiled.

"This was taken two years after I came home." She swallowed the lump which had formed in her throat. "It was just before Mama got her cancer diagnosis."

She felt him still beside her and he asked, "Did she make it?"

Her heart grew heavy as she shared, "It was breast cancer. Mama beat it once, but it took everything out of her. She was never the same physically. She grew quieter. It came back when I was fifteen. Ferocious and fast. Mama didn't have the strength to fight it off a second time."

A tear rolled down her cheek. "She died when I was sixteen."

Again, his hand covered hers. "I'm so sorry, Paige."

"She was only thirty-seven when she died. Nana and I clung to each other. I lived with her until I was twenty-five." She mustered a smile. "Then she kicked me out. Told me I had a job and a life to live, and it was time I was on my own." Shrugging, she added, "So, I bought this place."

His gaze traveled along the room. "It's nice. Cozy. It looks lived in."

She chuckled. "That's a nice way of you saying that all the furniture is worn and obviously secondhand."

"I wouldn't have guessed that. Things look well cared for."

"I redid a lot of it, with help from my friends Vivi and Sarah."

A silence fell between them, but it wasn't an awkward one. His hand still covered hers, and it felt good. Right. But she had never physically been close to any man and abruptly stood, confused by the feelings rushing through her.

"Can I get you something to drink? Coffee? Iced tea?"

"Actually, coffee would be great."

"Give me a few minutes then."

It surprised Paige when he followed her into the kitchen and took a seat at the table, watching her turn on the coffee maker.

"Would you like some breakfast? If you drove here from Owens, I doubt you stopped along the way because nothing would have been open."

"Do you have bacon and eggs?" he asked.

"I do, Hollywood. Are you telling me you know how to cook them?"

That earth-shattering smile appeared again. "Breakfast is one thing I can make. Scrambled or fried? Dealer's choice."

She laughed. "Over easy for me. And two pieces of bacon."

While Paige got out a skillet for him, he moved to the refrigerator, removing what he needed. As the coffee brewed, he cracked eggs and flipped sizzling bacon while she toasted bread, setting out butter and jam on the table. She couldn't get over how easy things seemed between them. He was a stranger—and yet he had played the most important role in her life, helping her return to Sugar Springs and her loved ones.

Tanner dished up the bacon and eggs and brought their plates to the table, taking a seat.

"I said it before, but I feel as if I need to say it again. I want to thank you for being so brave that night. If you hadn't intervened, I don't know if I would be alive today," she revealed.

He gazed intently at her. "You think he would have killed you?"

"I know he would have. He was getting tired of constantly being on the move and on guard. He told me that he didn't love me. That he'd only taken me to piss off Mama. They had divorced a few months before it all happened. He was the kind of man who didn't want her to be happy."

He reached for her hand, turning it so her palm faced up. He searched for the message he had once seen, and his fingertip traced the faint letters still showing.

"I was scared for you," he admitted. "I watched you in the parking lot and when you came into the diner, something was off."

"I appreciate you doing what you did. Speaking up. And your mom and dad, too. I'm sorry I got him shot."

A fierceness came into Tanner's eyes. "Never say that. Your dad is the one who shot mine. You are blameless."

"Your mother was very kind to me. I'll admit that I haven't thought much about that night. I didn't want to dwell on it. It's mostly a blur, as are the months I spent with him on the run. After I came home, I never wanted to talk about it, and I didn't. Seeing you has brought it all back now. I can't believe I never recognized you all those times I was sitting in a movie theatre. Your eyes are so distinctive. I wonder why I didn't remember that."

She shook her head. "But I pushed away every memory of that night. I had to—to survive—and to keep Mama and Nana happy."

He squeezed her fingers. "You never had any therapy? Or talked about it with anyone?"

Paige withdrew her hand, placing it in her lap. "Come on, Hollywood. You grew up in Owens. Did your school have a psychiatrist or someone who did talk therapy with students, much less with a traumatized child kidnapped by her own father?"

"No, you're right. Have you ever thought about seeing someone now? Talking about what happened to you?"

She lowered her gaze and softly said, "No. Those services still aren't available around here. No one ever suggested it. For me, the fact that I was home with a loving mother and grandmother was therapy enough. Mama and Nana never brought it up—and neither did I."

"Well, it seems like you turned out all right. I know you're a teacher. I Googled you. And obviously, you have a side gig which you are very good at. I saw the Knox Monroe indie film. And that you got a Spirit Awards nom for writing it."

She met his gaze again. "Other than writing the script, I had nothing to do with that film. Hailey sold it, and that was the last I heard. I finally saw it when it came to Netflix."

Surprise filled his face. "You didn't go to the movie premiere? Or drive to Dallas to see it?"

"No," she informed him, ashamed that she didn't go anywhere. "Hailey's sold another screenplay of mine. It's in pre-production now. Once again, it's out of my hands. I suppose that's why I was shocked that you wanted to meet with me."

"I needed to meet with you," he said earnestly. "I told you this will be my directorial debut. I've been a student on every set I've worked on for years, trying to learn as much about my craft and that of others, preparing for this day. When Hailey sent me your script, I knew it was the one I had to do."

He raked a hand through his thick, dark hair. "We both come from small towns, Paige. We understand that vibe. I meant what I said earlier. I would like to go through every page of your work with you and pick your brain. Get your thoughts. I want to merge your vision with mine and create the best film I possibly can. I think directors who ignore or don't work close with the writer are fools."

Tanner cleared his throat. "I know you're on your spring break and might already have plans."

"I don't," she admitted, not sure why she told him that. In fact, she had shared more about herself in a handful of minutes than she had with anyone else her entire life. Even as close as she and Vivi were, they had never once talked about that night in Owens.

He smiled warmly. "Then I will pay you for your time this coming week, Laramie Fisher."

She smiled, hearing him call her by her pseudonym. "Well, Hollywood, I don't know if you can afford me," she teased. "And I'm not sure if your check has cleared or not."

Tanner grinned. "Hailey told me I could pursue

things as if it had. Once her legal team drafts the docs, it'll be a done deal. Will you trust me enough for us to start working on the project this week?"

He stuck out his hand. Paige hesitated a moment and then took it. They shook hands and tingles rippled through her.

Don't fall for him, she told herself. *He may be a boy from a small town, but he's been a creature in Hollywood all these years. He's only making me feel special because he wants something from me.*

Determination filled her as she said, "I'll give you this coming week—and then we're done."

6

T anner stood. "Let me go and grab my copy of the script. I left it in my truck."

Paige looked at him, baffled. "You want to start *now*?"

"If I only have you for a week, then the week starts immediately. I realize you have your own life. Teaching. Writing. Family and friends. If you're willing to give me a week of your time, then I need to squeeze as much out of you as I possibly can."

He left the house and went to his truck, claiming the script which Hailey Madison had delivered to him only a day ago. He wondered about Paige. While initially she had hugged him—that is, after knocking him flat on his ass—she had pulled away both times he had initiated physical contact with her, placing his hand on hers to offer comfort. Knowing the trauma she had experienced, as well as learning that she had never received any kind of therapy regarding it, told him she still had multiple issues to deal with all these years later.

And that he could never become involved with her.

Tanner had a policy of not dating anyone he

worked with. He didn't care if a woman happened to be the producer or his makeup artist. He never mixed business with pleasure.

Yet he felt such a strong pull toward Paige. Perhaps it was merely because they had experienced something together which left an indelible mark upon both of them. Their own interaction had been brief, but the incident had marked them in ways that could never be comprehended by others. While he had gone on in a stable environment with two loving parents and a supportive sister, as well as a town which cheered his every achievement, Paige's life had been torn apart. The man she had called father had betrayed her in ways she would never understand. She'd had to deal with the death of her mother, as well. She'd bottled up everything that had happened to her and stored it in a place which she was now having to revisit with him coming to Sugar Springs.

It had to be unnerving for her to have him here, out of the blue, much less working with him. He admired her strength and courage, as well as her creativity.

Returning to her doorstep, Tanner opened the door, finding Paige in the same spot on the sofa where he had left her. She had a faraway look in her eyes, as if she didn't even realize he was present again.

Clearing his throat, he asked, "Do you have a highlighter? And a pen I can use?"

She came out of her reverie and stood. "You're asking a teacher for supplies?" She smiled. "Already coming unprepared, Hollywood. That's a strike against you."

He laughed as he took a seat again and she left the room, returning almost immediately with a package of highlighters and several pens and pencils.

"I don't have a copy printed out anymore," she informed him. "But I usually print one several times during my writing and editing process. I use various highlighters to note passages I need to revise."

"Then we'll simply have to share."

He settled his back against the sofa, and she sat, closer this time. He thought of her as a feral cat. One had shown up on their ranch when he was about seven or eight years old. His mom had begun feeding it, explaining to Tanner how the cat wasn't tame and could even be dangerous. She said it might have been born in the wild or had been dumped and had to learn survival skills on its own. The cat was thin and wary but obviously hungry. Over time, Mom was able to reduce the distance between them and the creature. After several weeks, Helen Haddock finally got the cat within petting distance. It took another month, but the cat eventually would come to his mom when called. Only her, though.

It remained with them for many years, acting as a mouser in the horse barn. But it always remained a little wild, disappearing for days at a time. It would only allow Tanner to pet it if his mom were present.

Paige reminded him of that feral cat from long ago, teetering on the edge of fleeing every time they had an encounter. He needed to make sure he remained all business with her.

Even though the urge to kiss her grew stronger by the minute.

That thought knocked him on his back as much as she had done. He never had to approach women. They always came to him. Even back in elementary school, the girls flocked to him, passing him notes, asking him to check a box if he liked them or not. He had dated many women over the years, most casual relationships, a couple of times deeper ones which hadn't lasted, but he'd never found a woman he wished to spend the rest of his life with. His gut told him to leave Paige Laramie alone.

Yet the thought of her tugged on his heartstrings. He didn't know if it were because they had shared an experience so unique that most others would never understand or if he were truly physically attracted to her. Still, he tamped down all those feelings and used his acting skills to play his current role of a first-time director meeting with his screenwriter.

"You've called it *Midnight in the Shadows*," he began. "I love the title, but I was toying with something else."

She shrugged, retreating within herself. "You bought it. Call it whatever you want. I remember reading a story once about an old TV show called *The Love Boat*. The producers fell in love with that title, but there was a nonfiction book with the name *The Love Boats*. They bought the book for that title. Do whatever you want with the screenplay. You own it now."

"And I've told *you* that I'm looking for a collaboration. Yes, I have some ideas that I want to run by you. I have a few things I'd like to tweak, but I want to get to know your characters. I realize everything about them didn't make it to the page. That you have a lot of stuff in your head that I can use when I'm prepping my actors for a scene and helping give them the motivation they need. I don't want to change your work, Paige. I only want to enhance it."

Tanner cleared his throat, hoping to transition now. "I said I liked your title, and I mean it, but I have another one in mind." He paused. "What about *Shadows of the Past*?"

He let the title change settle in with her and could almost see the wheels turning in her head.

"You're right," she agreed. "I like the idea of shadows because they're so fluid. They can look like one thing and be something totally different. That's Peter Willoughby's character to a T. But Gwen only knows him as the guy from her past. She comes to discover who he truly is, what he truly was, even all those years ago. Gwen knew the best parts of him, but he kept his darkness hidden from her."

Paige was on a roll, and Tanner let her continue, soaking up every word she uttered.

"You see, I don't believe an antagonist is all bad. Same thing with a protagonist. A hero isn't all good. He can't be. Humans are complex beings, made up of so many different parts. While Peter is a serial killer, one with a traumatic past, he's been able to cover it up. He's hidden it from everyone, even himself, for a long time. It's only after he leaves their small town that other terrible things happen to him. He lashes out, allowing the evil within him to flourish."

She paused, and he nodded. "Go on."

"Peter somehow still salvages the parts of him that Gwen brought out. The best parts. She's pure. Innocent. She loved him in the past. Sure, she only loved the parts he let her see—but she loved him, all the same. No one else ever has. That first teenage love can be extremely powerful. I know adults think of it as puppy love, but it really was real to these two. It marked them. When they went their separate ways after graduation, she took that relationship and what she had learned from it, using it to become a better person, while he dwelled on his loneliness and the fact he'd lost her. Losing Gwen was something that fed the darkness within him. He let her go because it was what *she* wanted, but possession became an incredible idea to him. When he kills, yes, he does experience the thrill of the kill. More than that, however, Peter experiences ultimate possession—power—over these women."

He took a moment to take in all that she'd said. "I'm blown away by what you're revealing about both these characters. Some of that made the page, but a lot of it didn't, just as I'd thought. You've already given me insight into both of them. It will shape my thinking about them. How I'll cast them."

Tanner scribbled a few notes on the first page of the script. "I have never played a villain. I've always been the good guy. One who saves the day. Or the world. One that saves a woman and falls in love with her. I've never had to climb into the skin of an antagonist. As a director, I need to do so. Your point about Peter being not all bad resonates with me. It humanizes him. I think if I can bring that out, audiences will connect with him. They won't want him to be bad—even when he is. They will understand him more, though, because of all the shades of gray within him. The darker shades will dominate, of course, turning him into something frightening."

"Hailey mentioned that you might want to play Peter. Are you still considering it?"

Tanner blew out a long breath. "Actually, I haven't had time to think much about it at all. My focus is on directing the film."

"Don't you see how you'd be perfect for the role?" she insisted.

He laughed. "You think I'm a serial killer in the making?"

"Be serious, Hollywood. You have an image. You could play off that image. Audiences *do* think of you as the ultimate good guy. They are supposed to have mixed feelings about Peter. Your reputation could feed into their ambivalence. They'll want to like our heroine. They'll want to make her happy. She's suffered a tragedy in her life and is finally looking for love once again. She understands the healing power of love. If you are Peter, audiences will immediately trust you the moment you appear on screen."

Excitement filled him. "I see your point. Then they'll grow—as will their horror—when they begin to see exactly what I'm capable of. Peter, that is."

"Yes," Paige said enthusiastically. "You're beginning to understand. Play against type. Sucker them in. Make them trust you. Then let Peter's true colors peel away like layers of an onion. They come in loving you. They'll feel Gwen's hurt and want Peter to make her world right. Their feelings for you transfer to Peter. And then you lower the boom. Gradually, of course. Tease it. Make them doubt themselves, just as Gwen doubts herself at first when things with Peter don't quite add up."

Once more, Tanner furiously scribbled down several thoughts, hoping he would be able to read what he'd written.

"I read it straight through on the plane yesterday. For plot—and to see if I might be interested since Hailey was so high on it. Last night, I read it again, still quickly, but making some notes. I'll need to read through it numerous times more slowly and expand upon those notes. For now, can we move through and discuss my first impression and generalities?"

"It's your rodeo, Hollywood. You said you're paying for my time. I'm all yours."

A part of him wished she could be.

He turned the page and a few beyond that before

getting to his first notation. Tanner asked her a question, and she clarified a point for him. He made new notes, writing as quickly as he could, thinking he might need to record their conversations instead so he wouldn't miss anything. Something told him, though, that Paige Laramie would object to that.

They went through the entire script, addressing the major questions he had, based upon his notes from the two times he'd read through the material.

"Many more questions have come to my mind," he told her. "I need to do another pass through it before I can vocalize them, though. A slow read. A deep dive. I do one after accepting a role, trying to get to know the characters as much as possible, mine and the ones I interact with."

Tanner glanced at his watch. "It's a little before noon now. I'd like to adjourn and regroup. Maybe come back around six. I could pick up some dinner, and we could work tonight if it's all right with you."

Paige's brow furrowed. "Actually, I'm due at Nana's at six tonight. We have dinner every Sunday."

"Could I invite myself along? It's been a long time since I've spent time in a small town. I want to soak up Sugar Springs as much as I can. Something tells me that your grandmother would be an excellent cook, as well as a great resource on small town life."

"Nana adores cooking for others, especially baking. She would love to have you for dinner. But did you bring a week's worth of clothes with you when you left Oklahoma this morning?"

Tanner cursed under his breath. "I hadn't thought about that. I do need to go home and get some clothes. Explain to Mom and Dad and Alana that I'm going to be in Texas for at least a week. Where's a good place to stay?"

She didn't speak for a long moment and then said, "I have a spare bedroom. It's not much. Actually, it serves as my office. There's a daybed in it. You're welcome to stay with me. In fact, I think it would be best if you did so."

"You seem to be a very private person, Paige. I don't want to overstep and invade your space."

She rolled her eyes at him, and he thought she resembled her students when they heard a pop quiz was coming up.

"Do you even realize who you are, Hollywood? The minute you went to our one motel or a local bed and breakfast, news would spread like wildfire throughout Sugar Springs and beyond. You have one of the most famous faces on the planet. We would never get any work done." She paused. "Besides, no one knows that I'm Laramie Fisher."

That surprised him. "Not even your grandmother? Or Vivi and Sarah?" he asked, naming the two friends she had mentioned previously.

She pursed her lips, only making them look more kissable. He shoved that thought aside.

"I'll give you this. You do listen. That alone will make you a good director in the long run. The answer to your question, however, is no. I teach. I grade papers. I run. I participate in a few community activities. No one has a clue I've written, much less sold, two screenplays. I took a pseudonym in order to maintain my privacy. Draw a line between who I am here in Sugar Springs and the person who writes on the side. I made peanuts on the first screenplay, but the one in pre-production now was a great payday. I paid off my mortgage and bought Nana and me new iPads. Nana is crazy about the Internet."

Paige gazed steadily at him. "I prefer to remain

anonymous. I don't want students distracted and asking me about movies when I've got a slew of material to get through before the state testing starts. I don't want others to gawk at me in the grocery store. And I sure as hell don't want people coming out of the woodwork, asking for loans." She took a deep breath. "Okay, you can come to dinner tonight. I'll even share with Nana what I've been up to. But that's as far as it goes, Hollywood. You've got to lie low while you're here because I still want to have my life when you leave here."

"I can do that. I look forward to meeting Nana. I can make it back to Owens a little after two. Take an hour to talk to Mom and Dad and pack a few things. I could be back here by five. Five-thirty at the latest." He smiled. "In time to make it to Nana's to dinner by six. Or should I say supper?"

Paige laughed. "You are in Texas. Small town people eat supper. All right, Hollywood. Go back to Oklahoma and grab your things. I'll see you here when you get back."

"Thanks for letting me bunk with you. You're right. My staying in town would be a distraction and hard to explain when I started hanging out with you eighteen hours a day."

Tanner stood. Paige did, as well, walking him to the door.

"I appreciate you agreeing to work with me over your spring break. I believe that our collaboration will make the difference in this project being successful."

He bent and brushed his lips against her cheek, the contact between them causing a rush of desire to flood him. He sensed her shiver.

"See you soon," he promised, hurrying out the door.

As he got into his truck, his heart pounded in double time. He told himself he would not make a mistake and kiss her. He would keep things professional and friendly.

At least until filming ending. It might be a year or longer before that happened.

When it did, he would see if Paige Laramie might like to explore the possibility of seeing what was between them.

Because she had to be feeling what he did.

Paige finished printing out a copy of *Midnight in the Shadows*. No, *Shadows of the Past*. Tanner had called that one perfectly. It kept the word shadows in play, which she liked, but it also would hint at how the past colors the present. And future.

What was in her future?

For years, Paige had rolled along a calm river, stroking her oar occasionally, letting the flow of the water do all the work. She liked her low-key, uneventful life. Excelled at teaching. Mentored other faculty members. Did volunteer work. Had a few close friends and Nana.

When that hadn't proved to be enough, she'd taken up her pen and begun writing. Fiction, at first, and then she'd branched out, taking an online course on screenwriting. She liked the terseness of that art form. How one page of a script equaled one minute of screen time. How she had to capture everything possible while using only a few words. It was challenging. Rewarding. Screenwriting filled a hole that she hadn't known existed.

Until Tanner Haddock showed up—and she realized she had a way bigger hole inside her.

Until her father had kidnapped her, Paige had been a friendly, outgoing child. An excellent student but full of mischief and playfulness. When she finally came home after those harrowing months, her entire personality had changed. She still wanted to excel in the classroom, but she was reserved. Watchful. Even timid. Being back in Sugar Springs helped her heal, though. She became more confident—but never let her guard down. She kept only a handful of friends and was fiercely loyal to them.

Then her mother had grown fatally ill, and Paige had withdrawn even more deeply into herself. She grew impatient with shallow small talk. Being around others, other than Vivi, caused her to feel irritable and emotionally and physically drained. She hadn't dated much and when she did, she preferred double dating with Vivi and her boyfriend, feeling safer in a small group. Her high school years had been a lot of studying and working at the local library, especially after her mom's death.

She'd earned her degree and continued to remain in Sugar Springs. Teaching had taught her to act, what she called doing five live shows a day in front of what sometimes could be a hostile audience. While she was an introvert, Paige had forced herself to become an ambivert, something she'd studied about in a psych class. Ambiverts fell into the middle of the social spectrum. While most enjoyed solitude and quiet, they could adapt in social situations and become open, even gregarious.

That was her school persona. She was friendly, open, and welcoming to all, students and faculty alike. Paige always had a ready smile and helping hand for anyone. She was personable and outgoing with her students and doubted any of them would suspect her introverted tendencies. When she arrived home after a day of teaching, though, she craved the quiet and time alone, so much that she had never even gotten a pet for company. She cherished her house and not having to share it with anyone. She could unwind. Change into an oversized shirt and leggings. Eat cereal for dinner. Grade papers and then binge on the latest Netflix series.

Then writing began to consume her. It became the focus in her life. Though she was still an excellent teacher, she soon lived to write. It was fun, having this secret, creating worlds from her imagination all on her own. It didn't matter that she'd never had a serious boyfriend or that she wasn't married with kids. Her kids were her characters.

Tanner Haddock had changed all this in one meeting.

She'd watched his long, lean fingers as he pointed out something on the page. Listened to the deep rumble of his voice. Stolen glances at his perfect profile. Inhaled the subtle cologne lingering on his tanned skin.

For the first time in her life, Paige wanted a man. She wanted to kiss him. Hold him. Be held by him. She wanted to touch Tanner's incredible body, exploring every place she could find. She understood the basics of sex. She'd read about it in books. Watched it on the screen. But at thirty, she was a never-been-kissed virgin, à la Josie Geller, just like the old Drew Barrymore movie.

"It is laughable to think that a sexy, confident Tanner Haddock would ever think of you in a romantic light, Laramie," she told herself aloud.

Hearing the words made her thoughts laughable.

No man who looked like Tanner Haddock would ever be the least bit interested in her.

"Focus on the work," she said. "The screenplay. That's what's important. Help him understand Peter and Gwen. Help him realize his dream of directing. His success might very well reflect and become her success. If his directing debut hit the right notes, it could only encourage others to seek out her work."

She agreed with every word she said—and still felt miserable.

What if *she* kissed *him*? Once. Or maybe twice. Of course, it would have to be at the end of this week. He would waltz out of her life at that time. She'd never have the kind of access to him in the future that she did now. Maybe she could play it off as a goodbye kiss. Maybe that was a Hollywood thing. Didn't people in Tinseltown go around smooching or air kissing one another as a greeting and farewell?

"Oh, this is so frustrating!" she shouted, aggravated that she was thinking such crazy, stupid thoughts.

She went to do something productive, putting clean sheets on her bed, a Sunday habit. She was going to offer him her bedroom. Having him stay here would keep their work private, but the daybed would never be comfortable for his long frame. It would easily fit her, though.

After she'd tidied the house, Paige jumped into the shower, finally washing away the morning run. She couldn't believe she'd sat next to Tanner after having run for a couple of hours. She must have reeked. Again, another embarrassing reason to add to what would most likely be a growing list of things that would turn off a man such as Hollywood's leading star. Nope, there would be no kiss at the end of this week, friendly or otherwise. Paige would merely smile and wish Tanner Haddock the best in working with her material. For her, it would be back to school and picking up with the unit covering the1960s. Her students enjoyed that turbulent time in the nation's history, with hippies, the Vietnam war, and feminism. They appreciated the songs she played from different eras and the books which were popular during that time. She would immerse herself in school and maybe start fiddling with ideas for her next screenplay.

She didn't bother with makeup. Why do that? She did apply lipstick, though, knowing Nana liked her in it, and Paige blew her hair dry, using a round brush to help it curl under slightly.

Her next stop was the grocery store. That had been her original plan for today. With a houseguest, she would need to have plenty of food on hand. She worried that he might eat tofu or want all the fruits and vegetables to be organic. She snorted, thinking he was in her neck of the woods now. He would take whatever she gave him, like it or not. Since he'd grown up in Oklahoma, he'd known plain and simple food. He could revert to it for a week. In fact, that's probably what he got when he visited his parents, plenty of home cooking and no pretention. Well, that's what Mr. Haddock would also get here in Sugar Springs. He might have star power, but she would remain immune to it.

Paige put away the groceries and then found herself at loose ends. It was four-thirty. Tanner would be back within the hour. She didn't feel like she had enough concentration to read a book or write. She certainly didn't want to sit and daydream about a hot, unattainable Hollywood guy because that would amount to a big, fat nothing.

Instead, she pulled out her iPad and went to the Sporcle website. She played a few games on it every day, trying to keep her mind sharp as she explored the various quiz categories. It didn't work, though. Her concentration was shot. Usually, she could play the quiz naming all the countries in the world within eight minutes. Today, time ran out when she still had another thirty to go.

It hit her that people would wonder about an unfamiliar truck sitting in front of her house. It had been there all morning. Some of her neighbors would have seen it when they walked their dogs or left for church. Tanner had been gone before noon, so maybe no one had seen him drive away. But he couldn't park the large, expensive vehicle there for a week without someone checking on her. Everyone on the block knew one another. Their comings and goings. When they had friends over or out-of-town guests.

Grabbing her phone, she started to text Tanner and then wondered if he would answer a text while driving. He had in his movies, but he might actually be more responsible in real life. Instead, she called him.

"Hey. I'm close," he said. "Should be there in ten minutes or so."

"I'm going to park in front of my house. Pull into the garage and don't get out. I'll close the door."

He chuckled. "Hiding me from nosy neighbors?"

"You've lived in a small town. You know how people talk."

"Owens is incredibly small, but we lived on a ranch outside of town. Yes, I do know people gossip, but I didn't even think about your neighbors questioning a strange truck parked on the street all week."

"Just pull in the garage and park," she ordered, hanging up and grabbing her keys.

Paige went to her sedan and hit the button to raise

the door, backing out of the driveway and moving her car directly in front of her house. As she got out, she saw Mrs. Dunaway and her black poodle coming down the front porch stairs. Her neighbor waved, and Paige got out of her car, locking it, and then headed toward the woman. She hoped she could keep the conversation short and sweet because Mrs. Dunaway was a huge gossip.

"Hello, Paige. How are you? I see you're parking on the street."

"Yes, ma'am. I'm going to do some deep cleaning during spring break," she lied. "In the house to start, but I really need to clean out the garage. I'll probably leave my car at the curb all week and put trash sacks of clothes and other things I want to get rid of in the garage. At week's end, I'll—"

"I'd be happy to help you with a garage sale, dear. I know you teachers don't get paid nearly enough. Why, I could help you mark all the items. I could do the same. We could have a joint sale." The old woman brightened. "We could even have a street-wide yard sale!"

She'd have to shut down this idea. Fast.

"No, I'm not really interested in that, Mrs. D. I have a lot of schoolwork to do, as well. I just want to clear some things out. I don't really have time for a garage sale." She glanced at her watch.

"Expecting someone, dear?"

Paige tapped her watch. "It's been running a little slow all day. I was just checking it. It probably needs a new battery." *Come on, Mrs. D. Leave!*

"Well, if you change your mind, Paige, I'd be happy to help."

Feeling bad, she said, "Let me clean out and see what I've got. If it's enough for a sale, I'll consider it."

"Oh, good."

The poodle yipped.

"All right, Precious. We'll go finish our walk. I'll see you later, dear."

"Bye."

She moved to the porch and saw her neighbor turn the corner. Paige's head swiveled the other direction. Sure enough, she saw Tanner's truck turning the other corner.

That had been close.

And she still didn't know if any of her other neighbors might glance out their windows and see the most bankable American actor's pickup pull into her garage.

Tanner signaled and turned into her driveway. She motioned him to continue on and then rushed into the garage as he cut the engine. Before he could get out, Paige hit the switch, on the wall, closing the door. He waited until the door shut fully before getting out.

"A little subterfuge," he said, his eyes dancing with mischief.

"I just lied to my seventy-five-year-old neighbor," she complained. "I never lie. But Mrs. Dunaway is the biggest gossip on the street. Nice but way too chatty."

"I'll take the hit if she finds out I'm here. I'll tell her I asked you not to share that information with anyone."

"What if she does find out? How am I supposed to explain that I have a famous actor staying with me for a week? Oh, I forgot. We need to get to Nana's. Get back in your truck."

"Yes, ma'am."

Tanner climbed inside as Paige opened the garage door again. She went to her car and retrieved her remote. Returning, she told him to stay put while she went into the house and grabbed her purse and keys before going back to the garage and getting into his truck.

"I'm tempted to have you ride lying in the back seat," she told him.

"Is it really that big a deal?" he asked, looking doubtful.

"Do you ever really go out in public?" she demanded. "To the post office or the dry cleaners?"

He looked at her sheepishly. "Well, no. I'm usually on a set. Or in Oklahoma at the ranch. Or at home in Malibu. I do swim and surf and jog on the beach. Early, though. And it's private," he admitted. "The only time I'm out in the wild, as my security head calls public outings, is usually attending a premiere. My doctor and dentist see me after hours. The girl who cuts my hair comes to my house. So does my masseuse." He sighed. "You're right. The few times I'm out, I cause a stir."

"And that's in L.A., where famous people outnumber the civilian population. In Sugar Springs, it would be a disaster if word got out you were here."

"Then how will we get to Nana's? I'll have to get out of the car when we arrive. Unless you want me to stay here."

She waved away his concern. "That's easy. Nana has a long driveway and a freestanding garage at the end of it. I always go down the entire length of the driveway and duck in the kitchen door. Easy-peasy."

"You're the boss. Want to drive? I can get in the back seat like you suggested."

"Would you? I don't want to ask too much of you."

"Hey, you're the one doing me the favor. We need solitude to work in and not have a dozen reporters hanging around your front lawn, along with half the population of Sugar Springs."

Paige nodded. "Okay. Back seat, it is."

Tanner got out from the driver's seat of the truck and into the back, stretching out.

"Ready," he told her.

She slid behind the wheel, slipping the remote onto the visor before adjusting the seat and mirrors to accommodate her.

As she backed the truck from her garage and closed the door, she said, "You realize this truck cost more than what I make in a year as a public school teacher?"

"I do. Teachers are notoriously underpaid. That's why I'm going to handsomely reward you for your time this week and pay you an obscene amount of money."

Without thinking, Paige said, "Exactly how obscene an amount of money are we talking about? Profane—or really offensive?"

"Really offensive," Tanner smoothly replied, not missing a beat.

She laughed. "You know lines from *Pretty Woman*?"

"Heck, yes. That scene with Mr. Hollister and Edward is one of my favorites," Tanner replied, laughing, referring to the lines they had just exchanged. "So many good scenes and dialogue in that movie." He paused. "This baby must corner like it's on rails. Big mistake. Big. Huge." He paused. "What's your name?"

"What do you want it to be?" she replied automatically, almost purring. "That's one of Julia Roberts' best lines in the whole picture."

"I'm glad we have a love of *Pretty Woman*, Laramie."

"Welcome to Hollywood. What's your dream?" she said, mimicking the voice and tone of the last line in the film.

What she didn't say was the line in the movie that hurt every time she heard it.

I want the fairy tale . . .

Because she was living a crazy reality right now. Driving Tanner Haddock's sleek, black truck. Trading bits of dialogue with a famous movie star. Ready to spend a week in the company of a sexy, charming man.

And unfortunately, Paige Laramie *did* want the fairy tale. But she was no leggy, drop-dead gorgeous Julia Roberts. She knew whenever this magical week ended, she wouldn't be swept off her feet and live the fairy tale. She'd be back to being Miss Laramie, history teacher, while Tanner Haddock would move on and never think of her again.

She told herself to enjoy it while it lasted—because fairy tales didn't exist. At least for people like her.

8

Paige wondered what Nana would say about her bringing Tanner Haddock to dinner. Not that Nana would gossip and spill the secret of Tanner's presence in Sugar Springs, but Paige worried how to keep the superstar hidden from view for an entire week. Not a lot of people left Sugar Springs over spring break. It wasn't like those who lived in Dallas or Houston, people who could afford to take vacations to exotic places over spring break. Still, not everyone remained in town during the holiday. Spring break had become a time to visit relatives and take children camping at Tyler State Park.

From the back seat, Tanner said, "You know, you're going to have to tell your grandmother that you're a writer now. Otherwise, how are you going to explain me?"

"I could tell her that I've become the new president of your international fan club, and you decided to stop by in person and thank me," she said drily.

His deep laugh sounded from behind her, sending chills along her spine. She spied Mrs. Dunaway and Precious and was able to turn the corner and head in the opposite direction before she came too close for the older woman to recognize her. Mrs. D would definitely be one who would spread rumors of Tanner's presence at Paige's house. Hopefully, her neighbor might think the visitor in the black truck was now leaving town. Once again, she hoped they would be able to accomplish a good amount of work before his presence became known in Sugar Springs because it was bound to leak. She imagined a mob of adoring fans trampling her front lawn, waiting for a glimpse of him.

"We're almost there," she told him. "When the weather is good, I usually walk over for Sunday dinner because we don't live far from one another."

"Is Nana your mom's mother?"

"She's my maternal grandmother. A Fisher, through and through."

"The picture you have on the mantle of the three of you really shows a strong resemblance between them. I favor my dad quite a bit," he volunteered.

"Maybe that's why you always seemed so familiar to me anytime I went to see one of your movies."

"You've seen my work?" he asked, sounding pleased.

She laughed aloud. "I don't know any woman on the planet who hasn't taken the opportunity to see a movie of yours, Hollywood."

As she signaled and turned into Nana's long driveway, he said, "It still amazes me. Where I came from. How far I've come. That people pay money to see my films."

It surprised her how normal—and humble—he was. "You've made Owens, Oklahoma, proud, I'm sure. Even if you claim that your mom is the superstar in your family."

"Mom keeps all the Haddocks in line. She's the

rock in our family. I know she and Dad would like to see you again. Maybe at the end of this week, you can come up to the ranch with me. That is, if you think you could go back there."

Her blood chilled at the thought of not just leaving Sugar Springs, but going to the place where things ended so tragically.

Even though she wasn't a parent, Paige gave a, "We'll see."

Parent code for *Hell, no.*

She would put him off for now about making such a trip. By week's end, she would tell him she was too busy. That she needed to prepare for the upcoming week of school since she'd spent her entire break with him.

Paige brought the truck to a stop and cut its engine. "Stay down," she warned, climbing from the vehicle. She glanced about and didn't see anyone on the sidewalk at the front of the long drive.

"Olly olly out free," she told him, and Tanner climbed quickly from his hiding place, joining her as she moved swiftly to Nana's back door.

He opened the screen door for her, and she went in without knocking, seeing Nana stirring something at the stove.

"Hello, Paige," her grandmother said. "I hope you're hungry for—"

Nana's jaw dropped, and she released her grip on the wooden spoon she held, turning to face them.

A choice expletive escaped her lips. "My word, you look the spitting image of . . . no, you *are* Tanner Haddock!" Nana beamed at the actor. "Well, I hope you're hungry, young man."

"I smelled the fried chicken the moment we stepped into the house, Mrs. Fisher. It's so nice to meet you." He stepped forward and offered her his hand.

Her grandmother took it and smiled coyly, causing Paige to bite back a smile. "I am Nana to everyone. I expect you to use it when you're in my home."

Tanner gave her his megawatt smile. "I can do that, Nana."

"Well, Paige accuses me of making enough to feed an army each week. I usually send her home with leftovers and a couple of other things I've made to help get her through the week. She's a very conscientious lady and the best-loved teacher at Sugar Springs High."

"I'd like to hear more about that, Nana." He leaned over, looking at the stove. "You better stir that gravy before it burns."

After another colorful curse, Nana went back to stirring, adding a bit of pepper to the cream gravy as she did.

"I don't how big your appetite is, Mr. Haddock. That'll depend upon if leftover chicken goes home with you or not. But I did make a baked ziti and some stuffed peppers for Paige. And banana bread." She paused. "That is, if you'll be around for a few days."

"If dinner tastes half as good as it smells, Nana, I am your devoted fan for life," Tanner said.

"I believe I'm the fangirl, Mr. Haddock. I've seen every one of your movies."

"If you want me to stay for dinner, Nana, you better start calling me Tanner. Mr. Haddock is my dad."

"Yes, I remember what a lovely man he was."

Paige's jaw dropped. "You knew? That the police chief was Tanner's father?"

Nana smiled benignly. "Well, I met him, didn't I?

Chief Haddock was wonderful to your mother and me. You, too. And Mrs. Haddock was such a wonderful, calming presence."

"You never said anything, Nana," Paige protested. "Not once. And how many movies have we watched together of Tanner's?"

Her grandmother shrugged. "I guess I just assumed you knew who he was. He's from Owens. He's the spitting image of his daddy."

"We never talked about Owens. About that night. Or about all the time I was gone," she said quietly. "I barely remembered anything about that night in the diner until Tanner showed up at my doorstep. A lot has come back to me, in bits and pieces."

Nana put down her spoon and enveloped Paige in her arms. "I'm sorry, honey. I had no idea. You never brought it up. We thought it best to ignore it because you did. You never had nightmares. You never cried. Ever. You never once mentioned that asshole who took you from us. We kept quiet because you did."

She released Paige and went back to the pan, giving it a finally stir before pouring the contents into a bowl.

"Set another place if you would, dear," Nana said. "Then I want to hear all about how the famous Tanner Haddock wound up at my table this evening."

Nana opened the oven and removed a pan of lightly browned biscuits.

She had known she would have to finally come clean with Nana, bringing Tanner with her this evening. He gave her a sympathetic look as he asked, "Can I bring that in for you, Nana?"

"Why, of course, young man. Everything else is already on the table. Hope you like mashed potatoes, corn on the cob, fried chicken, and biscuits."

"You may have named my favorite meal, Nana. And if an apple pie magically appeared, it would be heaven."

The old woman laughed heartily. "We'll see," she said.

They gathered at the table, Tanner allowing them to fill their plates before he did his own. Paige saw why. He took portions so large, they would have fed two-and-a-half men. She didn't know if he did so to be kind until she watched him dig in, happy murmurs of approval coming from him.

"This may be the best fried chicken I've ever eaten—and that includes what my mom fries up," he declared.

"Why, thank you, Tanner. I'm glad I could get a home-cooked meal in you. I doubt Veronica Pierce serves those up."

Nana had named a famous actress. Paige frowned, not understanding why she did so.

"Don't you ever read the gossip columns, honey?" her grandmother asked. "Why, Tanner here has been dating Miss Pierce off-and-on for a while."

He snorted. "I hate to disappoint you, Nana. We did a movie together about a year and a half ago. I haven't seen her since, much less spoken with her. She may be one of the most beautiful women in show business, but she's got a nasty temper."

Nana eyed him speculatively. "I saw those love scenes, Tanner Haddock."

He dabbed his mouth with his napkin. "It's called acting, Nana. And I'm damned good at it."

The old woman roared with laughter.

The meal passed pleasantly, with them switching topics easily, from gossip in Sugar Springs to world affairs. When they finished eating, Nana started to rise, but Tanner told her to keep her seat.

"You did all the heavy lifting, Nana. You're cooking is nothing short of spectacular. The least I can do is clear the table. I haven't washed dishes since I was a kid, but I still remember how."

"Just rinse and set them in the sink, honey," Nana encouraged "I like to load the dishwasher my own way." She turned to Paige. "If you'd bring in the pie and fetch the Bluebell, we'll be set."

"Did I hear you say Bluebell?" Tanner asked, a smile tugging at the corners of his mouth.

"You did," Nana informed him. "Is there any other kind of ice cream in this neck of the woods?"

While Tanner removed their plates and the serving bowls and brought them to the counter, Nana instructed him where the Tupperware was. He put the leftovers in containers while Paige cut them slices of pie and placed a dollop of vanilla ice cream atop each one.

He returned to the table and sighed after biting into the pie. "I may need to let my cook go, Nana. What are your thoughts on moving to Malibu and living at the beach with me?"

"I've never seen a beach in seventy-two years. I think I better stay put here in Sugar Springs." She paused. "Isn't it about time the two of you tell me what you've been up to?"

Paige hesitated and then nodded at Tanner to go ahead.

"While I enjoy acting, I've long held the desire to branch out and direct. Maybe one day even produce. I've been on the lookout for a screenplay that spoke to my heart. Your granddaughter has written one which did so. I bought it, and I'm here in Sugar Springs for a week to help understand her characters more. Paige created them, which means she's got insight into them. Insight that's critical for me to have. I've spent years being a student of every director I've worked under. It's time I put that knowledge to good use with *Shadows of the Past*."

Nana nodded approvingly. "Paige always was an excellent writer. She wrote short stories when she was young and worked on the school newspaper for several years." Turning to her granddaughter, she asked, "When did you start writing for the movies?"

"You remember that Knox Monroe movie you liked so much?"

Nana's face softened. "Oh, we watched it together once. I've probably seen I half a dozen times now because I liked it so much." She paused. "Did *you* write that, honey?"

Paige nodded. "That was the first screenplay I sold. I've sold one more since then. They'll begin filming it sometime this summer."

Nana smiled. "I knew you had a talent. I just didn't realize how good you were." Suddenly, a knowing look crossed her face. "Is that how we both got new tablets? I never bought that story about a school bonus. That was hogwash. Teachers in Texas make peanuts."

"The first indie film didn't pay much, but the second one made up for it," she revealed.

"What about this third one? Has Tanner here bought it? Or did some studio?"

"I bought it outright, Nana. Paige's agent is a close friend of mine. She knew I've been on the lookout for something special. She brought it to me before pitching it to any of the studios. I own the rights. I'll direct it. If a studio won't take me attached to the project, then I'll simply go the indie route and produce it myself."

He hesitated and then told them, "And I think I'll be shooting *Shadows of the Past* right here in Sugar Springs."

brilliant idea had begun forming from the time Nana Fisher tossed out her first curse word.

He would film his movie in Texas. Right here in Sugar Springs.

Tanner had listened to the older woman with interest. She was feisty and funny. Entertaining and interesting. She had a kind heart. He knew she would be a natural on screen.

His gut told him he needed to go all the way indie on this film. Even if he could get the backing of a major studio, its executives would most likely hang over his shoulder during the entire shoot and then linger in the editing booth, making what they deemed helpful suggestions to a first-time director. If he wanted to make *Shadows of the Past* his own film, he would have to have complete creative control. Filming in a small town, using it as the background for scenes and casting several of its locals, would save time and money. Of course, for the few major roles, Tanner would have to go with seasoned pros. He already had a few ideas whom he would hit up to play Gwen Foster.

"Are you insane?" Paige asked, looking at him as if he'd gone off the deep end.

"Let the boy say his piece," Nana urged, nodding encouragingly at him.

He took a deep breath and blew it out slowly. "Filming here in Sugar Springs means I wouldn't have to waste time scouting locations. You two are familiar with the area and can tell me what's here. Answer my questions. I wouldn't have to build sets. I could just rent a few houses for interiors. I'll bet some of the proprietors of shops in town wouldn't mind me shooting scenes in their stores."

"Where would you put the crew?" Paige asked. "We've got one motel. A pretty small one, at that."

"How far is Tyler?"

"Less than half an hour," she told him.

"Good. Big enough to house cast and crew. Actually, I could put a few key players in the motel in Sugar Springs or a B&B," he said, thinking aloud. "It would be less expensive to shoot here than other states, and Sugar Springs would catch the ambience of a small town. To me, a setting can be a character. Sugar Springs could give my movie the flavor I'm looking for."

"I think it's a good idea," Nana declared. "It would help the local economy. Maybe even bring some tourists here once the movie came out. You know, Tanner Haddock ate an ice cream cone at this store. He and his leading lady sat on this bench in the park."

"I'm also thinking about using some locals as actors," he said, wading into those waters. "No one can capture the people of a small town like those who've lived in one." He smiled at Nana. "There's a great role for you in it, Nana."

"Me?" she asked, looking dumbfounded. "I don't

think I could act. Learn lines and say them while cameras filmed me. I'd be too self-conscious."

Tanner glanced to Paige, who nodded approvingly. "You want her for Gloria, don't you? Nana, you would be absolutely perfect for the role."

"Is she smart and beautiful?" Nana asked, patting her hair before cackling loudly.

"Gloria is a key piece to the puzzle," Tanner assured her. "A good chunk of solving the mystery hinges on Gloria."

"Would I have someone to do my hair and make-up?" Nana pushed.

"Yes. But you don't need much done to your appearance, Nana," he said. "You are a fine-looking woman as it is."

"Flattery may get you what you need, Tanner Haddock," she proclaimed. "I want to read it, Paige. See if it's something I could do or not. Email it to me. In fact, go home right now and send it."

He laughed. "You're kicking us out?"

Nana stood. "I have homework to do, something I haven't said in over fifty years. Let's get your food to take home."

The old woman packed a canvas bag with containers of food. It was just past eight o'clock, and the sun had recently set.

"It's been a pleasure meeting you and eating your food, Nana," Tanner said, hugging her.

"Remember, Nana, no talking about Tanner being here," Paige reminded. "No telling anyone what I've been up to outside of school hours."

Nana cursed. "I'm not a blabbermouth, Paige. I get it. Top secret. Go home and send me that script."

They said their goodbyes and went to the car.

"Do I need to duck and cover again?" Tanner asked.

"It's dark, but it wouldn't hurt," she said. "I don't think we can be too careful."

They arrived home a few minutes later, Paige closing the garage door before either of them got out. Tanner brought his duffel in from the truck and set it on the kitchen table.

"I'll put the food away," he volunteered. "You email Nana. We don't want to keep her waiting."

He found a place for everything in the refrigerator and found Paige at her computer in a small room which looked like her office. He eyed the bed and hoped he'd be able to get to sleep on it.

"I'm going to do my slow read now," he told her. "So, you've got the rest of the night off." He glanced around. "I'm assuming this is my space."

"Actually, I'm giving you my bedroom," she said. "I'm five-three and will fit the daybed better than you could. I've put fresh sheets on my bed. We'll have to share the bathroom in the hall, though. It's the only one."

"I can't take your bed."

She gave him one of those womanly, don't mess with me looks, one his mother and sister had perfected and trained their men to respect.

"Okay, I can take your bed. What time do you want to start tomorrow?"

"Is seven too early for you?" Paige asked. "I'll probably run at four-thirty or five."

"Can I go with you? I may go stir-crazy staying inside for an entire week."

She frowned. "I guess so. It's still dark then. I just don't want anyone to see you."

"I brought a ballcap and can wear dark glasses. You know, a typical Hollywood disguise."

She laughed. "Yes, wear the cap. I think you can leave the sunglasses at home that time of morning. If we see anyone, which I rarely do on my morning runs, just keep your head down."

"Sounds like a plan. Let me grab my stuff."

Tanner retrieved his duffel bag and took it to the bedroom she pointed out. He felt guilty taking her room but relieved that he wouldn't have to attempt to sleep on the day bed. It took him a few minutes to unpack, and then he brushed his teeth and stripped down to his boxer-briefs back in the bedroom. Usually, he slept naked, but being in a strange place with an attractive woman and a bathroom down the hall, he knew he better keep something on.

Turning back the comforter and sheets, he climbed into bed, propping pillows behind him. A good, strong light came from the lamp on the nearby nightstand. He picked up a pencil and the script and set to work, knowing it would take him three to four hours to go through it. Hopefully, he would finish up by midnight and then get in a few hours of sleep.

He lost himself in the script, sinking deeply into the characters, knowing things about them from his discussions with Paige that he hadn't known the first couple of times he'd read through it. Tanner jotted more notes in the margin as he went. Not as many as he thought he would have because things were already taking a clear shape in his head. Still, he separated questions he had for Paige from notes to himself, thinking the first thing they could do after tomorrow's run would be to address his questions.

He finished at a quarter till midnight and set the

script on the nightstand, rubbing his eyes. So much had happened in the last two days. He'd gone from having no idea when he would start his next project to finding a script he was passionate about, as well as locating its writer and deciding on where to film the bulk of it.

And discovering Paige.

She was a complex person, living a double life as an ordinary member of the Sugar Springs community while she secretly wrote and sold screenplays. Paige Laramie was definitely an onion, someone who had dozens of layers to be peeled back—and a hundred more beyond that.

Tanner decided to hit the restroom before bed and grabbed his shaving kit. Opening the bedroom door a crack, he saw Paige had left on the hallway light. He puttered to the restroom across the hall, finding a post-it note attached to the mirror.

TOWELS IN THE LINEN CLOSET. If you've forgotten anything (toothpaste?), use mine or look in the medicine cabinet. If you're up too late reading, don't worry about getting up to run.

Charge for staying here? You cook breakfast each morning. I'll handle the rest.

A WARM FEELING settled inside him. He was getting to know her characters, the ones she had created from scratch.

More than them, Tanner wanted to get to know the real Paige Laramie.

He finished his business and returned to the bed she'd given up for him, wishing she were in it. Borrowing one of Nana's expletives, he muttered it under his breath. He couldn't mope around. He had business to accomplish in Sugar Springs. This week would be productive, but he would need to kick things into high gear once it ended. He had a million and one things on a To Do List which he had yet to start. Wasting time thinking about Paige was not on that list. Not on the top or bottom or anywhere in between.

Tanner had never had problems falling asleep, and he burrowed into the pillow, the covers only pulled to his waist because he always ran hot, summer or winter.

A mournful wail caused him to sit up abruptly. He blinked, shaking the sleep from his head, wondering what ungodly noise had disrupted his sleep. He paused, listening. Nothing. Reaching for his phone, he saw it was a little after two in the morning. Maybe he'd had a bad dream. But he rarely dreamed and couldn't think of the last time a nightmare had come.

He shook it off, lying back against the pillow. Listening.

It sounded again. Louder this time. Turning from wail into a piercing shriek.

And it was coming from Paige.

Tossing back the covers, Tanner threw open his door and went to the bedroom next door. The door was closed. He didn't think knocking would do any good. He opened it and spied Paige fidgeting and flinching on the daybed, thanks to the nightlight burning in a nearby socket. Tanner went to her and stared down at her.

She frowned deeply, mumbling something he couldn't make out. Then her eyes opened. Sheer terror was in them, and the unearthly noise came from her again.

He perched on the bed, touching her shoulder. "Paige?" he asked softly.

Her eyes, which had been open, closed. She started murmuring again, the words unintelligent. Then the thrashing began. Her entire body whipped from side to side. Tears streamed down her cheeks.

Tanner grabbed her shoulders and brought her to an upright position. He wrapped his arms about her.

"You're safe. You're safe. I'm here. It's Tanner. I'm here, Paige. I won't let anything happen to you."

She wriggled, her head whipping back and forth a few times, still talking in her sleep. But she was calmer now. He kept his arms around her for a few minutes, murmuring to her, telling her she was going to be fine. She calmed further. The talking ceased.

But Tanner was afraid to leave her alone again.

Since there wasn't room for both of them in the daybed, he scooped her into his arms and carried her back to her familiar bed, placing her in it and then climbing in beside her. He brought the covers up as she turned on her side, away from him. Undeterred, he slipped his arms around her.

Paige was ice-cold. He threw a leg over hers, hoping his body heat would warm her. He rubbed a hand up and down her arm and then enveloped his arms around her slight frame, pulling her flush against him. Gradually, her chilled body began to warm.

He pressed his cheek into her hair, which smelled like warm sunshine.

Tanner couldn't think of anywhere else he'd rather be.

Her breathing was slow and even now, her body relaxed against his. She'd ceased talking. In fact, she was stone-still now, in a dead sleep. He brushed his lips against her hair and closed his eyes.

"I'll protect you," he whispered. "You're safe with me."

Tanner fell asleep, guarding the precious bundle in his arms.

10

P aige awoke, luxuriating in the warmth surrounding her. Then she started to stretch —and realized she wasn't alone in her bed.

What was she doing in her bed?

With Tanner Haddock?

The last thing she remembered was climbing onto the daybed and falling asleep quickly, which was her usual pattern. Had she somehow been sleepwalking and returned to her bed out of habit? Whatever had happened, she needed to extricate herself. Now.

Yet the feel and smell of this man kept her from moving. Here she was, a thirty-year-old virgin who had never been kissed, in bed with one of the world's sexiest men. She realized there was so much more to Tanner than what the public thought. On the surface, he was the ultimate in cool, a man who could charm any woman with his magical smile, and yet someone men also wanted to be friends with. What didn't show was deep at his core, his small-town roots and values. He was a hard worker and had spent years learning how to attain his next goal, directing a film. Paige was honored he had selected her screenplay.

Beyond that, they might have a friendship. At least

during this week while they worked on the script to-gether. But all the longings she now felt—the desires this man was awakening in her—were pipe dreams. In the long run, she was an average-looking high school teacher, while Tanner was a worldwide sex symbol.

Paige wondered how to get out from under him since they were tangled together. She didn't want to wake him, but she needed to move away. Soon.

Or she might kiss him.

More than anything, she needed a hard run to clear her head and knock some sense into her. Slowly, she pulled one arm away, causing him to stir. As he did, he clasped her more tightly as if he knew she'd tried to leave him.

This was never going to work. He covered her like a blanket, and his intoxicating male scent and mus-cled body was putting things into her head which she couldn't act upon. Paige pushed against his broad chest and wriggled again. This time, his eyes opened. They were face to face, so close that if she'd leaned in an inch, she might find her lips brushing against his.

"Morning," he said sleepily. He didn't release her.

"Good morning, Tanner," she said formally, as if she weren't wearing just an oversized T-shirt and his chest wasn't bare and hot and they weren't tangled to-gether. "I apologize for somehow making my way back to my bed and invading your privacy."

"You didn't. I brought you here."

Paige stiffened. He quickly added, "Nothing hap-pened. But you were having one helluva nightmare."

"I was? I don't ever recall having one, much less last night."

"You were loud enough to wake me up. I went to check on you. You were thrashing about and cold as ice. I wanted to help you. The only thing I could think of to get you warm was to bring you back to bed with me."

"Thank you," she said softly. "I have no recollection of any of that. I've seriously never had any nightmares."

Shouldn't he be letting her go now? Shouldn't she ask him to since he hadn't?

"I'm afraid my coming to Sugar Springs may have awakened some of the dark memories hidden within you. I'm sorry for that, Paige."

"Don't be sorry. I liked reconnecting with you. Besides, I think writing *Shadows of the Past* has had a lot to do with it. My state of mind. I always knew there were dark things lurking within me. Memories I couldn't quite recall. I let those subconsciously spill onto the page."

He smiled lazily. "Well, you've crafted a damn good script, Laramie Fisher. I think it's cool you took your pseudonym's surname from your grandmother."

"And mother. Mama was a Fisher before she married my father. She and Nana were cut from the same cloth."

"I like Nana," he told her. "Quite a bit."

"Do you really believe she could be Gloria? Nana has never acted a day in her life."

"I think your Nana embodies the character. Maybe you wrote Gloria with Nana in mind and didn't even know it."

"You might be right," she admitted. "Of all the characters in the script, Gloria rings the most true for me. But are you really serious about filming in Sugar Springs?"

"It would save a ton of money, and I'm thinking I don't want the fingerprints of a studio on this film. I only want mine. If I'm going to sink my dollars into this production, I want total control. I don't want to cut corners, but I need to be frugal and fiscally responsible when I can. When you think about it, many of the characters in your script are merely window dressing. They let the audience glimpse what small-town life is like. Most of them only have a few lines or a scene or two at most, interacting with Gwen Foster. At the bakery. The bank. The florist. I'll cast a professional actor in Gwen's role. It needs an actress who can display great vulnerability but also a reservoir of great strength, both emotionally and physically."

"You didn't mention Peter Willoughby. Have you decided to play him yourself?"

Tanner nodded. "You were right when you said audiences have a relationship with me. They come in already liking me. Trusting me. Just as Gwen does with Peter. I can use that to my advantage. I want their suspicions to unravel at the same time Gwen's do. The horror of seeing me in this type of role will only add to their watching experience."

He chuckled. "Besides, I can pay myself peanuts. My salary can be small and a tax write-off."

"Do you have anyone in mind for Gwen?"

"Maybe. We can talk about it. After our run. Once we go through the script today."

He slowly released his grasp upon her, and they untangled themselves from one another. Paige pushed aside the emptiness which suddenly filled her.

"You take the bathroom first," he suggested.

She left her bedroom and retrieved the running clothes she had set in her desk chair. She brushed her teeth, horrified to think she'd been inches from Tanner, and they'd had such a long discussion. Glancing into the mirror, she did her best Cher imitation from *Moonstruck.*

"Snap out of it!"

Tanner Haddock didn't care what her breath smelled like. He had no attraction to her. He had simply acted as the good guy he was and rescued her after a nightmare. She knew his arrival had stirred up the past and decided it might be time to talk to someone about it. The school district had a psychologist on staff, someone not on the payroll twenty years ago during her crisis. She would talk with Brynn Mattson and see if she might have a recommendation for someone Paige could see. Or Brynn might even agree they do a few sessions together. Either way, Paige realized it was time to address the shadows of *her* past.

While she traded with Tanner and gave him the bathroom, Paige checked her emails on her cell. Sure enough, Nana had sent one. Paige opened it.

FIRST OF ALL, honey, I want to say how proud I am of you. Your work touched me deeply. You've captured the workings of a small town, but more than that, you've created a taut thriller.

I see a lot of you in Gwen Foster. You were brave as a child. Even braver as a teenager when your mother went through her hard times. You've turned out to be a wonderful woman. I'll tell you now that while those kids at school adore you, that time with them has passed. You've found your true calling in writing. I plan to go back and watch that Knox Monroe movie again today, this time thinking my incredible granddaughter wrote all that snappy dialogue!

I noticed you're using the name Laramie Fisher as your screenwriting name. Your mama would be so proud of you, adding to the Fisher legacy.

Second thing, my darling girl, is that I find myself wanting to be Gloria. I'm not nearly as wise as she is, but I think I could do justice to this role. I'm not an actor, but I don't think that's what Tanner wants. He wants the real deal—and I plan to give it to him.

Call me when you have a chance. I love you, honey.

PAIGE BLINKED RAPIDLY, tears welling in her eyes. She had spent twenty years not crying, yet the past twenty-four hours, she'd been a watering pot.

Tanner appeared in the doorway. "You ready?"

"Let me drink some water first and stretch."

He followed her into the kitchen and retrieved glasses of water for both of them. As they stretched, she glanced at the time on the microwave. It was almost five o'clock.

Outside, Sugar Springs was still dark. The morning paper hadn't even been delivered yet. They started at an easy pace for half a mile, and then she kicked things up a notch. Tanner kept stride with her. After another half-mile, Paige turned on full steam. Once again, he matched her without any trouble.

They ran along the quiet streets of Sugar Springs, arriving at the town square near the end of their run. After circling it and turning up Elm to head to her house, she slowed to a jog. They had seen no one, for which she was grateful, but she wanted them to leave earlier tomorrow morning if he still chose to accompany her. They reached her house, and she jogged around the house to the back gate, opening it so they could enter through the back door. They stopped in the small mudroom. She had old hand towels stacked there and tossed him one.

They both rubbed the sweat from their face, neck, and arms.

"You certainly know how to haul ass," Tanner joked. "How far do you run each day?"

"I'm not really sure how far I go. Normally, I run sixty to ninety minutes. Sometimes, longer on the weekends, when I have more time. You kept up nicely."

"Barely," he said. "I do jog along the beach near my house, but I also lift once a week and do some yoga for flexibility. What I'd really like to do is see how you trained in Krav Maga."

She chucked. "Still upset I dumped you on your back, Hollywood?"

"More fascinated," he said, following her into the kitchen.

Paige got them fresh glasses of water, and they drank those down. Tanner went to the sink and filled his glass again, drinking another full one lightning fast.

"I think a couple of rewrites are in order," he suggested. "Gwen needs to pull Krav Maga out of her bag of tricks and use a little of it on our killer."

"Already talking rewrites?"

He grinned. "Not until we go through my notes first. Then we can see if we can work in some Krav Maga magic for our heroine."

"Do you want to eat first or shower?" she asked.

"I'm ravenous. The owner of my B&B told me I'd be responsible for breakfast each morning. I hope you don't mind a repeat of yesterday. My repertoire is limited."

"Could I have my eggs scrambled this time? I've got some bell peppers, onions, and cheese you can add to it."

"That I can do."

While he worked on the eggs, Paige made them cups of hot tea and poured them tall glasses of orange juice, along with toasting English muffins for them. They ate breakfast and surprisingly didn't mention the script once. Instead, he asked her about school, and she entertained him with education stories, the kind every educator could trot out.

Tanner shook his head. "I don't see how you do it. Teenagers are a plague upon mankind. I know. I was one. Thankfully, my sister didn't hit her teen years until after I'd left home. Mom said Alana was hell on wheels. You are an unsung hero, Paige Laramie, for being in the trenches with teens every day."

She laughed, shaking her head. "No, that honor goes to all those elementary school teachers. I can't imagine little people clinging to me. Give me a hormonal sixteen-year-old any day of the week, and I'll whip him or her into shape."

He asked her what she taught, and she explained she split her time between US and World History, saying that US history actually became world history, starting in the twentieth century.

"How do you keep your students interested?"

Paige elaborated on a few of the upcoming projects her students would be asked to complete. Tanner nodded with interest as she spoke.

"If I would've had a history teacher like you, I would've appreciated it more when I was young. As it is, it took being in my thirties before I did so. I watch a lot of the History Channel and NatGeo in the little spare time I have."

"You do seem to be quite prolific as far as your career goes."

"I always have half a dozen balls I'm juggling.

Filming one movie, while another one is in edits and a third is playing at your local cineplex. I'm also reading scripts as they come in, deciding what I want my next role to be. I stopped all that, though, during this last shoot. I only read for what I could direct, not act in."

She had too many yearnings as she listened to him and abruptly stood.

"Let me clean this up while you go shower. I know you don't want to waste any more time, so we need to get started."

Tanner stood. Surprisingly, he took her hand. "I don't think I've been wasting time with you, Paige. Far from it. I enjoyed hearing your school stories. I enjoy being with you."

She felt her cheeks grow warm under his intense gaze.

He tugged on their joined hands, pulling her next to him. His free hand cupped her cheek, his thumb lightly grazing it.

"I want to kiss you, Paige. I have pretty much from the moment we met."

Her insides melted even as her heart began beating in double-time. Still, she couldn't believe what he was saying.

"Men like you don't want to kiss women like me."

His thumb stilled. "What do you mean?"

"You know exactly what I mean."

His brow creased. "No, I don't. Spell it out."

She dug her fingernails into the palm of her free hand. "You look like . . .well, like the superstar you are. I'm just an ordinary—"

"You are far from ordinary," he interrupted, framing her face with his large hands. "You are special, Paige Laramie. You were the first time I laid eyes on you. And you still are."

Tanner's head dipped, and his lips touched hers. An instant spark shot through her, a sensual tingling she'd never experienced before. It made her dizzy, and she grabbed onto his T-shirt, bunching it in her fingers. His mouth smiled against hers and then pressed harder. Her heart sped up, beating so violently inside her chest that she was afraid he would hear it.

One hand slid from her face to her nape, and he held her in place as he stepped into her, their bodies pressing against one another. His mouth grew more insistent on hers, his kiss demanding something that she also wanted but didn't understand how to give him, thanks to her lack of experience.

Then his tongue danced along the seam of her mouth, teasing it open. His tongue swept inside her mouth, finding hers, mating with it. A rush of heat filled her, engulfing her. Paige thought she might burst into flames as Tanner continued kissing her. His arm had come around her, holding her against his muscular chest, imprisoning her. But she had no intention of fleeing.

Instead, she tentatively brushed her tongue against his, hearing his low moan. He drew her even closer, until she felt they were almost one being, one body. He kissed her until she was breathless. Senseless. Until her legs began to give way, causing him to sweep her into his arms. Her arms looped around his neck, wanting more of him, as much as he might give her in this one moment of bliss.

Paige kissed him unabashedly, with enthusiasm and longing, not quite understanding how it had started or how it might end.

Then she found herself on her feet, Tanner's strong hands steadying her as he gripped her shoulders.

As he rested his forehead against hers, his words caught her by surprise.

"I should never have done that," he apologized. "I won't do it again," he added firmly.

Tanner released her and walked away.

She stood there, her body like limp spaghetti. Her lips felt raw. Her body continued to tingle. Between her legs a painful throbbing pulsed.

Paige heard the bathroom door close. The shower starting.

And had no idea what had just happened between them.

11

"Who's the A**Hole now?" Tanner asked himself as he angrily scrubbed his body.

He wasn't on social media and tried to limit his time on the Internet. The one thing that had always hooked him, though, was Reddit's *AITA—Am I the A**Hole*. Everyday people posted on the forum. Women complaining about their unwavering mothers-in-law. Parents griping about their college-bound kids. Employees elaborating on their bosses' bad behavior. Tanner found the situations fascinating, usually agreeing that it wasn't the writer who posted but the person they were complaining about who was the problem.

For the first time, *he* was the problem.

He prided himself on being the consummate professional when filming. He was always on time. Took direction well, even if he didn't agree with it. He didn't yak on his cell during costume fittings or when he was in hair and makeup. He was cordial to everyone on set, from his fellow actors to the prop assistant to craft services. Tanner knew the producer might be the one who took home the Oscar for Best

Picture for a film, but every job on a film crew was a vital one. Everyone did his or her best to make him, the star, look good. In turn, he was pleasant and friendly to everyone, trying to help the cast and crew by being kind and prepared. He'd seen too many stars throw temper tantrums, holding up the shoot while they acted like toddlers on crack. That was not his style.

In his personal life, he was a *go with the flow* type person. He never made demands of his tight circle of friends. He went out of his way to be a regular guy and not pull out his fame card the few times he was in the wild. He tipped well. He had a ready smile for everyone. He tried to be a good friend by being a decent listener. With his family, he was his regular self, pitching in on the ranch, helping to feed the livestock and exercise horses or run an errand in town for his mom or Alana.

He cursed as the water sluiced over him, knowing he had most likely ruined things between Paige and him.

All because he couldn't keep his hands—or his lips—to himself.

And yet all he wanted to do was jump from the shower and kiss her again.

She had held back at first. A little. But she'd quickly warmed to him. She didn't seem all that experienced to him. He supposed living her entire life in Sugar Springs, she had a limited dating pool to choose from. If it were like Owens, young people in Sugar Springs fled as soon as they graduated. Few people stuck around Owens after they finished high school. Even fewer went away and came home with a degree. Paige must be one of the few who had returned to Sugar Springs after graduating from college. He couldn't imagine there being a large number of single men to date.

The thought of her with another man caused jealousy to flare within him. It actually calmed his temper because he laughed at how absurd that idea was. He had no rights to her. No idea if she were even dating someone, like a beefy football coach or the principal. Or the town vet or cop or hardware store owner. As much as he thought he knew about Paige, the truth was that he knew very little about her. Yes, she was smart—despite what she'd said earlier about herself. She had a quick, sarcastic sense of humor. She was a dedicated teacher who truly cared for her students.

But he knew zilch about her love life.

Was she dating anyone? Had she been married before and was now divorced? Or did she even like men? He was such a fool. His policy of not becoming involved with a co-worker had sailed out the window. It was obvious he would have to show a whole lot more restraint if they were to work together this week. Maybe he shouldn't work with her. In her experience, both her previous scripts had been bought, and she hadn't been called to the set, much less been in contact with the directors. Maybe his idea of a collaboration was foolish. He'd bought what she'd written. It was up to him to spin it into gold.

That's not what he wanted, though. He wanted to delve deep within her and find out everything she thought about the characters she'd created. He wanted to bounce ideas off her and come to a decision on a scene. He wanted her input in casting. Actually, he wanted her onset as he filmed. Not as a crutch, but more as a second pair of eyes to help him take everything in. Keep him on track.

Tanner turned off the water and reached for the

towel hanging on the towel rack next to the shower. As he dried himself, his thoughts swirled. He didn't know what he would say to Paige. Maybe he should let her take the lead. He would take his cues from her.

He dressed and shaved, emerging from the bathroom and heading to her living room. No Paige. He tried the kitchen and saw her sitting at the table, turning the pages of a newspaper. She looked up—and he saw the questions in her eyes.

"Look, I'm sorry," he began.

She scowled. "The last thing a woman needs to hear is that a man is sorry that he kissed her. I get that I didn't know what I was doing. That you've probably been kissing women since kindergarten. How was I to know my first kiss would be with—"

"Your what?" he demanded, stunned by what he thought he'd heard.

Color flooded her face. She crossed her arms defensively. "I've never kissed anyone before," she said evenly, her voice shaking. "I apologize that my ignorance—"

He cut her off again. "You've never been kissed?"

Her eyes narrowed. "Oh, let's just keep hammering home that point, Hollywood. I'm already humiliated enough as it is." Her face flamed by now. "It's obvious you . . .you . . ." Her voice trailed off. She lowered her head.

Tanner went to her, taking her chin in hand and raising it so their gazes met. "You have nothing to be ashamed of, Paige. Nothing to be embarrassed about. I thought you were a great kisser."

She jerked her head free. "Don't patronize me, Hollywood."

He took her by the elbows and brought her to her feet, feeling her tremble. "I'm not," he said softly. "I didn't know I was your first kiss. Actually, I want to be the only one who's kissing you. I was thinking I should've asked if you had a boyfriend or something."

"No boyfriend. Ever. I went on a few dates in high school. Mostly double dates with my best friend Vivi and her boyfriend. But no real boyfriend then. Or now."

He took her by the waist, anchoring her so she wouldn't flee. "Why? You're a beautiful woman."

Paige snorted. "No, I'm not. You're flattering me. Yes, my hair is a nice shade. And I have good calves from all the running I do. But I wouldn't call myself beautiful."

"I would," he said softly. "I remember the girl you were—and now see the woman you've become. You may not be confident in your looks, Paige, but they're there all the same. You've got beautiful skin. Your hair is like silk. Those emerald eyes draw me in in a way I can't explain. Your lips are the most kissable I've ever touched. Soft and inviting. Your frame is compact. Physically, you're the entire package."

His hands slipped to her waist. "But you're even more beautiful inside. You're creative. Bright. Nurturing. Loyal."

He brushed his lips slowly against hers, his insides going liquid.

"I'm quiet. Too sensitive."

"Is that why you haven't kissed anyone before now?"

Paige nodded, color flooding her cheeks. "I've never . . .felt comfortable with the thought of being physically close to someone. I don't trust many people. I have a small circle of friends. Lots of acquaintances, but not many true friends."

His thumbs stroked her. "What were you like in high school?"

"Focused. Even before what happened in Owens, I was the best student in my grade. Competitive. Hardworking. I became more so after that. Mama was sick then. When I wasn't in school, I was by her side, holding her hand as I studied. Then she died. I lost finding the small pleasures in life. I studied. I worked. I knew I had to because I wanted to go to college, and Nana didn't have the money to send me."

"I never went to college and wish I had," he admitted. "The day after I graduated from high school, I set out with a duffel bag and a backpack and hitched my way to California. I wouldn't have appreciated a college education back then."

"It was all I wanted. Nana finished eighth grade. Mama finished high school and a year of community college but never went beyond that. Everyone always told me how smart I was. I loved learning. I wanted others to love it like I did."

"Is that why you became a teacher?"

Paige nodded. "It was all I knew. All I wanted. At least, back then."

"But you want more now?" he asked.

"Yes," she whispered, her gaze meeting his. In it, he saw a woman who didn't have much confidence in herself. One who was beautiful and talented and yet didn't know just how special she was.

Tanner decided he would make certain Paige Laramie knew exactly how remarkable she was.

"You are extraordinary," he told her. "One of the most exceptional women I've met."

She bit her bottom lip, causing desire to race through him. "But not enough to kiss me again."

He kissed her softly to prove her wrong. A long,

slow, sweet kiss. His insides did things they'd never done before. A deep need swept through him, unlike anything he'd ever experienced.

Breaking the kiss, he said, "I want to do more than kiss you, Paige. It's always been a Tanner Haddock rule, though, not to get involved with someone I'm working with. *That's* why I told you it wouldn't happen again."

"Oh." She thought a moment. "So, you didn't think I was a terrible kisser."

"Not at all."

Tanner kissed her again, taking his time. He teased her lips open and swept his tongue inside her mouth, sensually stroking hers, feeling her shiver in his arms. He drew her against him, kissing her for a long time. It was funny. He had kissed more women than he could count, most having as much experience as he did. The sex it had led to had usually been enjoyable.

But these kisses he now traded with Paige Laramie were the sweetest, most satisfying of his life. Maybe it was knowing she'd never done this with another man, and he was exploring unchartered territory with her. Or maybe it was because he'd found a woman who made his heart race and his blood sing, something unique. And surprising.

He slipped the ponytail holder from her hair, pushing his fingers into the golden waves. Hearing her sigh into his mouth brought a rush of lust through him.

Breaking the kiss, he captured her face in his hands. "I want you, Paige. All of you. But I know that's a big commitment. You haven't known me long. I'm not going to ask you to give yourself to me. Yet. Let's keep getting to know one another. Continue working on your script. I need you to help me start visualizing it. I want to take it slowly. I'm not going anywhere."

"But you said you'd only be here a week."

"That's before I decided to film right here in Sugar Springs," he reminded her. "I want to spend this week with you. Then yes, I'll have to go for a while. Work on putting a crew together. Casting. Making arrangements for the company to come to town."

Tanner kissed her again, deeply, feeling his soul fill with Paige.

"But I'll be back. I'm breaking all my rules for you. I'd told myself I would wait until filming was over before I said a word to you." He smiled, smoothing her hair. "But you're so tempting in so many ways. I couldn't keep quiet. I couldn't keep my hands off you."

"It's hard to believe you were thinking what I was thinking. I was attracted to you from the moment I opened my door and found you standing there, Tanner." She shook her head. "Every woman under ninety finds you sexy. It's just hard for me to believe you are attracted to me."

"Believe it, babe," he said, his mouth seeking hers again.

Tanner kissed Paige tenderly, wanting her to understand it wasn't all physical attraction on his part. Yes, he was drawn to her, but it was more than that. He was taken with her as a person.

He broke the kiss. "I could kiss you all day—or we could start working on the script."

"I need a shower," she told him. "How you can find a sweaty mess in an old T-shirt and gym shorts appealing is beyond me."

"You could wear a potato sack, and I'd want to kiss you," he declared. Kissing her swiftly one last time, he said, "Go. I'll get everything set up so we can start the minute you're done."

He watched her leave the room, fighting the urge to join her in the shower. Images of her naked, him taking her against the shower wall, water pouring over them, filled his brain.

"Cool down," he told himself.

He wasn't about to have sex with Paige anytime soon. Hell, she'd just been kissed for the first time. It was important to him to take his time. Let her see if he were truly what she wanted.

Because he knew Paige Laramie was exactly what he'd been looking for. He just hadn't known it.

Until now.

12

———

Charles Dickens had been right. It was the best of times. It was the worst of times.

Paige couldn't help but think of the opening lines of *A Tale of Two Cities* and how it reflected the past several days with Tanner. Their collaboration had been nothing short of astonishing. After that third reading, the actor seemed to know her script even better than she did. The questions he asked her regarding plot and characters showed his insight and understanding of the screenplay. He forced her to delve deeply into the motivations of both Peter and Gwen. Talking about it aloud, it made these inventions of hers become even more real. What Paige had written with *Shadows of the Past* was completely different from the two rom-coms she had first produced. She realized now that it was a result of some of the lingering darkness within her—and how she wanted to resolve it, even subconsciously.

They had gone through the script, with her answering all Tanner's questions about character, structure, and tone. Then they had gone through it again, literally scene by scene, line by line, picking everything apart. She had taken the role of Gwen and he had become Peter as they read the dialogue aloud to one another. Paige was pleased that most of it rang true, but there were a few times when something sounded hollow or hit a false note. Together, she and Tanner had worked, crafting just the right word or line which would make the scene flow seamlessly. She'd even teased that he would need to place his name on the script, along with hers, since she felt he was contributing so much.

Tanner had entirely disagreed, saying they were merely tweaking what was already on the page. He wanted Paige to have sole credit for the writing.

Their only disagreement had occurred when he had told her she needed to put her true name on her work and not hide behind a pseudonym anymore. She had been adamant in keeping the Laramie Fisher name, saying she wanted that layer of privacy.

Tanner had told her those days would soon end. With him shooting in Sugar Springs, somehow—some way—word would get out regarding her involvement. Paige worried that her students would no longer take her seriously as a teacher if it did, and she couldn't imagine how parents might respond. Something told her that learning about history would take a back seat in everyone's mind as they pressed her for more information about Hollywood and movie making.

She knew she stood on a precipice and would have to make a decision soon. She had talked to Nana twice this week. Both times, the subject had come up. Her grandmother had pushed for her to resign at the end of the school year, telling Paige that she needed to devote herself full-time to writing. She wanted to do so, but fear held her in its grasp.

What if she weren't good enough? What if she

couldn't make a living through her writing? She might be the new It Girl for a nanosecond, and then the Hollywood bandwagon would pass her by. Still, she owed it to herself to try. After all, she could always fall back on her teaching degree if she needed to.

As she dressed for their daily run, Paige also wondered what might lie in the future between Tanner and her. He had not kissed her again, which had been the hard part of this week. Being physically near him almost drove her insane. She wanted to reach out. Glide her hands along his firm body. Wrap herself around him. Kiss him until her lips grew numb. She knew he bided his time, sensing what was between them and refusing to act on it. Yet doubts plagued her. She might just be convenient since she was here. He might think he had true feelings toward her, but once his movie finished shooting, Tanner Haddock would go back to his life as a Hollywood superstar.

Paige didn't want to play any part in that life.

Absently, she picked up a glass sitting next to her computer. She still left half-empty glasses of water scattered about the house. Tanner had teased her about doing so and asked her why she did it. For the first time, Paige had lied to him, telling him she was simply lazy and didn't want to get up and fill a glass with water. That it was easier to leave one lying around for her to sip on, no matter what room she might be in.

The truth was that it hearkened back to the time she'd spent on the run with her father. Paige had always been a water drinker, encouraged by her mother to stay hydrated. Her father had used both food and water as a weapon against her, withholding both in order to control her. She could remember nights lying on the floor next to his bed, burrowing into her pillow, the thirst unimaginable. She had tried to drink from the faucet in the bathroom, but he had caught her doing so and punished her severely. She learned to live with the hunger, but the thirst plagued her. Once she was rescued and back at home in Sugar Springs, she swore she would never go thirsty again.

That was the reason behind so many glasses of water scattered throughout her house. She wanted to enjoy the freedom of taking a sip wherever she might be.

She downed the water and took the glass to the kitchen, where she found Tanner waiting for her. Going to the sink, she refilled her glass before drinking its contents. She set the empty glass on the counter, knowing once they returned, she would refill it and leave it next to her computer again.

They warmed up their muscles and set out on their morning run. Today was Thursday. They had already accomplished so much, going through the script with a fine-toothed comb. She couldn't imagine what was left to do in the next two or three days. The thought of Tanner leaving brought a deep sadness to her. She had had the actor to herself all week long. They had spent sixteen-hour days together, working, talking, laughing. They had eaten off what Nana had sent home with them, and Tanner had grilled burgers for them last night in her back yard. She had never spent so much time in a man's company, other than her father. Paige had never truly been comfortable around men, but Tanner proved to be the exception. It seemed as if they never ran out of things to discuss, well beyond her screenplay. He was interested in sports, architecture, and current events, and their conversations flowed with ease.

They started their run at a steady pace.

"Nana texted me," Tanner told her.

"She did?"

"She wants to bring dinner to us tonight. Manicotti. I told her that I love Italian food and that was nice of her, but she said she had ulterior motives."

"Nana said *that*?"

He grinned. "She wants to pick our brains about Gloria. Said she's already been learning her lines and wants to understand her character better."

"I know you've talked about wanting to hire locals for a majority of the roles, Tanner, but Gloria has a ton of lines. She's key to the entire piece. Do you really think it's a good idea to hire my grandmother to play such a pivotal role?"

"Do you really think at this point I could tell her no?"

She burst out laughing. "Probably not. When Nana sets her mind on something, she makes it happen."

Tanner was the one who increased their pace after that brief conversation, and they didn't speak again for the rest of their run. They turned into her driveway just before five and quickly entered the house. So far, no one other than Nana seemed to know Tanner was in town. The fact they had kept his presence a secret amazed her.

They went to the kitchen and settled into their usual routine. Paige put on water to boil for their hot tea, while Tanner provided the bulk of breakfast. When it was ready, they sat at the small café table.

"You've spoiled me this week," she said. "I usually make do with a protein shake or have some yogurt and blueberries for breakfast. A hot meal every morning has been a nice change."

She saw a thoughtful expression on his face. "What are you thinking about?"

He bit into a slice of crispy bacon and chewed thoughtfully. "I'm thinking about how to approach you about an idea I've had."

"I thought we've been pretty open with one another. Just ask."

"Can teachers take a leave of absence?"

Paige wondered where this was going. "It's not unheard of. One of our science teachers in is the National Guard, and he had to have a sub for two months last semester because he was called to active duty. Why?"

"I've told you this is going to be a Tanner Haddock production from beginning to end. I'm not taking this project to a studio. I plan to fund the bulk of it, and I have an idea of a few people I'll ask to be investors, as well. I can't do it all myself, though, Paige. I need someone I can trust. Someone who has intimate knowledge of this project. Someone who is organized."

His gaze met hers. "Someone who will always tell me the truth." He swallowed. "Would you think about taking a timeout from school and acting as my co-producer?"

His question floored her. "What would that even mean? I don't know anything about producing a film."

"You'd keep an eye on the production schedule and budget. Help book rooms for the cast and crew and deal with ground transportation. Work on getting craft services set up. Make sure we don't go over budget and come in on time. Basically, you'd collaborate with me and make sure between the two of us that we coordinate, supervise, and manage everything related to the production."

Tanner paused, letting the information sink in.

"I think you would be perfect for it. Teachers are organized people. That's what it takes to keep a production running on schedule. You know the area. You'll know most of the players once we cast them. We're already at a point where I don't think we can take the script any further. It's polished to perfection. I'm ready to start storyboarding today, and I'd like to scout locations tomorrow. I've already had some ideas based upon what I've seen on our runs, in and around town."

Paige sat, dumbfounded. "I never thought about producing. I'm not sure I'm up to the task if I'm being truthful."

"Your knowledge of the script and this area, along with the people who live in it, is invaluable. I know you're dedicated to your students, though. How many weeks are left in the school year?"

"Nine," she said without hesitation. "Every year after spring break, I keep a count on the board of how many days we have to go." She bit her lip, thinking on his idea. I don't know about a leave of absence, but I definitely have accumulated enough sick days to request time off. I would have to run this by Joe Bob Milton, my principal. The sooner, the better."

"Do it today," he encouraged.

For the first time since he had last kissed her, Tanner took her hand, causing a myriad of sensations to rush through her. If just a simple touch put her into such turmoil, how would she be able to work alongside him daily?

"I need you, Paige. I can't do this without you. This shoot's got to be lean and mean. If I have you by my side, keeping me organized, I can do this."

The faith he had in her surprised Paige. It also felt awfully good.

"All right. I'll talk to Joe Bob this morning." She glanced at the time on the microwave and saw it was now five-thirty. "Joe Bob has breakfast at Ida Lou's six days a week, come rain or shine. He's usually there from six to seven and then heads over to school. With it being spring break, he may linger a bit. I can shower and run over to the diner and talk to him there."

Tanner squeezed her fingers. "Are you sure you're comfortable doing this?"

She laughed nervously. "Well, I'm a bit of a control freak, so handing my classroom over to a sub for the rest of the year is going to be hard to do. I have someone in mind, though. A teacher who retired last June in order to care for her sick husband. He passed away in late January. When I ran into her at the grocery store not too long ago, she mentioned she might want to do some subbing. I can check with her and see if she could cover the rest of the year for me."

"I can't tell you how much I appreciate this." He grinned. "This production—this movie—feels like giving birth, in a way. I think our project needs two parents there, guiding it along."

"Hmm. Maybe I should ask for a co-directing credit," she teased.

He laughed. "You'll get a co-producer one. That should be good enough." Then he grew serious. "I mean it, Paige. I appreciate you putting your regular life on hold and taking this on. Taking *me* on."

Her heart beat faster as his hand went to the back of her neck, pulling her closer. Tanner kissed her softly and then released her.

"I won't start something we can't finish," he said.

"Right now, Joe Bob Milton takes priority. But after we get home?"

The heat in his eyes told her this would be the best day of her life.

13

Showered and dressed, Paige was ready to leave the house when Tanner asked her to wait for him.

"What do you mean?" she asked, confused.

"I want to go with you."

"No. No way," she said emphatically. "Ida Lou's Diner is a gossip hot spot. It's where most people get their news about things going on in town. I'm not going to subject you to that. Or me, quite frankly. It may come out in the next few weeks that I've written and sold a screenplay, but I want to cherish the quiet while I can."

"I'll stay in the car," Tanner volunteered. "No one will see me."

"What is the point of you going?" she asked. "If no one will see you, why bother going at all?"

He took her hand. Bringing it to her lips, he pressed a kiss on her knuckles. "Because I don't want to be apart from you."

Paige visibly trembled. His words made her knees go weak. "Damn, Hollywood. That's so . . . romantic."

He grazed his teeth against her knuckles, causing a

shiver to travel up her spine. "What can I say? I'm just a romantic kind of guy."

She took a deep breath, slowly exhaling. "All right. But you don't get out. Period. I don't want any Tanner Haddock sightings in the wild."

"Give me seven minutes. I'll be back."

He hurried off to the shower. Paige sat on her sofa, still a bit dizzy from both his touch and words. Could he possibly be telling the truth? That he really didn't want to be out of her sight? Having never dated, she didn't know if he might be spinning some kind of fantasy—or if this was the real thing. Either way, she would take it. Take him.

Even as she wondered what might pass between them after she spoke to her principal.

Her phone rang, and she saw it was Nana. "Hey, Nana. Up early as usual, I see."

"Good morning, honey. I was wondering if I might come for lunch instead of dinner this evening. Tanner did tell you about dinner?"

"He did. Manicotti. Really, Nana, you're pulling out all the stops. You usually make manicotti once a year, for my birthday."

"I thought Tanner would appreciate my recipe. I forgot that I need to meet with the altar guild this afternoon. By the time I get out of that meeting, it won't leave enough time for me to make the pasta and simmer the sauce. You know I like my meat sauce to simmer a good hour or more before baking."

"Lunch would be terrific. Whatever time is good for you, just come over."

"I'll aim for twelve-thirty. See you soon, honey."

"Bye."

She'd thought they could order a pizza from Romano's tonight, but there would be plenty of manicotti left over. Nana's recipe fed at least a half-dozen people. Maybe they could still get pizza and save the leftovers for tomorrow. Romano's reminded her of Vivi.

What would her friend think of Paige hiding her writing? Up until now, they had told one another anything of importance. She hoped keeping her screenwriting a secret wouldn't cause problems with her longtime best friend. Paige determined to call Vivi, maybe after she and Tanner did whatever he had planned for them today.

Tanner appeared in jeans and a navy, long-sleeved T-shirt. It made those crystal blue eyes of his pop. For a moment, Paige was spellbound and couldn't even move.

"Earth to Paige. Calling Paige Laramie."

"I'm here," she said, shaking her head. "I'm deciding whether to take your truck or my car. If I'm seen driving your truck, there'll be questions. But if we walk out to my car, someone might see us."

"It's barely after six in the morning," he protested.

"Small towns start early, Hollywood. No lazing about."

"I've had my share of early morning calls, Laramie. And I grew up on a ranch. I had chores to do before I could even think about breakfast or leaving for school. Shall I put a paper bag over my head and have you walk me to your car?"

"I'll pull my car into the driveway and open the garage. Dash out and get in as fast as you can."

"What about coming home? It'll be daylight by then. Won't Mrs. D be watching out her window?" he asked, referring to her curious next-door neighbor she had told him about.

"I'll think of something," she said, having no clue what might work. Already, her gut told her someone would see him, whether in town or as they returned to her house. "Actually, it might be a good thing to get it out in the open."

"Is that Paige Laramie talking? Or has some pod person taken over your body?" he teased.

"I think we've done all the work we can on the script," she said carefully. "I know you're eager to get rolling on things. Lining up financing. Casting. It might be better if you leave town today and get started on those things."

She turned and picked up her keys, but he whirled her around. "What's going on? You know we still have a ton of things to talk about." He paused. "And do."

Nerves flooded her. "Tanner, I'm thinking you were right to begin with. Becoming involved with a co-worker is not a good idea. I—"

He cut her off, the sudden kiss fierce and demanding. Paige pushed against his chest, wanting to finish what she was saying, but he was having none of that. His arms held her hostage—and she became a willing captive as his mouth grew more insistent on hers. The kiss was meant to be possessive and certainly got the point across.

Breaking it, he gazed down at her. "It was my rule to start with. It was a smart one for all these years. It kept an inexperienced, immature me from jumping in and making some bad decisions. It allowed me to be friendly and yet keep my distance with everyone I worked with.

"But I don't want any distance between us, Paige. We're so in tune, it's a little scary. We finish each other's sentences. We know what the other is thinking. I need you with me every step of the way on this film, but I'm not going to sacrifice the relationship I want with you because of a rule I set for myself more than a dozen years ago."

He kissed her again. "Believe me, not being involved with a fellow actor or anyone else on set worked a long time for me. I know my own mind now. I can handle it. I look at you as my equal. I need you along for the ride, every minute I'm on set working and a lot of the off-set time, as well. We'll need to watch the dailies. Make adjustments. This film will consume me, and I hope you, too. But I plan to make time for us to be together, no matter how busy we get. I want my commitment to you to be strong before we tackle this project as a team."

He cradled her face in his hands. "Yes, I'll have to leave soon and fly to California to do a few things. But you promised me a week. I plan to use every minute of that week to be here, with you. Got it?"

Paige nodded, slightly overwhelmed. She kept telling herself just because he said he was committed to her now didn't mean that commitment would continue down the road. In the long run, she figured she would be hurt pretty badly when Tanner walked away and returned to his old life. But she would have him now—and in the weeks to come—as they planned every detail of the shoot and then filmed. He had outlined the process to her, and she knew because of the small cast involved and the filming all taking place on location here in Sugar Springs, he would be able to complete the film by the end of summer. She would return to school and her life after that. He would go home and edit his first directorial effort.

Just enjoy the here and now. Soak up the experience. Find the joy in being with this man, if only for a little while. She could deal with heartbreak later.

Right now, *carpe diem* would be her philosophy for the rest of this week.

"Got it," she responded.

Tanner slung an arm about her shoulder. "Then I'll drive."

He led her to the garage and opened the passenger door for her. Paige tried to calm the loop-de-dos circling her stomach as he backed the truck from her garage and drove the few short blocks to the square. The time on the clock tower said it was almost six-thirty as Tanner pulled into an open parking spot a few places away from the diner's door.

"I'm coming in," he said, his tone even. "We're a team. We'll do this together."

She didn't protest as he came around and helped her from the truck, lacing his fingers through hers. In fact, she was a tiny bit proud as he led her to the door, and they entered.

Ida Lou's was about half-filled at that time of the morning. Paige didn't know if this was a normal crowd or not because she was usually on her way to school at this time when it was in session. She spied Joe Bob and tugged on Tanner. As they made their way across to the far side of the diner, she glimpsed the startled faces and then caught the buzz spreading through the diner as she slid into the booth, followed by Tanner.

Opposite them, Joe Bob Milton was chowing down on a short stack of pancakes and sipping coffee, an open newspaper next to his plate. He glanced up.

"Why, good morning, Paige."

Joe Bob's eyes flicked to her companion, and his jaw dropped. He tried to say something, but no sound came out.

"Good morning, Mr. Milton," Tanner said affably,

extending his right hand. His left still held hers under the table. "I'm Tanner Haddock."

The entire diner had gone silent, straining to hear whatever was said in the conversation about to occur.

Somehow, Joe Bob set down his coffee, though it sloshed a bit, and offered Tanner his hand.

"I know you. At least, I've seen you enough on the screen, thanks to my wife."

"Joy runs the furniture store we've passed," Paige volunteered, hiding her smile at her principal's reaction. "Her parents own it, but Joy manages it."

Joe Bob turned his gaze back to her. "What in tarnation are you doing with a movie star, Paige? At six-thirty in the morning?"

"I'm a screenwriter," she said proudly, happy to be openly admitting it for the first time. "Tanner has bought something I've written and will be filming a large part of it in Sugar Springs."

"You don't say," Joe Bob said, shaking his head back and forth in disbelief.

Tanner turned on the charm. "Joe Bob, I really need Paige's help with this project. I'll be directing for the first time, as well as starring in the film, and I can't do it alone. Paige understands these characters. After all, she created them. I was hoping you might grant her a leave of absence so she can help with the film."

For the first time, Joe Bob frowned. "I've got to put my principal's hat on, Mr. Haddock."

"Tanner," the actor prompted, smiling broadly. "I'm sure you can work something out. Like you did for the science teacher who had to pull guard duty."

"You know about that?" Joe Bob asked, perplexed.

"I know a lot about Sugar Springs. And Paige," Tanner said, releasing her hand and slipping his arm around her shoulders.

She heard the gasps coming from patrons throughout the diner.

"I need her help, Joe Bob," Tanner said earnestly. "I'll also be bringing in a film crew. It could be good for the businesses. Even good for tourism. I know a smart guy like you wants to help Sugar Springs in any way he can."

"Let her take the time off," Ida Lou prompted, having arrived at their table, coffee pot in hand. She topped off Joe Bob's coffee. "Tommy would be grateful."

"Tommy is Joe Bob's brother and mayor of Sugar Springs," Paige said quietly to Tanner.

"I'm thinking of asking Marge Echols if she'd be willing to sub for me," she told her boss.

"I'll do it!" a voice called.

Paige turned and saw Marge leap to her feet and rush over. "I've been marking time, Joe Bob. Even thinking about coming back to teaching full-time. Already have a call in with TRS, seeing if I can un-retire."

"It's called retire/rehire," the administrator said. "The process can get complicated."

"But I can sub now for Paige if she wants me to." A bright-eyed Marge looked at Tanner. "Marge Echols."

He did the megawatt smile. "Tanner Haddock. You'd be doing us a big favor, Marge. Thanks for volunteering."

"I'm happy to help," she said, her voice going dreamy.

Paige turned and coughed, trying to hide her laughter at seventy-year-old Marge mooning over a man half her age. Then again, what woman wouldn't do the same?

"Let me sweeten the pot, Joe Bob," Tanner added. "Not only could businesses in the town see a boost, but I'm also thinking of hiring local actors to play the small roles of people in the fictional town, similar to how *Nomadland* hired a number of real-life nomads as actors." He paused. "There might even be a role for you."

"Aw, hell," Joe Bob said good-naturedly. "I don't need a role, but if you have one for my wife, then Paige can take the damn LOA."

Tanner smiled. "I'll see it happens. It'll be small, but Joy will be on set. I'll make certain to get a picture with her."

"I need one now of you and me, else she's never gonna believe this," Joe Bob said, climbing from the booth.

They took the picture, and Joe Bob made Paige promise she would show up that final week in order to administer exams to her students and input final grades, which she agreed to do. By the time they left the diner, it was packed. Ida Lou helped clear a path, announcing Tanner and Paige had work to do, and he'd pose for selfies another day.

"You owe me," the diner's owner said as she got them to the door. "I want a part in your movie."

"Done," Tanner said. "There's a diner owner. You'll be perfect for the part."

More people had gathered outside on the square, apparently because those inside had texted them. Tanner hurried them to his truck, seeing her inside it and going around to the driver's side, stopping for one selfie with two giggling teenaged girls from her fourth period class. As Tanner jumped into the vehicle, she saw the teens squealing, jumping up and down as they looked at the picture.

"Welcome to the wild, Hollywood. East Texas style, that is."

He leaned toward her and gave her a lingering kiss. "I think we'll take a walk on the wild side ourselves now, Laramie."

Paige couldn't wait to get home.

14

The closer they got to her house, the more Paige's nerves ramped up. *Seriously* ramped up. As in she thought she might have a heart attack because the pounding was so violent, she thought her chest might explode. The blood had rushed to her ears, making her lightheaded. Her body trembled.

"You okay?" Tanner asked as he hit the remote and pulled his truck into the garage, cutting the engine and quickly lowering the door.

He faced her, his concern obvious. "You're white as a ghost, Paige." He reached for her hands. "And as icy as one."

Her teeth chattered as he rubbed her hands to warm them. "How many ghosts have you been around, Hollywood?" she teased, but her eyes filled with tears.

She pulled away from him and exited the truck, hurrying into the house. She grabbed a tissue and dabbed her eyes and then blew her nose. A glass stood next to the tissue box, about a third full, and Paige grabbed it, downing the water, telling herself to chill out as she placed the glass on the table again.

Tanner came up behind her, slipping his arms around her, pulling her against him. "We don't have to do anything, sweetheart."

She grasped his muscled forearms. "But I want to. I'm eager to explore . . .things."

"I understand you're nervous. Even a little afraid. I won't push you to do anything you don't want to do."

Paige let out a frustrated breath. "I'm not even sure what we'll do. I feel utterly foolish, Tanner. I'm thirty years old. Intellectually, I understand what's involved with sex. I've read romance novels. I've seen some pretty sexy movies. I just can't picture *me* doing any of that. With you. Besides, you've done it a lot. You're Tanner Sex God Haddock. Every woman wants to be with you. Every man wants to be you. I've barely learned how to kiss this week."

He turned her in his arms and gave her a deep, wonderful kiss. He broke it, gazing into her eyes, a ghost of a smile on his sensual lips.

"And look how good you've become at it after only a few times."

"You think so?" she asked, feeling zero confidence.

Tanner caressed her cheek. "Do you think I would have kissed you if I didn't like it? If I didn't like you?"

Her breasts tingled. So did the back of her neck. And a low throb had begun at her core.

"I do like you. I like kissing you." Paige rolled her eyes. "I never thought I'd say that to any man."

"Don't think. Just do," he urged, his mouth coming down on hers again for a kiss that curled her toes and caused her heart to palpitate.

Breaking the kiss, he said, "See? That was easy. We just kissed. We did what came naturally to us."

She swallowed. "You think sex will be the same? Even though I have no idea how to even get started?"

His lazy smile caused her heart to slam against her ribs. "First, we aren't going to have sex. We'll be making love with one another. To one another."

His words send a shiver running through her. A good kind of shiver. Not one of fear.

But of desire . . .

Tanner slid his hands down her arms slowly, making her heart skip a beat. He took her hands and raised them to his lips, tenderly kissing them.

"We do what makes us feel good. We stop if you want to."

Paige nodded, her throat thick with unshed tears.

He led her to her bedroom and closed the door. The blinds were already closed. He'd made the bed but went to it now, pulling the throw pillows from it and turning back the comforter.

"This is our world now," he said softly. "One we're creating for each other. One where we try to please one another."

"All right," she told him, stepping to him and slipping her hands around his waist. Paige rested her cheek against his chest and felt his heartbeat. It was fast, probably as fast as hers.

Raising her head, she asked, "Are you nervous? What if we . . .aren't a good match?"

Tanner's fingers slid into her hair. "Babe, we're going to be a perfect fit. Yes, I'm a little nervous because I want to make this good for you. But I'm more excited than nervous. More importantly, I know you want me *for me*. Not because I'm some guy on a big screen or because I make a ton of money. This week with you has shown me you aren't all that impressed with that stuff."

He took a deep breath. "For the first time in too many years to count, I'm with a woman who sees *me*.

Who wants *me*. Not the movie star. Just the guy who comes from a small town. The guy who wants to be with you more than anything else, Paige."

"Kiss me," she suddenly demanded. "If you kiss me, I think I'll be okay."

His fingers massaged her scalp. "Oh, I promise you'll be better than okay."

With that, his mouth came down on hers. The kiss was greedy, taking from her, branding her, causing her insides to spin until she was dizzy with desire.

She answered his kiss with everything she had. Everything she felt. Everything she wanted from him. From this moment.

Tanner was right. Kissing him had become the most natural thing in the world to do. Her favorite thing to do. What lay ahead might also become her new favorite activity. Paige tamped down the nerves and let her desire wash over her. It—and this beautiful man—would guide her.

He kept kissing her but unzipped the warm-up jacket she wore, pulling it from her shoulders. His hands slid beneath her T-shirt, warm and sure as they moved along her skin. His fingers found the clasp to her bra and undid it. Tanner lifted her shirt, briefly breaking the kiss to let it pass between their lips, and then his mouth seized hers again as he pulled the shirt over her head and tossed it aside. He slipped the straps from her shoulders and then the bra, too, was gone.

Bare to the waist now, she felt the cool air against her skin, along with his warm hands, kneading her breasts, causing her heart to speed up and her core to pound unmercifully. He pulled her against him, his lips trailing down her throat, nipping at the pulse point. They slid to her shoulder, and he continued nibbling it, sending surges of need through her.

Paige broke the kiss. "Fair is fair, Hollywood," she managed to breathlessly say, grabbing the hem of his T-shirt and bunching it in her fingers, sliding it up to reveal the six-pack and muscular chest she had gawked over during more than one movie.

He bent slightly so she could pull it over his head. Before she could even release it, Tanner had already wrapped her in his arms again, warm flesh pressed against warm, bare flesh, her breasts tickled by the matting of hair on his chest. She dropped his shirt, looping her arms about his neck, and initiated a kiss with him for the first time.

It felt good. It felt right.

It felt real.

His hands stroked her back up and down. She caught the tang of his cologne as she pushed her fingers into his thick, abundant hair and held onto it as his mouth overwhelmed hers, greedy again, taking, taking, taking until Paige was breathless.

But in a good way.

He walked her to the bed, the back of her knees bumping into the mattress, and then she was against it, flat on her back, her legs dangling from the bed. He remained on his feet, bending to unlace her sneakers, pulling them and her socks from her feet as she stared up at him hungrily. The thing was, he stared back with the same need in his yes.

Need for her . . .

Paige had always thought herself average-looking, but the way Tanner gazed at her now made her feel like a goddess. Her confidence began to soar.

Until he unbuttoned her jeans and began sliding them down her hips.

Panic filled her. She suddenly couldn't breathe. This was wrong. All wrong. She was wrong for him. He needed a tall, leggy, gorgeous creature who oozed sex appeal. Not a short high school teacher with small breasts and no experience in the bedroom.

"Disney?" he murmured, chuckling.

No. Oh, hell, no.

She had not thought today was the day she would be having sex for the first time. She'd flung on the first pair of underwear that she'd dug out of the drawer, hurrying so she could get to Ida Lou's and talk with Joe Bob. Her face flamed with humiliation as she saw Tanner grinning down at her Disney boy-short panties. They were covered in Pluto, Mickey, Daisy Duck—you name it. Vivi had found them on Amazon and thought they were a hoot, buying each of them a pair several years ago.

Tanner was still kneeling. He'd slid off her jeans and now his fingers brushed against her belly, slipping into the waistband.

"I figured you more for the Disney Princess type," he drawled, his fingers sliding beneath the cotton.

"They're comfortable," she said defensively. "Vivi bought both of us a pair for Christmas one year."

He dropped a kiss on her belly, causing her to tremble. "We'll find you a pair with Belle on them. Or I'll have some made up for you with your picture and the label *My Disney Princess*." He waggled his eyebrows at her.

Paige laughed, relaxing. "Doesn't that sound a little lecherous, Hollywood?"

Grinning, he said, "Maybe."

Then he slipped them down her thighs. Her calves. Her feet. She squeezed her eyes closed, not wanting to see him looking at her. She was naked. He wasn't.

"Ah. Perfection," he said, resting one hand on her flat belly, his thumbing stroking it. Then he slowly ran a finger along the seam of her sex.

Paige almost came off the bed.

Nudging her back down, Tanner said, "We need a warmup act before the big show."

"Do you mean foreplay?"

"I mean by the time I enter you, I want you hot. Panting. Out of your mind, screaming my name."

"Oh."

He smiled—and the warmth of that smile did her in. That and those crystal blue eyes.

Tanner stood, unbuckling his belt and opening his jeans. He pushed them down his legs and stepped from them, slipping a condom from his pocket and setting it on the nightstand. His boxer-briefs were a dark gray, the bulge in them obvious.

He touched it. "This is for you, babe. All yours. But I'll take my time."

She swallowed. "Okay." Now, she worried about how big he must be and how much it was going to hurt.

Don't think about that. Just enjoy the moment, she told herself.

Joining her on the bed, he went to work like the master he was. He worshipped her breasts, kneading them, licking them, sucking them until she was panting and tingling all over.

Then his tongue glided down her belly—and kept going. She tensed and then forced herself to relax as Tanner took her hand and gave her fingers a squeeze.

He reached his destination, taking her thighs and

opening them. His hands rubbed up and down them, sending shivers through her. He touched her core, sliding a finger inside her and stroking her deeply.

"Oh. Oh!"

"Good?"

Paige raised her head. "Better than good. Leaning toward great—but I don't want your ego to overinflate, Hollywood."

That magical smile again. "Ah, Laramie. What am I going to do with you?" He paused. "I know."

A second finger joined the first. His gaze locked on hers as he caressed her. She began trembling, dropping her head back onto the pillow, closing her eyes and giving over to the new, marvelous sensations. She'd never been someone who experimented. Had never touched herself intimately. So everything he did was new and wonderful, and incredible.

Then he licked the seam of her sex, and she whimpered. His hands went to her knees again, steadying her, as his tongue plunged inside her. Paige cried out. In wonder. In awe. Because it felt so damned good. Everything he was doing was amazing.

His tongue and teeth worked her into a frenzy. She was gasping. Panting. Raising her hips to meet him.

Then colors burst and collided. Her orgasm exploded, unlike anything she'd ever felt.

"Ride it, babe. Ride it. Master it," Tanner encouraged.

She'd always followed instructions well and did so now, reaching a peak of pleasure so great that tears leaked from the corners of her eyes. Before she could thank him—kiss him—touch him—Tanner was knocking at heaven's door again.

"You are wet for me. And wild," he told her, slipping on the condom.

"Yes," she said, gasping, as he plunged inside her with one, swift thrust.

A moment of pain. Hardly that. She didn't question it because he began to dance with her. An age-old dance of love performed for thousands of years between men and women. He kissed her deeply as he stroked her body. All the while he danced, moving in and out. She caught his rhythm. She wrapped her arms about him and caught him. She would never let go.

Never . . .

Then the feeling rose in her again. She moaned. He groaned. Their dance spiraled higher and higher and then out of control as they hit their climax at the same time. By now, Paige had wrapped her legs around Tanner's waist, which allowed him to drive more deeply into her. She rode the waves of pleasure, laughing, crying. Coming back down to earth.

He stilled above her after making a very satisfied sound and collapsed atop her. She welcomed his weight, which drove her into the mattress. Paige absently stroked his back with one hand, the other toying with the hair at his nape.

Rolling suddenly, she found herself on her side, face-to-face with him. Tanner. The man she'd just had sex with.

No, the one she had made love with.

Brushing a lock of hair from her face, he cupped her cheek. "How are you?"

"Over the moon. How about you?" she asked worriedly.

He brushed his lips softly against hers. "As good as it gets, babe."

Tanner turned her and spooned with her, his front to her back, their legs tangled, his arms secure around her. He dropped a kiss on her shoulder, one she felt to her soul.

"I love you."

Paige stiffened in his arms. "No. You don't. That's just the after-sex glow talking, Tanner. We barely know one another."

His arms tightened around her. "No. It's as if I've known you forever, Paige. I knew what you were feeling the moment I saw you through the glass all those years ago. Walking across the parking lot, being guided by your father. I knew you then. I know you now."

She shook her head. "No. You just think you do. It's only been a few days. I can't have you telling me—"

"That I love you?" She sensed him shaking his head. "I wouldn't have thought I could either. But feelings don't lie. I *do* know you. I know I have a lot more to learn about you, but I know you in my heart. I know you prefer quick showers over long baths. That you eat ketchup on your fries and your cheeseburger but never on a hot dog. You like animals but have never had a pet. You run because if fills a need in you that doesn't have a word to describe it. You write because while teaching is your heart, writing is your soul."

He kissed her shoulder again. "I know you because we both come from small towns. We have core values in common. We're both hard workers. Creative. Loyal. We're friendly but have few friends, preferring to keep the world and most people at arm's length."

Tanner turned her in his arms, so they were facing one another again. "And there are intangibles that are so elusive and ethereal that I can't put a name to them yet. Maybe you, the writer, can classify those feelings one day when we're old and gray and rocking on the porch in our matching rockers."

Paige looked deeply into his eyes. "You're painting a picture of us that I don't think you really understand."

"I understand that we're kindred spirits. That you make me laugh. That you challenge me." He smiled, his thumb caressing her bottom lip. "And you're sexy as hell. Like an onion, you've got layers and layers for me to pull back and explore for years to come."

"But I'm not of your world, Tanner."

"What world? Hollywood? It's just a name. A place. Yes, I have a house there because I film in California a lot. But my true home is the one on the ranch in Oklahoma, away from Tinseltown and its flash and lies."

He smoothed her hair. "No, that's not exactly true. I just realized something." He paused. "Home is when I'm with you."

Paige burst out in tears.

Tanner held her, letting her cry, saying nonsense to her. She'd never felt such a depth of emotions before. To be honest, she'd never let herself feel much of anything after Mama died. She didn't experience lows or highs. She simply rode a small wave that didn't bump up or down too much. With Tanner, he had brought all of himself to the table and laid everything out for her to see. No pretense. Just him. And she loved that about him.

She . . . loved him . . .

Gritting her teeth, she closed her eyes. "I love you, too."

He chuckled, kissing her brow. "Is it that hard to say? You look like you're in pain, Laramie."

Paige opened her eyes, seeing the teasing light in his. "I'm confused."

"About what? I want to be as transparent with you as possible."

"I don't get how someone like you could feel the way I feel about you."

He kissed her. "You act as if you're some nine-headed hydra, babe. You are a very attractive woman. You're intelligent. Creative. Sensitive. Nurturing. I have the feeling everyone around you loves you to pieces—and you have no idea they do so or why they would."

Tanner had hit the nail square on the head.

"I've never felt good enough," she admitted. "I pushed myself hard in school to be the best. To stand out. I tried so hard to make Mama proud and then to ease her suffering when she was sick. I put in long hours at school, trying to come up with lessons which will make my students appreciate and enjoy learning. Not just history but about life and people and themselves."

He kissed her again. "You are my ideal woman, Paige Laramie. If I have to spend every day for the rest of our lives convincing you of that, I will."

"What are you saying?" she asked, her guard coming up again swiftly.

"I guess I should've had some writer put the words down on paper for me to memorize. I'll speak from my heart, though." He framed her face with his hands. "I love you. I want to spend all my time with you. The rest of my life. Our lives. I want to work together. Have kids, if you want them, too. I want to push myself—and you—to make some great movies. With you, I'm happy. No, more than that. Content, just being with you."

Warmth filled her. "You really mean what you're saying, don't you?"

"I do," he confirmed.

"Why are you so sure?"

"Aren't you?" he countered. "If you're not, say so. But for me, I've never felt this relaxed in someone's company and yet excited at the same time."

Paige saw the love in his eyes and gave into it. "I have zero experience, Hollywood. I've let the first gorgeous, athletic, funny, smart, perfect man turn my head. That's you. It's all you. I can't imagine it ever being anyone but you."

Tanner began kissing her again, and their passion flared. He made love to her tenderly, lovingly, letting Paige know just how much she meant to him.

They lay in one another's arms afterward, talking, drifting into sleep, awakening and talking some more.

Then the doorbell rang. Both bolted up.

"I guess someone finally worked up his courage and decided to ring your bell," Tanner said.

She giggled. "Nope. It's not that. I forgot to mention that Nana said she was coming for lunch instead of dinner."

"Then we better get out of bed and greet her."

Paige scrambled from the bed, tossing on her clothes. "Let me get the door. If anyone is out there, I don't want them getting a glimpse of you."

She hurried to the front door and opened it, startled by what she saw.

At least two hundred people were on her front lawn. Flashes from cameras exploded, and she realized it just wasn't Sugar Springs residents but others who had arrived. It was a surreal, *Notting Hill* kind of moment, when Hugh Grant's roommate opened the door to see the swarm of press gathered outside their flat.

Nana pushed past Paige and jerked on her arm, pulling her back into the house and slamming and locking the door.

"You and Tanner can't stay here, Paige," Nana declared. "You've got to leave town."

15

Tanner realized he had been living in an idyllic world with Paige ever since he'd arrived in Sugar Springs. It surprised him that they'd kept his presence quiet for as long as they had. He had forced the issue, though, by accompanying her to the diner this morning.

What had occurred between them once they got home was the most moving and magical experience of his life. He was right in distinguishing for Paige the difference between having sex and making love. He felt he had made love for the first time today and looked forward to the years ahead he would spend with this incredible woman.

For now, though, they needed to deal with the present situation.

He went to the window and eased a slat of the blinds up, seeing Paige's yard filled with people, who also spilled out into the street. Two police officers tried to hold back the group, while a third man stood in the center of the sidewalk leading up to the house's doorway.

Tanner turned and asked Nana, "Are you all right?"

"A little rattled," she admitted. "But I'm fine. I'm pissed because I was jostled and lost the manicotti I was bringing you for lunch." She used one of her colorful expletives to explain the loss of the oval Corning Ware dish, one of her favorites.

"I'll replace it for you, Nana. I promise."

"I don't want you to think Sugar Springs is a bad place, Tanner," the old women told him. "Yes, I saw some people I know in the crowd, but the majority of them have come in from other places surrounding the town. Your impromptu visit to Ida Lou's this morning spread like wildfire. When you come here to begin filming, I guarantee you that the town will close ranks, especially if you are serious about putting residents here in your production. Right now, Police Chief Hamilton is out there with two of his officers trying to manage the crowd."

She turned to her granddaughter. "I meant what I said, honey. For both your sakes', you need to get out of town for a while."

"You know I can't do that," Paige said through gritted teeth.

Concern filled him. She had gone white, no color in her face. Gone was the laughing, carefree, sexy woman who had more than satisfied him in bed the last several hours.

"I think the best thing to do is head to Dallas," Tanner suggested. "I usually stay at The Mansion when I'm in town there. They know me. They'll protect my privacy. Their suites have a nice-sized living room, along with a kitchenette and two bedrooms. We can work on the storyboarding and then—"

"No," Paige said emphatically. "You go on. Without me. In fact, why don't you head back to California now? You were going to at the end of the week anyway. You can start working on casting. Pulling together your crew. Obtaining the additional financing you wanted. I'll stay here and start scouting locations. Investigating housing for the cast and crew. Things I can do easily because no one will be following me around."

"I hate to break it to you, sweetheart, but I'm sure pictures of us from the diner are already flooding the Internet and fan sites right now. I put my arm around you and held your hand in there for a reason. I wanted the world to see you were my girl and that you make me happy. That means the press is going to dog you. At least for a little while."

Paige let a few choice expletives of her own fly from her lips. If the situation weren't so serious, Tanner would see the humor in it because Paige so resembled Nana in this moment.

"Go pack a few things, and I'll call The Mansion. Reg, too. I think I've mentioned him to you before. He's head of my security team."

"I'm not going with you," she said flatly and stormed from the room.

Moments later, he heard the bathroom door slam and the lock being thrown.

His eyes cut to Nana. "What's going on?"

The old woman shook her head slowly, sinking to the couch. Tanner went to join her, taking one of her hands in his.

"Talk to me, Nana. I need to know what's going on with Paige. Why doesn't she want to go to Dallas with me?"

Tears swam in her eyes. "She doesn't leave Sugar Springs, Tanner. Ever."

"What do you mean, ever? I don't understand."

"I don't know how to say it more clearly. Ever since my daughter and I brought Paige home from Owens, she hasn't left this town. It's as if Sugar Springs became her refuge. Her anchor. Her fortress of solitude. The only place she felt safe."

Nana's words hit him like a physical blow. "But . . .what about college? I know she earned her teaching degree."

"We have a local community college. Paige attended it. Then she took online classes offered by the university over in Tyler. She did her student teaching right here in Sugar Springs, and they hired her after she graduated. She doesn't leave this place, Tanner."

Anger surged through him. He released Nana's hand. "You should have gotten her therapy. She was just a little girl when all the bad things happened to her."

Nana eyed him with her infinite patience. "We're a small town, Tanner, and it was twenty years ago. Paige told her mother and me that she didn't want to talk about it. That it made her feel bad when we brought it up. We respected her wishes and didn't. She thrived. Was always the best student in her class. She does have trust issues, and I can understand why. She's never been close to any man. Never dated. Then you came along, and I saw the sparkle in her eyes finally return. I haven't seen it for many years."

Nana placed her hand atop his. "You're good for her, Tanner. This writing. It's good for her, too. She needs to leave the confines of Sugar Springs. There's a big world out there. I know my granddaughter can tackle it. That is, if she has someone she trusts by her side. Not someone propping her up and pushing her along. Or dragging her. A man who can be her equal and walk next to her in the journey of life."

"I want to be that man, Nana."

Her gaze met his. "Then help Paige take those first baby steps. Be there when she falls. When she fails. Because she will."

"I can do that," he solemnly promised. He rose. "I'll go talk to her now. You might want to head home."

"I think I'll stick around until the two of you leave," Nana said. "The crowd will follow you. I'll deal with any damage outside. Trampled flowers. That kind of thing. So Paige won't have to."

"Then at least let Chief Hamilton know that Paige and I will be leaving in the next half-hour."

For the first time, Nana smiled saucily. "I'll do that, Tanner. And just to let you know, I know all my lines and most everyone else's, too."

He chuckled. "I see overachieving runs in the family."

Tanner left the living room and went down the hall, pausing to collect his thoughts before he knocked on the door. What he would say to Paige now had to be strong enough to convince her to come with him after a lifetime of being tethered physically and emotionally to Sugar Springs.

Knocking on the bathroom door, he said, "Paige, I want you to let me in."

Silence.

Gathering his courage, he continued. "I want you not only to let me in the bathroom now but for you to let me into your heart. I thought you already had because you told me that you loved me. I love you. I'm ready to stand by you. With you. I need you to know that we are a team. That we tackle everything together, the good and the bad."

Tanner waited patiently, praying she would open the door to him. this physical door—and the one to her heart.

When he heard the lock thrown, hope sprang within him. The door slowly opened. Paige was still void of color. She visibly trembled. Opening his arms, she stepped into them. He held her for a few minutes, not saying anything. Then he released her, capturing her hand and leading her to her bedroom, where he closed the door.

He took her other hand, facing her, and said, "Nana told me you never leave Sugar Springs."

Paige nodded. "I know it sounds crazy, Tanner, but it's my haven. I left it once—and horrible things happened. It's foolish, I know. I just can't help it, though."

"It's not foolish. It's been your security blanket all these years, but your mom is gone, Paige. You know she's not coming back. And as spry as Nana is, the day will come when she's no longer with you either. But I will always be here for you. I want us to create a home together. I know your heart is telling you the same thing mine is, Paige, and that is wherever we are together, *that* is home."

He tugged on her, bringing them closer together, and tenderly kissed her.

She pulled away, and he saw resolve in her eyes. "I can do this," she told him. "For me. For us."

"Would Dallas be too much for you?"

"Yes. I can't imagine being in that large a place so quickly. Even if Vivi, my best friend, is there." She hiccuped. "She doesn't even know about you. Neither does Sarah, my friend from school."

He smiled. "I have a feeling Vivi and Sarah are going to hear something about us, but I hope you'll speak with both and let them know your version of things versus what's been splashed across social media." He paused. "Since Dallas is a little too much to start with, I have an idea.

"We'll go to Owens. To my parents' ranch."

~

PAIGE BEGAN PACKING. She was numb inside. The thought of leaving her home, much less Texas, terrified her. The fact she would be returning to Owens caused her to quake in fear. Then she remembered how kind Tanner's parents had been to her all those years ago. He had said their ranch was outside of Owens. They might not even go into town at all.

"I can do this," she said aloud, suddenly knowing that she could. That Tanner would be by her side. He had made a commitment to her. He wouldn't let her down. If anyone could help her become whole again, it was Tanner Haddock. The boy who had saved her once.

She hoped the man he had become would save her again.

She quickly packed for a few days, all casual clothing, not seeing a need for anything dressy. She supposed after they left Owens that she would return to Sugar Springs, while Tanner flew home to California. He had talked a little about living in Malibu. How the ocean calmed him. How he ran along its beaches and swam in the waters. She had never seen an ocean in person. Perhaps it was finally time she did so.

She gathered her backpack, which she used to carry things to and from school, and placed her laptop and chargers inside it. She assumed they would keep working on the movie while in Oklahoma.

Paige pulled out her cell and called Marge Echols.

"Hi, Marge, it's Paige Laramie."

Marge chuckled. "I was expecting to hear from you sooner, Paige. I'm sure you're calling to tell me everything I need to know come Monday. After all, you have the reputation of being the most organized teacher in the building."

Quickly, Paige explained where her seating charts and lesson plans were located.

"Every day of the rest of the year is planned out, Marge. You can make adjustments as you go, but try to stick to my plans as closely as possible, so my kids will be ready for state testing next month. Quizzes and tests are locked in the cabinet. Other handouts such as project parameters, worksheets, and maps are on the two shelves behind my desk. Other than that, you know the drill."

"Thank you for giving me this opportunity to be back in the classroom, Paige," the retired teacher said. "I've been lonely since my husband passed. I wasn't quite ready to leave teaching when I did, but he needed me home full-time to care for him. Either this long-term sub assignment will let me know I still need to be in the classroom, or it will convince me my time is up and I should find new things to do with my life. Besides, I'm looking forward to having a very small role in your movie."

She chuckled. "Text me anytime you have a question, Marge."

"I don't want you to worry about school, Paige. You already have quite a bit on your plate. And as far as returning to administer finals, that won't be necessary. If it were anyone but me, I could see you coming back to wrap up things. You and Joe Bob can trust me to make sure I handle final grades and all the end of the year tasks for you."

"Thank you again, Marge. I'll be in touch to see how things are going."

Paige took her suitcase and wheeled it to the living room, where Tanner was on his phone. She held up a hand and mouthed, "Five minutes," quickly going to her bathroom and collecting her toiletries.

When she rejoined Tanner, he had a duffel bag at his feet.

"Ready?" he asked.

She nodded, tamping down the rush of fear that bubbled within her.

They went to the kitchen, where Nana was bustling about, wiping down counters. Her grandmother assured Paige she would stay behind and lock up after they had left, as well as move Paige's car into the garage. Tanner took their things and went into the garage to place them in his truck.

Nana kissed Paige's cheek. "Let me know when you get there, honey. I know this is a huge step for you."

"Leaving Owens—or trusting Hollywood?"

"Both," Nana said emphatically. "Tanner is a good man, Paige. He'll understand you. And you'll grow together."

Tanner returned from loading their things into his truck. Nana lifted an insulated bag and handed it to him.

"I packed some waters and a few snacks for you," she told them.

He accepted the bag, slinging the strap over his shoulder, and then enveloped Nana in a bear hug.

"I'll take good care of her, Nana. You can count on me."

"She'll take care of you, too, Tanner. Please tell your parents hello from me."

"Will do. Maybe next time you can come up to the ranch with us."

Nana beamed at him. "Why, I would like that, Tanner. Oh, Chief Hamilton said once you make it past the square, a squad car will be waiting to escort you to the highway. He said give it the gas and keep up with the car. The siren and flashing lights will do the rest."

Paige hugged her grandmother again and accompanied Tanner to the garage.

"We won't have to run the gauntlet. The doors will be locked," he assured her. "Be prepared for people to swarm the truck, however."

Tanner leaned over and kissed her. "Let's do this."

He hit the button on the remote to open the garage and started his truck, backing out slowly once the door had been raised. Paige braced herself, not exactly sure what to expect. As they moved slowly down her driveway, she heard the squeals. The shouts. And saw the blur rush toward them.

She hadn't signed up for this.

Panic streaked through her, causing her heart to race and her mouth to grow dry. She squeezed her eyes shut, forcing herself to take slow, deep breaths and exhaling as she counted to ten. A few bumps shook the truck.

Then she opened her eyes. She had survived being kidnapped by a man who had wanted to make her mom suffer. He hadn't cared a whit about her. Paige had been a tool her father had used to hurt his ex-wife. She had come back to Sugar Springs and thrived. She had a wonderful job at the high school. She had written a script so good that none other than Tanner Haddock had plucked it from who knows how many other screenplays, wanting to make it his directorial debut.

And she had found love. Real love. From the moment she had seen Tanner all those years ago, her gut had told her he was someone she could trust. She still felt that way. The boy had matured into a thoughtful, talented man. One who loved her with all her many flaws. She'd always thought things were meant to be circular, and nothing demonstrated that more than Tanner coming back into her life. They were committed to one another. They had a future together.

Paige was going to enjoy every minute of it.

They reached the street, backing slowly in order not to hit anyone and risk a lawsuit. Chief Hamilton and his cops were pushing the crowd back as much as they could. Women were screaming. Crying. Shouting Tanner's name as he put the truck into drive.

Their gazes met. He took her hand in his, threading their fingers together.

"Let's make a run for it." He smiled at her, one which made her grow warm all over.

"When in doubt, go the Nike route—just do it," she told him.

Tanner nudged the truck forward and those gathered parted. Some began running, either to their cars to give chase or simply after the truck itself. Thankfully, no one had thought to jump into the truck's bed.

He made it to the square and circled around it, exiting the other side, where a waiting Sugar Springs police car eased from a spot and moved in front of them. The cop turned on his lights and siren, and Tanner fell in behind him, speeding in order to keep up. Soon, thanks to their escort, they reached the highway. The cop driving waved and moved to the right lane, easing his speed and cutting the siren and lights.

"Owens, here we come," Tanner said, squeezing Paige's fingers. "Anytime you need me to stop, I will.

We do have to go through town when we get there. I hope that's okay."

Before, she would have protested. Now, with this incredible man by her side, Paige felt she could do anything.

"I'll be fine," she assured him. "I'm with you."

"I called Mom to let her know we're coming. She's invited us for dinner. In the meantime, I'm hungry. Can you break into the snacks Nana packed for us?"

"Will do."

She opened bottled waters for them and removed sandwiches and chips, telling him there were also grapes and cookies.

As they ate, her phone rang. Looking at the Caller ID, she laughed.

"It's Vivi. I need to get this."

Answering the FaceTime call, Paige said, "Hey, Vivi!"

"Paige Laramie, the Internet is going bonkers. Are you having Tanner Haddock's love child? The tabloids say you've been secretly seeing each other for months now. If you have, I am absolutely going to murder you."

"Relax, Vivi. The tabloids didn't get it right."

Her friend sighed dramatically. "Well, there are pictures circulating everywhere, and the girl with him looks exactly like you. Of course, I know how easy it can be to alter things digitally. I just wanted you to be aware of what's out there. I don't want you worried about it."

"I'm not worried. There's no love child. At least not yet. And I haven't been seeing Tanner for months. Just this past week."

Vivi sputtered, "What? What?"

Paige turned the phone so that it faced Tanner. He

glanced over, flashing his megawatt smile. "Hi, Vivi. I've heard awfully good things about you. I can't wait to meet you. I hope you'll cook for me. Paige says you're the best chef in Texas."

She turned the phone back so that it faced her, seeing Vivi's jaw slack.

"He's even better looking in person," she bragged. "I can't wait for you to meet him. We'll talk later. I can't really say where we're going, but I'll call you tomorrow and explain everything."

"Oh, you'll do more than explain, Paige Laramie. You will give me every. Single. Detail. Starting with how he kisses."

"Bye," she said playfully, hanging up and turning off her phone, before slipping it into her purse.

"I like her," Tanner said. "She's protective of you."

"We've been there for each other since kinder-garten. She'll be my maid of honor." Then Paige gulped. "I didn't mean that. Well, she will be, but . . .what I'm saying is . . ."

"You don't want to assume anything. I understand. I've told you I love you and I want to be with you, but I didn't formally ask for a lifetime commitment. I'm sorry about that. I'm a dense kind of guy. I just as-sumed you knew I meant forever."

Tanner switched lanes and took the exit, going along the access road and pulling into a parking lot. It was a roadside picnic area, with two tables and re-strooms. No one was around. He stopped the truck and got out, coming to her side and helping her from the passenger seat.

"This will make for an interesting story for our kids," he said cheerfully, taking her hand and leading her to one of the shaded picnic tables.

Bending to one knee and taking her hands in his,

he said, "Paige Laramie, I wasn't looking for love—but it found me. Fate brought me to you twenty years ago. Now, we've found our way back to each other. I plan for us to never be parted again." He cleared his throat. "I don't have a ring yet, but I'm asking if you'll marry me. I want the fairy tale, Pretty Woman. I want us to rescue one another, over and over, for the rest of our lives."

"Yes," she said softly. "Yes," she told him again, her voice grew stronger. "Yes, yes, yes!"

Tanner sprang to his feet and pulled her into his arms, kissing her thoroughly. He broke the kiss.

"We better get back in the truck before anyone spots us," he said. "I want to get to the ranch so that we have some privacy. Sound good?"

Paige beamed at him. "It sounds great. Everything sounds great, Tanner."

They walked to the truck, hand-in-hand. He opened her door and helped her inside and then climbed into the driver's seat.

"A marriage proposal at a rest area, between ham and cheese sandwiches and cookies. Hope it was romantic enough for you." He started the engine. "How many do you want?"

"Cookies? Or kids?" Paige teased.

"Both," he said, reaching for her hand and bringing it to his lips. "For now, I'll take two cookies, though."

She laughed, opening the bag Nana had sent. "They're chocolate chip."

Tanner grinned at her. "Then maybe three. Cookies, that is."

Paige laughed, the weight she'd been carrying for so long magically lifted from her. This man would always protect her. Always keep her laughing. He would challenge her and stand by her.

All because of this one special man, life was starting to get very, very good.

16

They spent the time driving to Oklahoma getting to know one another even better. They played a quick version of Twenty Questions, covering a wide variety of topics. Paige revealed her favorite snack was cashews, while Tanner couldn't get enough of potato chips. He enjoyed bingeing on Netflix. She preferred reading a book before ever seeing the movie version of it. He was fond of Italian food but limited eating it, citing how he needed to stay in shape—and pasta and bread were rough on the abs.

"You have taken off your shirt in a good number of your movies," she noted. "I should know. Just to let you know, I've called you eye candy to Nana and my friends."

He laughed. "Well, you're *my* eye candy, Laramie."

Paige found herself blushing at the wicked smile he tossed her way and couldn't wait to be in bed with him again, yet a part of her still doubted how someone who looked like Tanner would want to be with an average-looking woman such as herself.

"I want to take you to Greece for our honeymoon," he said out of the blue. "I've traveled a lot for the films I've made. Unfortunately, I never get to act as a tourist in those places. I film and get in and out as quickly as possible. While I've shot movies everywhere from Tokyo to London, I haven't seen many of the sights. Greece is one of the few places that I took my time in, though."

"That was the spy film," she recalled. "Not much of the movie took place there. You hopscotched across the world in that one."

"It was the longest, most grueling shoot to date. But I loved the clear waters and skies of Greece. When filming ended for that movie in Sydney, I retreated to Greece for almost three weeks. Rented a villa on Mykonos for a week. Moved to Corfu and then Crete. My gosh, the pristine beaches there were breathtaking."

He glanced at her. "It was one of the happiest times in my life—and yet one of the loneliest. I was in paradise and had no one to share it with."

He turned back to the road ahead and added, "This time, I'll share it with the love of my life."

Paige was touched and yet she said, "You keep saying these incredibly romantic things to me, Tanner. I'm sorry. I'm plagued with doubts."

"Why? I've been nothing but transparent with you. I've made my feelings for you abundantly clear."

"It's just my insecurities talking," she admitted. "Hammering away at me. I've never felt good enough my entire life."

Tanner reached for her hand and brought it to his lips. "You never need doubt my feelings for you, Paige. You are the best thing that's ever happened to me. Actors are like gypsies. We live out of a suitcase, traveling all around. We make friends on the set, and I will admit that a lot of actors have brief flings while filming goes on. It's a way they connect and pass the down time. Then the shoot ends. Cast and crew go their separate ways. It's an interesting but lonely kind of life. It doesn't have to be anymore because I have you as my anchor. Thankfully, you have a job you can do anywhere."

He hesitated. "At least, I hope that's the case. That you can leave teaching to write full-time. When I go on location, I want you to come with me."

"Have laptop, will travel," she assured him, realizing that she had already spent her last day in the classroom and would resign at year's end. She wouldn't miss it, though. As much as she had enjoyed teaching and had made it her entire world, a new world was opening up to her, courtesy of her fiancé.

The man she loved. The man she would spend the rest of her life with.

"It may be a little hard for me because this is my first time out in the wild, as you call it. But I do love you, Tanner. I want to be with you wherever you go."

"If we can make a go of *Shadows of the Past*, maybe we won't always have to work on separate projects. Maybe we can partner professionally again. I haven't asked. Have you started something new?"

Paige shrugged. "I've been toying with a few ideas. Nothing solid yet. I've never written with anyone particular in mind, though. Maybe I will make you the protagonist in my next script." She grinned. "Or the antagonist again. No, you're already playing against type in *Shadows of the Past*. You'll need to reach and challenge yourself with something different the next time out. Mix things up. You might even enjoy directing so much that your next project might be totally behind the camera instead of in front of it."

They drove through Broken Bow, and Tanner told her they would soon arrive in Owens. She felt the tension build within her. She had come a long way in just a few hours, physically and emotionally. Leaving Sugar Springs. Accepting Tanner's marriage proposal. Talking about traveling with him when he went on location. Deciding to step away from teaching. Confronting the demons of her past.

But a large challenge loomed ahead of her in Owens, a place she'd never thought she would return.

Paige was determined to face those demons. Stare them down and conquer her fears.

"You said we would go through Owens to get to your parents' ranch."

"Yes. Why?"

"I want to stop in town. At the diner."

Tanner didn't respond immediately, causing her to question her idea.

She told him, "I couldn't have done this alone before, but I'm strong enough to stand up to my fears. Because I have you by my side."

Tenderness filled his eyes. "Babe, you'll never have to do anything alone again. If that's what you want us to do, then we'll stop."

They rode in silence for the next few minutes, and then Paige spotted the sign that told them they were entering Owens. The population was barely over two thousand people, tiny by Sugar Springs' standards.

Although it had been many years since she had been here, she got that eerie déjà vu feeling of knowing she was somewhere she'd been before. Yet when they pulled into the parking lot, the sign didn't look familiar to her. The parking lot was also paved, where before it had been merely gravel. She could still hear that crunching sound in her head and even feel her father's fingers tighten on her neck. Paige took a deep breath and blew it out slowly.

Tanner cut the truck's engine, and they sat for a moment. She glanced around the parking lot and only saw one car.

"It's three-thirty now," he said. "That in-between time. The lunch crowd is long gone, and the early birds for dinner have yet to arrive." He paused, their gazes meeting. "Are you sure you're ready for this?"

"I think so. I do know it's something I need to do for myself. If I walk in and walk back out immediately, I know you'll understand, though. Let's try."

He helped her from the truck. Joining their fingers together, he led her to the entrance and opened the door. They entered the diner, Paige's eyes sweeping across it. She spied one man at a table and a server behind the long counter. The woman looked vaguely familiar, and Paige decided she might very well be the server from that long-ago night.

"Tanner Haddock," the woman said fondly, coming to meet them. She looked to be in her mid-fifties, a little heavyset with light brown hair and kind eyes. "It's good to see you. And who is this young lady with you?"

"Annie, this is Paige Laramie, my fiancée."

While she thrilled at hearing Tanner refer to her as his fiancée for the first time, she noticed Annie's eyes widen in shock. The woman recovered quickly, though, and gave Paige a warm smile.

"Paige, it's so nice to meet you. Tanner is a favorite of mine."

A voice called out, "Hey, Tanner, come back here and let me show you a few new things."

She saw a man dressed as a cook standing at the pass-through, smiling broadly.

Tanner glanced to her. "I'll be right back, okay?"

Paige nodded. "Take your time. I need to go to the restroom anyway."

Annie asked, "Can I bring you anything?"

Tanner said, "Mom is making dinner for us, so I'll just take an iced tea." He looked to Paige.

"Make it two iced teas, Annie," she said and walked through the diner to the restrooms, nodding to the lone customer who dabbed his mouth with a napkin and then stood, ready to go.

Everything looked different from what she remembered. Not that she ever allowed herself to think about that night. The once fuzzy images which she had pushed into the recesses of her mind suddenly returned with startling clarity, branded into her memory. Now, though, the inside of this diner looked as if she had never been in it before. She remembered the padded booths having teal cushions and large windows which looked out over the parking lot. The floor had been a black and white vinyl check pattern, while the stools alongside the counter had chrome legs with a red circle cushion for the seat with no backs. Sometime in the last twenty years, this place had undergone a huge makeover. In fact, it looked more like a café than diner now. While it still had a long counter, the chairs next to it were of a good quality of wood and had backs to them. The booths had rust cushions, and the windows were smaller now. The floor looked like wood, but she guessed it was one of those vinyls which resembled wood. Still, the entire diner had a homier feel to it now, from its color scheme to the curtains hanging in the windows.

She entered the restroom and once more saw the entire place looked totally different from what she now recalled. Her heartbeat slowed from a racing pace to a normal one now. No boogeyman was here. The changes the restaurant had undergone made her memories of the past obsolete. Paige was glad she had asked to come inside, wishing to stand up to the demons haunting her. Those shadows of her past now seemed long gone, at least as far as this diner went.

As she returned and sat at a table, Annie arrived with two iced teas.

"I was here," Paige revealed. "A long time ago."

Sympathy filled Annie's eyes. "I know, honey. I thought I recognized you. When Tanner introduced you, it confirmed what I thought. You were the girl whose daddy took you." The server smiled at her. "I was here that night. My husband had passed away a week earlier, and it was my first day back. He was quite a bit older than I was and left me the diner."

"I remember you," Paige said. "But you've changed the place quite a bit. I suppose business has been good."

"No, that was all Tanner's doing."

Surprised filled her. "What do you mean?"

"He couldn't come in for a couple of years after what happened. When he started dating, though, this was really the only place to take someone for a bite to eat. He told me back then that one day he would help change things—and he did."

"Tanner is the one responsible for the updates?"

Annie nodded in confirmation. "Yes. About ten years ago, after he had his first leading role, Tanner came to me and asked if he could buy the diner outright. He wanted me to stay on and manage it. He offered a price too good for me to pass up. I told him he was the boss now and could do whatever he wanted with the place. He didn't consult me. Just came up with this design all on his own."

Annie looked contemplative and added, "I know

that night affected you, honey, but it did Tanner, too. I think he wanted to step in here and not see a place of nightmares. Not the place where he saw his daddy get shot and another man killed."

"I like the changes he made," Paige said. "It looks more like a café now to me. Very homey."

"I agree. I don't mind running the place and not having to worry about making ends meet at the end of each month. With the price Tanner paid, I won't ever have money worries again. He has an accountant that looks after everything. Of course, I still place orders for things, but Sam and I are relaxed and enjoy taking care of it for Tanner."

"Sam?" Paige asked.

The older woman smiled. "He's the fry cook. Makes the best chicken fried steak you'll ever taste. You'll have to come back sometime when you aren't going to be eating Helen's food."

"We'll do that," she promised as she saw Tanner approaching them.

"Would you like those teas to-go?" Annie asked. "You must be eager to take Paige home to meet your parents."

"Good idea," he said.

Annie retrieved the drinks from the table and told them she would be right back.

Tanner took a seat. "Sorry I was gone for so long. Sam had a few things to show me since the last time I stopped by."

"I know you bought this place," Paige said quietly. "You're the one who made all the changes to it. I feel in a way that you did that for me."

He nodded thoughtfully. "For the longest time, I couldn't step through those doors. Even though Dad was only wounded, that night I realized that his job could be dangerous. Everything about the diner reminded me of what had happened. When I was in a position to buy it, I did. I wanted a total redesign of the place."

She took his hand. "I like what you've done. It's inviting. Cozy. It looks nothing like what it did before. You're going to have to bring me back so we can eat some of Sam's chicken fried steak."

He beamed at her. "You're on. It's so tender. And Sam's gravy is smooth and peppery and the perfect accompaniment to it."

Annie returned with their to-go cups and said, "On the house. Or the owner."

They all laughed, and Tanner escorted Paige outside to the truck.

"How long until we reach the ranch?" she asked.

"It's about eight to ten minutes from town to the first gate. Maybe five minutes beyond that before we reach Mom and Dad's. My house is about a mile northeast of theirs, while Alana's is located another mile west of me. Do you want to go to my place first and freshen up?"

"No, I'm eager to meet your parents again."

"I told Mom I was bringing home someone. I didn't tell her who or why. She doesn't know that I've bought your script, much less that we're engaged. I wanted us to tell them the good news together. I asked for Alana and Karl to come to dinner tonight, too."

New nerves flitted through Paige. "I've never been introduced to a man's parents before."

"They aren't new to you. You just haven't seen them in a good, long while. They will embrace you with open arms, Paige."

She fervently hoped so.

17

Tanner had no idea how his parents would respond to all the news he brought. He had let them know he was leaving the ranch because he had a lead on a script he wanted to direct. They were among the handful who knew of his ambitions beyond acting, the others being George and Hailey. George was one of the people Tanner had asked to write an endorsement for his membership in the Directors Guild of America.

As he pulled up to the house, though, he experienced excitement in what he would share, coupled with a small bit of worry. His dad was methodical in all he did. If anyone thought Tanner was acting too quickly regarding his feelings for Paige, it would be Jeff Haddock. His mom, though, would get it. He might look like his dad, but his heart and personality were all Helen Haddock.

Glancing to Paige, he saw how still she was. She'd gone quiet ever since they went through the gates of the ranch. He tried to put himself in her shoes and couldn't imagine what she might be feeling. She'd already conquered something huge by wanting to go into the diner where they'd met. Tanner was pleased that the changes he'd made helped her to push aside the horrible events which had occurred there. He hadn't known when he bought the diner and made the changes that he would ever see Paige again, much less bring her home with him to Owens. Now, he was thankful he had.

"Hey," he said softly, smiling gently at her.

She blinked, coming back to reality. "If they don't like me, don't say anything about us. I mean, you can tell them about the script and our work together on it, but don't—"

"They will love you," he promised. "I'm not hiding my feelings for you from them or anyone else. Hell, they probably already know we're engaged."

"How could they?" she asked, clearly puzzled.

Tanner laughed. "Well, I did tell Annie that you were my fiancée."

Shock filled her face. "Would she have called your mom?"

"No, but she probably has already mentioned it to a few people. I can't promise none of them have called the house. I'm hoping not. I want us to be the ones to share our good news with them."

She bit her bottom lip, causing a surge of desire to flood him. He wanted to do the same to her. Tanner wanted to do all kinds of things to her. With her. For her.

"If they—"

"No ifs, Laramie," he said firmly. "We're running with it. Everything. No secrets."

An SUV pulled in behind them. He glanced in the mirror. "It's my sister and her husband. I guess we'll start with them."

He quickly got out of his truck and helped Paige out, going to the maroon SUV as Karl helped Alana from the passenger seat. His sister already had that pregnancy glow about her.

"Hey!" she called, immediately turning her attention to Paige. "I'm Alana, Tanner's sister. This is Karl, my husband."

Paige offered her hand. "It's so nice to meet you. Congratulations. Tanner shared your good news with me. I'm Paige. Paige Laramie."

Alana took it, the name apparently forgotten by his sister. After all, she'd only been six and not present at the diner that night.

Paige greeted Karl, who said, "Nice to meet you, Paige. I work on the ranch with Helen, helping to train the horses and working in breeding."

"Karl lives, breathes, and eats horses," Alana kidded. "I thought Mom was bad until I met Karl at OSU. Oklahoma State. I was an education major, and my roommate was majoring in animal science. So was Karl."

Paige laughed. "I have no idea what that involves."

"I studied domestic animals," Karl told her. "Livestock such as beef, horses, dairy cattle, sheep, and poultry. You learn about their nutritional needs. Genetics. How to keep them healthy and what their behaviors mean. I'd toyed with the idea of becoming a vet, but I did an internship here with Helen between my sophomore and junior years. She convinced me to come work with her full-time once I graduated."

Alana laughed. "I'd told Mom I was interested in Karl, but it surprised me when she offered him a job. Sometimes, I wonder if he loves Mom's horses more than me."

Karl snagged his wife about the waist and planted a healthy kiss on her mouth.

"Maybe it's me today," Alana said, a glint of mischief in her eyes. She wriggled from her husband's hold and slid a hand through Paige's arm. "Tanner has never brought a woman home. Ever. I'm ready to pump you for all the info I can get. Let's go inside and get something to drink."

Tanner watched the pair move away. When they were out of earshot, Karl asked, "She's the one?"

His eyes met his brother-in-law's. "She's definitely the one."

"Good. It's about time," Karl said, smiling with approval. "I hope she doesn't take shit from you because you're a big movie star."

"Paige doesn't care about that," he said. "She's the first woman I've met since I became an actor that's interested in Tanner Haddock, small-town boy from Owens, Oklahoma. Not Tanner Haddock, movie star millionaire."

Karl's smile grew. "Then I like her even more." He paused. "But . . .you already knew her. From before. I recognized her name."

"It's a crazy coincidence how we came together again after twenty years," he admitted. "Let's go catch up."

By the time he entered the house, he heard his mom bustling in the kitchen and followed Paige and Alana there, Karl trailing after him.

Mom looked up and froze, her eyes resting on Paige.

Paige closed the gap between them. "Hello, Mrs. Haddock. I see you recognize me."

"What?" Alana said, clearly confused.

Helen threw her arms about Paige. "Oh, my goodness!" She squeezed Paige and then pulled away. "It *is* you. Paige Laramie. You still have those luminous green eyes. You've grown into quite the beauty, my dear."

"You know Paige?" Alana asked.

His mom embraced her guest again before pulling away. "I do, Alana. We met years ago at Annie's diner."

Alana squeaked, suddenly putting things together. "You're the girl Tanner helped rescue?"

"Yes," Paige said bashfully. "He seems to have a habit of doing that."

"He saved you again?" his sister asked.

"Enough with the questions," Tanner said. "When will Dad be home?"

Mom consulted her watch. "Not for another hour."

"Then we're going to my house to unpack. We'll be back."

"You can't go," Alana pleaded. "I have so many questions." She shot a triumphant look at him. "For instance, when did my brother fall in love with you?"

Tanner just laughed off the comment. "We'll be back and talk then. Dad would kill us if we said another word."

Alana wrapped Paige in her arms. "We have a lot to talk about."

"Yes," Paige agreed. "I want to hear all about your baby."

Alana's jaw dropped—and then she burst out laughing. She hugged Paige as she looked at Tanner. "I like her. She'll be good for you."

"She is," he agreed, snagging Paige's hand and leading her from the house. "We'll be back," he called.

"If you're going home just to have sex, you better not be late for dinner because I'm starved," Alana hollered after them.

They laughed all the way to his truck. Once inside,

Tanner captured Paige's face between his hands and gave her a long, slow kiss.

"That might not be sex, but it's a promise of great sex to come," he teased. "Yes, fast sex can be fun, but I want to take my time with you tonight."

"Good. That sounds like a plan. Besides, I'd be too nervous now, knowing we're due back at your parents' house so soon."

"Alana will still probably sniff you," he said, laughing. "She can be incorrigible."

They arrived at his place. A surge of pride ran through Tanner. He quickly glanced to Paige to see what she thought of the single-story ranch.

"I love the limestone," she said, opening her door and climbing from the truck.

He retrieved their luggage from the back and accompanied her to the porch.

Lovingly, she touched one of the rocking chairs that sat on it. "I have always had a thing for porches. And rockers."

"I've sat out here more times than I can count and watched the sun set."

Paige eased into a rocker. "I can see how peaceful that could be." She gazed across the land. "I understand why you want to come back here between movies. Owens grounds you. Being with family does, too."

"Yes. Come inside. There's a lot of house to see. Not much furniture, though."

Tanner opened the door and as they entered, Paige asked, "Why not?"

"It's got five bedrooms. About thirty-five hundred square feet. I only use a few rooms, though. I built it with my future in mind." His mouth had gone dry. "One with a wife. Kids."

He dropped what he carried and reached for her, hunger for this woman burning within him. Their kiss was all-consuming as their bodies pressed against one another's, heat filling him. Taylor drank from her, wondering if he would ever completely get his fill of her.

Breaking the kiss, they both panted.

"You are some kisser, Hollywood."

He kissed the tip of her nose. "You aren't bad yourself, Laramie." Releasing her, he stepped away, knowing if he stayed too close, she'd be back in his arms again in seconds. "Let me give you a quick tour."

Tanner led them to the large den, which was completely furnished. The eat-in kitchen also was functional and had a table with four chairs. Beyond that, the entire downstairs, other than his bedroom and office, was empty.

"You weren't kidding," she said. "You have a lot of rooms to fill with furniture."

He shrugged. "I figured someday I would have a wife. That we could do that together. Pick out a dining table and hutch. Stuff for the guestroom. Then work on creating a nursery and slowly filling the other rooms." He hesitated. "Do you even want children? I guess we need to talk about that."

She stepped to him, slipping her arms about his waist. "I never admitted it to myself, but I have since I was a little girl. I always wanted sisters and brothers. And then kids of my own. I never thought that would happen. You know I've barely dated. I didn't let my thoughts go there. I vaguely toyed with adopting, but it would just have been me. I didn't want to do that to my own child."

He kissed her lightly. "You turned out fine under your mom's and Nana's hands. But I get it. I'm just glad to hear you do want a few. I guess we can negotiate how many down the road. Right now, the only baby is your script and this picture. Let's get that taken care of before we think about making babies."

Paige's fingers touched his cheek. "I'm a little old-fashioned. I'd like a ring on my finger before any kids come. I guess that's the small town coming out in me."

"Done. Let's get married once we finish filming *Shadows of the Past*."

"How long does it take to make a movie?" she asked, obviously curious.

"Starting tonight, we're going to storyboard the hell out of this one," he said. "That will speed things along. I think we can get everything involved with pre-production done this spring. By the time school is out, we'll be ready to film. I think six, maybe eight weeks of shooting, and we'll be done. I can wait to cut it. How does August in Greece sound?"

"Like heaven."

He wrapped his arms around her and kissed her again, losing track of time. Paige was the one to break the kiss.

"Let me put on some fresh lipstick and comb my hair. I don't want your family to think we've been up to . . .well, what we've been up to," she said, laughing.

"I'll get our stuff."

Tanner got their things and brought them to his bedroom. "We can unpack later."

"Give me five minutes," she said, taking her cosmetics bag and going into his bathroom.

He ran his fingers through his hair and glanced in the mirror. *Did he look any different to others?* He did to himself. Being in love for the first time was different than what he'd thought. Part of him was giddy inside, yet he had a calmness about him, knowing his future was secure.

Because Paige *was* his future.

He went to the closet and removed the shirt he wore, tossing it in the laundry basket, and then pulling one from its hangar. Buttoning it, he felt better. He was excited and yet a little bit nervous to tell his parents about their marriage plans, hoping they would understand that even though this relationship was new, it wasn't rushed. That it seemed fated. Meant to be.

Paige came out of the bathroom. She'd slipped a thin headband into her hair, pulling it away from her face, and had on a fresh coat of lipstick.

He softly pressed his mouth to hers, making sure not to smear it. "You look incredible."

"Casual," she responded, deflecting his compliment. "I see you changed shirts. I wonder if I should, too," she fretted.

"Nope. You look amazing just like this."

They returned to the house he'd grown up in. Just being home brought back all those warm, fuzzy feelings of being raised in a small town. Knowing everyone and everyone knowing him. He wanted that for their kids. The fact Paige also wanted them made him want to rush her back to his house to get started on making a baby as quickly as possible. But he was right—his next project was going to be like giving birth. It deserved all the time and attention necessary to make it a success. To help him reach his professional goals. To help Paige break away from the pack and come into her own as a screenwriter. Once the film was completed, though, he would be all about making babies.

He saw his dad's departmental SUV parked outside the house and went inside without knocking, hearing laughter coming from the kitchen. Brownie padded over to meet them, and Tanner introduced the dog to Paige. They entered the kitchen, and he took in the scene. Mom taking a casserole pan from the oven. Alana tossing a salad. His dad mixing up his famous guacamole dip. Karl pouring tortilla chips into a large bowl.

"Hey, everyone," he said, bringing all the activity in the kitchen to a halt.

He watched his father, who stopped stirring the dip. Dad left the spoon in it and came toward Paige, holding his arms out. She went into them without a word, and they embraced.

Dad broke the contact, taking Paige's elbows and pulling her slightly back. "Helen is right. You're all grown up, Paige. We're eager to hear what you've been doing with your life—and how you and Tanner reconnected."

"Let's take everything to the dining room table," Mom said. "We're ready to eat."

Tanner leaned down and whispered into Paige's ear, "It's a special occasion when we eat in there."

Soon, they were all seated. His mom served up her famous chicken enchiladas, and they filled their plates with the other side dishes.

"Make sure you get some of my guac," Dad told Paige. "It's better than restaurants serve."

She smiled at his father, and Tanner reached for her hand under the table. Paige smiled at him, too.

They started eating, plates full, and he opened the conversation with, "I've found the script I'm going to direct."

"I know you've spoken of your desire to do so," Mom said. "I'm so glad you've found something you feel strongly about, Tanner."

"Paige wrote it," he said, pride evident in his voice as he smiled at her.

"So, you turned out to be a writer," Dad said. "That's wonderful, Paige. How did you get into the film business?"

"Actually, I'm a high school history teacher, Mr. Haddock. I've been writing screenplays on spec for a few years now. I've sold two previous ones."

"Anything I might've seen?" Alana asked.

Paige mentioned the Knox Monroe movie, and Alana sighed.

"We've had to watch that one a few times," Karl said.

"The other is being filmed now," Paige continued. "It won't be out until sometime next year. And then my agent sold Tanner my latest one."

"I'll direct and take a leading role in it," he shared. "I went down to Texas to work on the script with Paige."

"Did you recognize her name when Hailey gave you the screenplay?" Mom wanted to know.

"Though she uses Laramie Fisher as a screenwriter, I put two and two together. Called Paige and asked if I could come visit her and work on it together. She hung up on me."

His fiancée blushed profusely. "I am sorry about that."

He lifted their joined hands and kissed her fingers. Alana sighed. The rest of the table grew quiet.

Looking at everyone, Tanner said, "You know I've never brought anyone home. I've never found love. Reconnecting with Paige has changed my life, though. Paige has taken a leave of absence from school to help me make this movie. She'll resign her position, as

well, because we are meant to be together. We're getting married."

Everyone began talking at once. Tanner let them,
glancing to Paige and grinning.

"They'll settle down soon enough because they'll
want to hear all about our plans."

"We don't really have plans," she pointed out.
"Other than making a movie and then getting
married."

"And going to Greece. Don't forget that part."

"You wouldn't let me," she joked.

"Then let's make our plans. Now."

The voices died down. Everyone looked at them
expectantly.

"I'll need to head to L.A. to sign some papers next
week with Hailey. Get some financing. Paige will return to Sugar Springs and scout locations because
we're going to film there, using quite a few locals in
small roles. I'll pull a cast and crew together, and then
we'll try to begin filming by the beginning of June."

"That's all nice, dear," his mom said. "But let's talk
about the important thing."

"The getting married part," Alana chimed in, grinning at him.

Paige squeezed his fingers. "I know this sounds terribly rushed. I would have doubts if it were my son
making such a sudden commitment to a stranger."

"But we're not strangers," Tanner pointed out.
"We've got this cosmic connection."

"You're beginning to sound like a contestant on
The Bachelor," quipped Karl.

"We've spent every waking moment together since
Tanner came to Sugar Springs," Paige said. "We just . .
.know that it's right. I suppose we can always change

our minds. Working together under intense scrutiny might alter the way we feel about one another."

"No, it won't," he said determinedly. "Paige doesn't realize it, but I'll never let her go."

He leaned over and kissed her in front of everyone, causing his mom to gasp and Alana to sigh dreamily.

Breaking the kiss, Tanner said, "We bonded all those years ago. I believe we had to grow and mature apart from one another before fate intervened and brought us together again. I look forward to our professional collaboration, but more importantly, I look forward to making Paige my wife."

"Your father proposed to me on our first date," Mom revealed.

"Dad!" Alana said, clearly stunned by this new information.

Jeff Haddock grinned sheepishly. "When you know, you just know. Haddock men have that in common. My dad asked my mom to marry him in the middle of their first date. She made him wait two months. Your mom here made me wait six. They were the longest six months of my life—but she was worth waiting for."

Dad stood and raised his glass. "To our wonderful son, who knows his mind, and his beautiful fiancée. Welcome to the Haddock family, Paige."

18

Paige awoke to a delicious warmth surrounding her, Tanner's lips nibbling at her nape. She began stroking his forearm and soon they were caught up in the frenzy of lovemaking. Though she still felt inexperienced, Paige was learning each time they made love. She discovered Tanner enjoyed having his neck and belly kissed. They made love now with enthusiasm, reveling in the fact they were together and happy, their future bright with promise.

"Want to go for a run?" he asked after they'd finished and she snuggled against him, inhaling the masculine scent that made her knees go weak.

"It would be a great way for me to see the property," she told him.

They spent over an hour jogging around the ranch. Paige enjoyed being outdoors and free. Free from the confines of Sugar Springs. Although the town had been her refuge for all these many years, it was nice to finally get out into the world. Even if it were only Oklahoma.

She wondered what it would be like to take her first plane ride. To stand at the ocean's edge in Malibu. To soak up the sunshine in Greece.

She turned to Tanner and smiled, knowing all those things would now come to pass, thanks to this amazing man who had healed her, dispelling so many shadows in her past which had not only lingered but dominated her life for far too long.

They returned to his house and showered together, making love in the large stall as the water sluiced over their bodies.

As they toweled off, Tanner told her he would have to make a trip into Broken Bow, which had the nearest pharmacy.

"Why?" she asked. "Are you out of aspirin or Band-Aids?"

He grinned wolfishly. "Condoms."

She felt the heat flush her face and said, "I suppose I need to do my part. See my doctor about going on birth control pills or getting an IUD inserted."

"No," he said, the backs of his fingers stroking her cheek. "Condoms are easy. Besides, once this film is over and we get married, I hope we can start on making a baby right away. I'm already thirty-four. I know you're thirty, but I haven't even asked when your birthday is."

"It's July Fourth."

Nuzzling her neck, he said, "We'll be sure to celebrate when it comes."

She thought of all the years she had ignored her birthday and found herself eager to acknowledge it for the first time since her mother's death. Still, they would be shooting his film when it occurred.

"Do film crews take off days such as the Fourth of July?"

"It depends. How does Sugar Springs celebrate the Fourth?"

"There's always a parade through town at ten that

morning. During the afternoon, booths are set up with games and food. That night, the high school band plays patriotic tunes under the stars while a small fireworks show takes place."

"If things are going well, I'll give the cast and crew that day off." He looked at her intently. "So that you and I can celebrate on our own."

Tanner kissed her deeply, and Paige thought she would never grow tired of his kisses.

They dressed and she told him, "It's time for me to earn my keep. I'll be the one who prepares breakfast while we're here."

"I'm afraid you won't find any herbal teabags in my cupboard. I've never been much of a hot tea drinker until this week, but I enjoy its soothing effects."

"I'll make coffee for you instead," Paige said.

"No, don't. It's been nice not having to depend upon a jolt of caffeine in the morning. I find a dash of Laramie and some OJ hits the spot just fine."

Paige made breakfast for them, pleased to see his refrigerator was stocked with fresh groceries. She served blueberry pancakes, with a side of sausage, and cut up a cantaloupe which was ripe and juicy.

Once the dishes were cleared and in the dishwasher, she asked, "What's next? We've gone through the script enough times. You know it and the characters forward and backward. I'm not sure how much more I can help you with."

"Ah, that's where you're wrong. We're going to have some pretty intense days ahead of us now, at least until I fly back to meet with Hailey and sign all the papers. We're moving into the storyboarding phase now, which I believe is the most important for a director. I've learned from the best, and George, Hailey's husband, has been my favorite director to work with. He storyboards each scene in his film so that he has a clear vision of the scene and the camera angles he wants to capture before filming begins. Alfred Hitchcock used to do such detailed storyboards that he said he was bored once filming began because he already felt as if he'd made the movie."

"Explain this process to me. What does it involve? While I've taken several online screenwriting classes, they never touched on this part of filmmaking."

"A storyboard is simply a visual outline of a film," he explained. "It breaks the action of a movie into individual panels and shows everything that will happen in the movie. Think of it as a shot-by-shot walk through the film."

"That sounds like a comic book. Or a graphic novel."

"You're right. It includes not only the picture but any relevant info regarding the action or dialogue. It even uses arrows to indicate the camera angle or the direction a character moves. It connects each shot to the next. It's all about flow and consistency."

Paige thought on his words. "So, you're picking key moments of each scene. Plotting the camera angles. You're crafting the script visually before the actors ever set foot on set."

"Exactly," he said, nodding with enthusiasm. "It's a lot of heavy-duty thinking. It cuts down on unnecessary shots so you don't waste time filming things you don't need. A good storyboard keeps you on track. And on schedule."

She shook her head. "It sounds like a lot of work. The thought that will go into it and then the actual putting this on paper. How do we even begin?"

"Most directors start with a shot list. Some work with their cinematographer on this, but I'm ready for us to knock this out together. Basically, we'll make a detailed list of every camera shot. Those show things about your characters and setting—even theme. It also specifies the camera angles to use. The right camera angle can reveal emotions and relationships between characters."

"I have zero experience in this area. This sounds complicated, Tanner. I'm not sure I'm the right person to help you with this project."

"I agree that it is a lot of work, but you know the script better than anyone. As an actor, I break down the scenes my character is in and turn them inside out. A director has to do that for every scene and each character in the entire movie. Our storyboard will give the exact specifics of every shot. It will let me, my cinematographer, and assistant director know what I'm trying to capture visually in order to tell the story and make each scene impactful."

He raked his fingers through his hair, something Paige found incredibly sexy but also knew he did when he was on a roll.

"Once the shot list is created, the actual storyboard is sketched out. It will include those camera angles—even the props needed—to convey the essence of each scene. Some directors add a few words below the images to help add context to the visuals, especially voiceovers. We've talked about how we'll use some of those from both Gwen's and Peter's points of view."

Paige mulled over the process. "You'll need to fly back Tuesday to be able to meet with Hailey on Wednesday. I don't think we'll have the entire movie storyboarded by that time. Besides the drawing, it'll take a lot of thought, especially regarding camera angles. It will be as if you're shooting the movie in your head and then capturing it on paper before you ever meet with the cast and crew."

"Exactly. We'll get as far as we can. Since it's not a huge group of actors, I think the process will go faster than you think it will. And I've got a lot of what I want to do already in my head. As I read, I've always run a movie in my head, and that's been helpful as we've gone through your script." Tanner paused. "You wouldn't happen to harbor any secret artistic talent, Laramie?"

"Count me out as far as drawing goes," Paige said. "I don't even draw a good stick figure."

"I'm a decent artist. I don't mind using a few stick people to get my point across. Some directors actually hire storyboard artists at this point."

Something occurred to her. "I may have something even better. Let me fetch my laptop."

When Paige returned to the den with her laptop and copy of the script, she saw Tanner had also retrieved his copy, as well as a legal tablet and pen.

"I wrote my first two screenplays in a Word document," she told him. "When I sold the second one for a decent amount of money, I decided to splurge and invest in a screenwriting program, which one of my online teachers recommended. He said it was the top seller in screenwriting software. I wrote all of *Shadows of the Past* using it. The software tools took care of formatting. I didn't have to bother with creating margins or worry about spacing or page breaks."

Tanner frowned. "I don't get how this would help in storyboarding."

She smiled. "I've only used a portion of the software. It also came with a bunch of other tools."

Paige pulled up and began running *Final Draft*. They spent a few minutes exploring what the software contained, finding it had many tools that helped in creating storyboards, shot lists, schedules, and even film budgets.

"This is fantastic," he declared. "We can even do printouts of what we create digitally. We won't have to create anything by hand." He kissed her enthusiastically.

For the next four days, they used the software to outline every scene in her script. The program was easy to use and organized everything, making it easy to find any given scene. They put in many hours, only taking breaks for food and sex. They did spend Sunday afternoon with Tanner's family, staying for a cookout. By Monday night, they'd completed their work. Tanner saved the last blocks of the final scene and closed the laptop, setting it on the coffee table in front of them. He leaned back, slipping an arm about Paige's shoulders.

"I don't believe I've ever worked so hard on something which has given me so much satisfaction," he said.

"I had no idea all that went into pre-production, but I understand now why it needs to be done. An organized director armed with detailed storyboards saves time and money."

"It will be the bible that will guide me in filming *Shadows of the Past*. Not every director does an in-depth storyboard for each scene as we've created. More experienced ones already have a bulk of it in their heads. Storyboards are important in intricate scenes, though, especially action-laded ones. It's important to get down the timing of complicated events, such as explosions."

"Will you meet with your cinematographer and camera operators and discuss the camera angles? I'd think they'd be some of the first people you'd want to hire for this project. I'm still fascinated how you already seemed to know the points of view for each scene."

"In part, that's thanks to you, babe. You've given me insight into these characters since we've been working together. As I got to know Gwen and Peter better, I could see the movie I want to make running in my head. I'm glad I've got it down visually now. These storyboards will guide me—and those I hire—throughout the production. They'll also help in putting together the filming schedule."

His face grew serious. "Paige, I couldn't have done any of this without you. I know there are directors who take a script and never meet with the screenwriter. That's been your experience so far. That's not the kind of director I want to be, though. Collaboration is key—and everything starts with the writing."

"You've opened my eyes to so many things about this business, Tanner. I think what I've learned from you will help me when I begin writing again."

His fingers ran through her hair absently. "I know you'll want to start on something of your own soon. I'm grateful you're giving me the kind of time you are on *Shadows of the Past*."

"You've changed my life in every way possible, Tanner. I won't even think about a new project at this point. I want to devote every waking moment to this film."

He cocked an eyebrow. "*Every* waking moment?" he asked suggestively.

Paige giggled, something she hadn't done since she was a child. This man had lightened every burden she carried. Her heart was full of joy each day now because of him.

She placed her palm on his chest. "Maybe not every waking moment. In fact, my next effort might be a love story. A very hot love story. With many bedroom scenes. I could stand to get a little research in. Maybe get some inspiration."

Tanner quickly stood and scooped her into his arms, carrying her to the bedroom. He made slow, deliberate love to her, teasing her in every way until she was frantic for him to enter her. When he finally did, she had the most explosive orgasm yet.

As Paige came back to earth, he gathered her in his arms. They lay there contentedly. He stroked her forearm wordlessly. It was enough simply to be together.

The next morning, Paige knew things would change. Tanner had arranged with Reg, his security head, to send a plane for him. He hadn't wanted to bother Ron, who was vacationing in Norway, telling her his friend and usual pilot deserved the time off.

"I won't need him until shortly before filming begins anyway. He's off the grid now, but he'll be in touch soon. I'll give him an idea of when we'll start since he serves as my stand-in."

They packed and stopped to tell his mother and Karl goodbye. Alana was at school and his father was at work.

They drove through Owens, Paige marveling at how much things had changed in her world. She could look at this town now without fear seeping through every pore of her body.

No words were spoken during the drive to Paris. Tanner held her hand the entire way, though. When they pulled up on the tarmac, his plane waiting, he cut the engine.

"I don't know what I'm going to do without you

these next few days," he admitted. "Dad was right. Haddock men know and commit. I'll miss you, Paige Laramie."

He leaned over and pressed his lips softly against hers. An ache formed inside her, knowing they would be apart. Tanner broke the kiss and gave her a wistful smile.

"I wish you were coming with me, but I know you need to take baby steps as far as traveling goes. We'll get you on a plane, though. Besides, you've got a lot to do from your end while I'm working on other things in California."

They got out of the truck, and he gathered her in his arms, holding her close, no words necessary.

"I'll call when I reach L.A.," he promised. "You take care, Laramie. I love you."

He kissed her a final time, and Paige said, "I love you, Hollywood." As he walked away, under her breath she added, "Maybe more than I should."

Despite his constant reassurances, she felt Tanner was settling for her. Yes, she did believe he loved her, but he was Tanner Haddock, Hollywood superstar. She was Paige Laramie, former teacher and budding screenwriter. It still amazed her that he could be interested in her. His confidence was so attractive to her. She knew her lack of it might grow to be a problem between them.

Tanner believed in her.

It was time Paige started believing in herself.

She got into his truck and waited, watching his plane take off. She saw him in a window, waving at her, and raised a hand to wave in return.

Then Paige started the vehicle and made her way back to Sugar Springs, wondering what might lie in store for her when she returned.

19

THREE MONTHS LATER . . .

Tanner woke and heard Paige breathing softly next to him. He was surprised he'd been able to fall asleep with everything swirling through his mind.

Today, he would lead a movie set for the first time.

It would be his creative vision, his stamp on everything done today. He had complete artistic control over the entire shoot and would make every significant decision. Already, he was used to making decisions which would impact his film. In pre-production, he had assembled his team, hiring an assistant director who had worked with George on several films, as well as a cinematographer, line producer, and production designer, meeting with each individually and then as a group to make certain they were all on the same page.

Casting hadn't taken long since he'd already cast himself as Peter and Nana as Gloria. He'd run lines with Nana, making certain the old woman was up to the challenge. She'd proven to be a natural. As she'd claimed, she knew every line in the movie. He would keep her on set to work with other actors, rehearsing with them and then letting Nana stand by to prompt anyone in trouble.

The greatest challenge had been to find the perfect actress to play Gwen. Gwen needed to appear fragile but have a strength within her to eventually stand up to the crazed, controlling Peter. She needed to be open and friendly and yet a bit mistrusting because of the recent death of her husband. Gwen was crushed by his death, but she's a resilient woman. The actress playing Gwen needed a vulnerability. She also needed zero Hollywood veneer. Gwen was pretty but not gorgeous. Some actresses would agree to strip off the makeup and wave away the hair people to play against type, such as Charlize Theron in *Monster*. Gwen Foster needed to have that small-town wholesomeness about her, something which could not be faked.

Tanner felt lucky to have cast Chloe Turner as his Gwen. She'd racked up two Oscar nominations by the time she was twenty-five and won Best Supporting Actress last year when she'd turned thirty the day of the awards ceremony. She was just coming off one of those large mega-productions. He couldn't recall if it were spies or superheroes, but Chloe had told Tanner she was ready for a quieter set and more thoughtful movie. A role which seemed simple on the outside, but one which she could layer in depth.

Chloe's screen test was magic. He'd sent it to Paige after he'd already signed Chloe. Paige agreed that Chloe seemed to have the chops for Gwen, but Tanner sensed a slight reluctance on Paige's part. He chalked it up to her not being able to see Chloe as anyone other than in the signature roles the actress had played.

He felt good about the casting of Chloe. She brought a ton of experience. They'd met several times over FaceTime and Zoom for him to help prepare her for the role of Gwen. Chloe understood what he was asking of her and had the range and depth he sought. She was also working for far less than she usually made and told him outright that she wouldn't be making the film if not for his involvement. She explained that she appreciated him and his choices as an actor and even had aspirations herself to direct someday. He agreed she could shadow him on the set and learn as much as possible, though he admitted he might be flying by the seat of his pants at some points, reminding her that it was his first time to helm a film. Tanner appreciated the opportunities he'd been given to do the same when he'd worked for other directors and wanted to help Chloe achieve her future dream, much as he was finding his footing as a director now.

He skipped employing a location manager. The bulk of that job description had been filled by Paige, who found and booked the locations where they would film. She'd secured permits, rented two houses which would serve as home bases for Gwen and Peter, and made sure everyone in Sugar Springs had been alerted about the upcoming shoot.

Paige had lined up people to work on set, being helped by her closest friend at the high school, speech and drama teacher Sarah Meinholdt. Sarah had been gone over spring break, taking a trip to New York to see an old friend perform in an Off-Broadway production. Once Sarah returned to Sugar Springs and Paige shared her role in Tanner's upcoming production, Sarah had gone out of her way to lend a helping hand. Many of the extras would be not only townspeople but Sarah's students. Several of these students were working as unpaid volunteers with the set designer and prop master, getting valuable experience in the art of filmmaking.

Paige stretched and yawned, turning toward him. "Hey, Hollywood," she said softly, her luminous green eyes tugging at his heart. "I guess maybe I should come up with another nickname for you, Mr. Director." She thought a moment. "I would call you Mr. D, but you might think you were paired off with Mrs. D next door."

"Please, no," he begged facetiously, thinking of the too-helpful neighbor who stopped by far too frequently.

"Okay, then it'll just be D. As in Director," she decided. "Does D need—"

He cut off her question with a kiss. Breaking it, he said, "D needs some love now. Hot, quick sex to energize him."

Her lips twitched in amusement. "What the D wants, the D will have to come and get."

Paige leaped from the bed, and Tanner chased her down, pinning her hands against the wall, his body leaning into hers, trapping her. Their kisses heated up, her fingers tangled in his hair, his mouth hot on hers. Tanner brought her legs up, and they locked around his waist. He thrust into her, greedily taking what he wanted, hearing her mewls as his lips trailed down her throat. He came quickly, burying his face in her hair, feeling her fingers comb through his.

"I'd say that was hot and quick," she quipped. "And very energizing."

They showered and dressed, Paige pouring hot water into cups and tossing a teabag inside each. Everything they needed was sitting on the kitchen table, and they each loaded a backpack with tablets, laptops, and printouts of what they would need for the first day of filming.

As Tanner pulled out of her garage, he saw signs in the yard and stopped. Sarah's students must have been responsible because they looked like the kinds of signs teenagers placed in yards.

"Good Luck. Happy Filming. Welcome to Sugar Springs," Paige read off. "That was sweet."

"Go, Knights?" he read, continuing to back down the driveway.

"We're the Sugar Springs Knights. I guess someone from the football team had to throw in a sports sign," she mused. "After all, I did hire a few athletes to be go-fers on set. They'll move things around. Do any paint touch-ups. I even have a couple who'll drive golf carts to take people around. They're all ready to pant over Chloe Turner."

"If I were sixteen, I'd be panting over her," Tanner said. "Probably half of them have a poster of her on their bedroom wall before I even hired her for the film."

"Oh, D, you are so out of it. Teenagers don't hang posters on their walls anymore. Chloe as a screen-saver, though? I've already told them—actually, all the high school kids, Sarah's included—don't speak unless spoken to. Don't ask for any selfies. Just do the job they were hired to do."

"D appreciates that," he said, playfully waggling his eyebrows.

"I also met with the locals who either have small speaking roles or are window dressing in background shots. They got the same lecture. They know it's a privilege being cast in your film."

"I promise I'll take time to take a selfie with anyone who wants one. Later. Not on the first day, but

I will do a few at the end of each day and get around to everyone eventually."

She smiled sympathetically. "Are you nervous? I was always nervous on the first day of school, no matter how many years I'd taught."

"A little," he admitted.

"You're prepared. Keep that in mind. You know the material forward and backward. Your hand is on the schedule. You'll guide the performances with ease. Just remember to give a little shout-out to everyone at some point. I found a little praise went a long way with hormonal teenagers. I'd think the same would be true with neurotic actors."

"I also have to keep track of each department. Make sure they're on top of things. I know communication is key." He smiled at her. "You've got my back. I've got nothing to worry about."

They pulled into the parking lot of the Baptist church, where the first scene would be shot this morning, the funeral of Gwen's late husband. Already, it was half full with vehicles and people.

"You know how to communicate," she told him. "Trust your gut. You've got this, D."

Tanner kissed her. "I've got you. That's what will make me successful."

He slipped on his ballcap, a Sugar Springs High School one, which Paige told him would go a long way with the locals. Getting out of the truck, they both claimed their backpacks and went to meet with the AD. He told them lighting was done and the sound had been checked, as well as walking them through what they already knew, but Tanner thought the more others were familiar with the schedule, the better.

Then he gathered the cast and crew to make a few opening remarks. Some directors did so. Others simply began filming the first scene. Tanner wanted to make that personal contact with everyone present, though, and motioned for the bullhorn.

"Thank you all for being here," he began. "It was your choice to be a part of this production. I appreciate how the citizens of Sugar Springs have welcomed us. I know filming will cause a few disruptions, and I appreciate the patience you'll show. I also appreciate the devotion you'll give to this production. It's a great story. Suspenseful. A slice of small-town life, with a bit of darkness coloring the edges. Thank you for learning your lines. Leaving your homes and families behind to be here. You know it's my first time helming a film. Let's make this one for movie lovers."

Cheers rang out. He handed the speaker back to his AD. Ron caught Tanner's eye and nodded his approval. Having his close friend and stand-in here bolstered Tanner's confidence. Paige also nodded at him.

"Take your places," he instructed, walking toward the church and entering it.

People began scurrying, moving into their positions. Camera operators stood poised to film. Actors took their places. Extras took up hymnals. The organist waited, hands poised above the keys. Chloe Turner approached him, looking lovely in her black widow's dress, her hair pulled back from her face, minimal makeup on. Nothing could hide her beauty, though.

"Any last-minute instructions, Tanner?" she asked, her voice low.

"No. Just do it as we rehearsed."

She went to her mark. The cast had spent the past week doing a read-through, while he and Chloe had rehearsed a good number of their scenes together alone. He knew she was as prepared as he was.

Chloe looked to him and nodded, signaling she was ready.

For the first time in his career, Tanner called, "Action!"

~

PAIGE DID NOT like Chloe Turner.

She had seen several of Chloe's films and thought the actress had been good in them, but Paige had been disappointed when Tanner had told her he'd cast the actress as Gwen in *Shadows of the Past*. While she didn't expect to be consulted on every decision her fiancé made regarding the film—after all, it was *his* film—she had thought Tanner would be interested in her input regarding Gwen.

Instead, he had called her and raved about Chloe's audition, saying she was at a point in her career where she didn't have to audition. Not after three Academy Awards nominations and a win. But the actress had asked Tanner if she could audition for the leading role in his movie. Word had leaked over the Internet this spring about him purchasing the Laramie Fisher script. Paige wouldn't put it past Hailey Madison to have been the leak. While she liked Hailey, Paige understood first and foremost, Hailey was an agent and wanted attention for her clients. The interest sparked had certainly brought attention to Laramie Fisher. Her Knox Monroe-led film was now number one on Netflix, and filming had been completed on her second screenplay. Rumors swirled about the movie, which would debut at the Toronto Film Festival in early September and was scheduled for release Thanksgiving Day.

While the attention her new career was receiving

was nice, Paige was focused on the film at hand. More than anything, she wanted Tanner to be successful as a director. He had been so happy working with her on the script and storyboards, and he continued to thrive with every challenge thrown his way regarding pre-production. He was organized and creative. She knew he would get the best from his cast and crew.

She just wished it didn't involve Chloe Turner.

Maybe she'd taken an instant dislike to the actress when they'd been introduced at a welcome dinner held at a local restaurant in Tyler, mainly because Chloe had barely spoken to Paige and clung to Tanner's arm. Paige had found herself at the far end of the table, watching Chloe laugh and play the star. Tanner didn't seem to notice the attention Chloe gave him, but Paige certainly did. While she'd never had reason to be jealous, she certainly was by the time they left the restaurant. She hadn't said a word to her fiancé, however, merely letting him tell her what she'd missed while she'd been at the other end of the table. Sitting with Tanner's AD that night, the young man had told her Chloe had a reputation for taking over a set. While the AD thought Tanner was a strong personality, he knew the director would bend a little in order to keep his big star happy.

Sitting in on the table reads, Paige thought Chloe had the chops to be Gwen. All the promise of her audition shone brightly during this read-through. Yet there was something Paige couldn't put her finger on, something that rang false about Chloe taking on this role. She couldn't say anything to Tanner. He was thrilled getting an actress of her reputation and caliber. Chloe had also agreed to work for peanuts, instead accepting a percentage of profits, saying she knew *Shadows of the Past* would be a big hit and turn into as good a payday as other films which paid her quite a bit up front.

Paige watched the take now, deciding that Chloe struck the wrong shade of vulnerable. She had written Gwen to be fragile. Susceptible to Peter's charm when he returned to their small town. Gwen was unguarded and open. Chloe was heading more toward a vulnerable that was weakness. A helplessness that Paige's Gwen didn't possess. Chloe Turner's interpretation was a woman who was powerless after losing her husband. At risk to be taken in by Peter's beguiling charm.

Chastising herself for being too critical, Paige kept her mouth closed. Tanner hadn't asked her opinion. If he did, she wouldn't hold back. As long as he seemed to be getting what he wanted, though, she knew he would stick with Chloe. It made her hate the wedge the woman was driving between them.

They finished the scene in the church and broke for the next set-up, which would take place in the church parking lot. Tanner was shooting the first scenes of the script in order for the next two days before he veered off the chronological order.

Standing near—but not too near—Tanner, she watched Chloe come toward her director. The change Paige witnessed knocked the breath out of her. While everyone around scrambled to new places, Chloe's face went from Gwen's to one of cold determination as she headed toward Tanner. Just before she reached him, it changed entirely, becoming concerned and a bit unsure.

"Tanner, I need help with this first scene between us," she said, her lack of confidence evident.

He turned his attention to her. "We've rehearsed it, Chloe. You nailed exactly the mood I'm looking for when we did so. Just stick to what we've done."

"One more quick rehearsal?" Chloe asked hopefully. "I just want this first day to be perfect, Tanner. I want to embody Gwen. Her sadness. Her despondency. And the hope that fills her when she spots Peter for the first time in years. Please. Come to my trailer and let's run through the scene once before we shoot it."

"All right," he agreed, removing his ballcap and handing it to an assistant. "But I'll need to also run to hair and makeup now. It'll be quick. I can meet you in your trailer in a quarter-hour."

He was already dressed as Peter. Paige had watched him go through different transformations in hair and makeup during pre-production, and his stylist and makeup artist had settled on an easy look which was quick to prepare, one which would help him seamlessly go from director to lead actor in a short amount of time.

"Sounds perfect," Chloe purred.

"In the meantime, Paige can accompany you to your trailer. I don't think the two of you have spent any time together. Paige might be able to answer any questions you're still struggling with even better than I can."

Tanner turned and saw she was nearby. He motioned her over. "Would you go with Chloe and walk her through the next scene with Peter?"

"I'd be happy to, D."

Turning, Paige saw Chloe was not happy at that prospect, however.

Which made her just a tiny bit gleeful.

As Tanner strode away, the actress coldly said, "I don't really need your help."

She smiled brightly. "It's what Tanner wants. I know neither of us want to disappoint our director."

Striking out toward Chloe's trailer, Paige only hoped the woman followed. She reached it and opened the door, turning and waiting for Chloe to climb the steps first. Paige followed the actress inside, closing the door behind them.

"I know my lines," Chloe said firmly. "I know how Tanner wants them delivered. I don't need you here."

She played dumb. "Then why did you need Tanner to work with you if you're so prepared? If you're comfortable with the upcoming scene, I'm happy to help give you any insight into Gwen."

Chloe's eyes narrowed. "You may think Tanner Haddock cares about you, Paige," she said dismissively. "In his way, he thinks he does. But he's using you. He's a first-time director. He wants this shoot to go as close to perfect as possible. He's cozied up to you and is collaborating with you. Honestly? He's milking you dry. And I'll tell you now, it will all come to an end. Filming in your little shithole town will be completed. He'll return to California and cut the footage. He'll think he's being sincere when he tells you he'll stay in touch. For you to stay here while he gets all the editing and post-production work out of the way. That you can be together then."

She snorted. "He won't think he's lying—but he will be. Because Tanner needs someone way better than you, Paige. You're pretty, but he needs gorgeous. You're smart, but he needs someone talented. More connected. You'll never challenge him enough. He'll grow bored quickly if he hasn't already. If you were smart, you'd end things now with him before you get hurt too badly. Continue working on the movie, of course. Be a professional, yada-yada-yada. But those claws you've sunk into him? They won't tear him. He'll merely turn on you and knock you away. He'll be ripped from your fingers, metaphorically speaking. Don't be a fool, Paige. You aren't woman enough to hold Tanner Haddock's attention for long."

She held her tongue, letting the anger wash over her. She wouldn't stoop to Chloe's level.

"Are you woman enough to do so?" she asked, interested in how far this actress would go.

"I want him," Chloe openly admitted. "It's why I agreed to audition for him. To work for close to scale. He's the biggest star Hollywood has to offer. The two of us together? It will be magic. You're just a small-town girl, playing on his past as a small-town boy." Her eyes grew wintry. "But he hasn't been that boy for a long time. He's a man who needs a woman who knows how to please him. I'm that woman. Stay out of my way."

She wanted to call Chloe Turner a bitch. She wanted to tell the actress that Tanner would never fall for someone so shallow. That he wasn't at all who Chloe thought he was.

Then Paige really looked at her rival. Chloe was beautiful. Famous. Talented. Lauded. The kind of woman Paige had always thought Tanner belonged with. Desperation filled her. Tanner was already slipping away, being pulled in a hundred directions each day. Chloe Turner came from his world. She understood it—and him—better than Paige ever could.

Still, she wouldn't go without a fight.

Putting a smile on her face, Paige said, "Let me know if you need any help with your character. Because you haven't captured Gwen's essence yet. If you don't, this movie will fall flat on its face. You'll go down, along with Tanner."

With that, she exited the trailer, her insides churning. Paige went behind the trailer and threw up, her throat burning as if acid had been poured down it.

If given a choice, would Tanner choose Chloe—or Paige?

She couldn't make the decision for him. She could only pray when the smoke cleared from the nuclear bomb she believed Chloe would eventually set off, Paige would be the one left standing.

20

They had a week's worth of filming in the can.

And something was missing.

Tanner sat back in his chair and mulled over things. No one else present said anything. It was Saturday, and they had broken mid-afternoon to give the cast, crew, and many volunteers a little extra time off, as well as allow him to view the dailies with his team and make a few decisions about how to tweak next week's schedule.

He turned to his cinematographer. "Everything is perfect on your end. You've captured the exact look I'm going for. You've incorporated Sugar Springs as a character into this film. That's exactly what I wanted, the feel of a small town.

"Lighting also has been superb," he added, turning to the lighting director. "I'm still not quite happy with that last scene we filmed today in the parking lot, though. We may need to reshoot it Monday since today was too overcast. Paige will get a revised schedule out to everyone. Look at the digital dailies again when you get home," he advised. "Text me if you have any ideas. Thank you, everyone."

The group gathered their things and began leaving. While he had watched the dailies with the key people in his crew each day, Tanner went home every evening and went through them again, trying to put his finger on what was lacking. He locked the trailer and headed to his truck with Paige. She was usually silent during these meetings, taking in what was said, telling him that part of his day he was surrounded by professionals and needed to hear their opinions, not hers. Her input had been invaluable to him, however. He had asked her advice on several things, and she was not shy about giving her opinion, despite her lack of experience in the industry. She was always right, too. Paige had an excellent eye for details and observed small things that others missed. He felt privileged to not only be filming her script but having her on set, a second pair of eyes which he trusted implicitly.

They got into the truck and were silent on the way home. He didn't know if it were because they were both tired physically or drained mentally and emotionally from finishing up their first week of intense filming.

Arriving at her house, Tanner couldn't help but be grateful for the short commute. When he filmed on location, it usually was anywhere from half an hour to an hour back to his accommodations. With everything taking place in the Sugar Springs area, though, they could make it to Paige's house in a relatively short amount of time, no matter where they filmed that day.

Going inside, they both deposited their backpacks on the kitchen table. Tanner pulled out his laptop and began charging it.

"I'm going to watch the dailies again. At least that last sequence we filmed today. Something isn't ringing quite right with me." He paused, studying her. "Do you have any ideas why?"

He noticed her mouth tighten and knew something was wrong. When she didn't speak, he pleaded, "Talk to me, babe. I trust your judgment. I value your opinion."

"Then why didn't you ask it when you were casting the most important role in this piece?" she demanded, a rare display of her temper flaring.

"What are you talking about? Your fingerprints are all over this casting."

"Not with the Gwen Foster role," she snapped back, picking up one of her scattered glasses of water and downing its contents.

He thought a moment, back to Chloe Turner's audition in California. How he'd been blown away by it. By her. He had called Paige and raved about the actress' performance and how right she was for the role, immediately sending Paige the audition footage.

But he hadn't asked her for her opinion on Chloe taking on the role of Gwen Foster.

"You don't think Chloe is right for the role, do you?" he accused, wanting to defend his choice for the role.

"No. I don't," she said flatly. "And I would have told you that if you'd asked me." Her face softened. "I know you are including me when you can, Tanner. You've spoken often of this being a collaboration. I appreciate that more than I could ever voice. I didn't expect to be involved in every single decision, but the casing of Gwen was important to me. Do I think Chloe Turner has talent? Without a doubt. But do I think she makes for the perfect Gwen Foster? That's a definite no."

"I thought you had worked with her a few times. I encouraged that."

Paige's lips thinned. "I tried to. She wasn't interested. Chloe Turner has her own agenda. She's going to do what she wants—and you don't even see it."

Her last statement baffled him. "No, I don't. Tell me what you mean."

Immediately, Paige gave him an example of a scene they had filmed yesterday, one in which he had given Chloe very specific instructions before the cameras began to roll. Chloe had completely ignored Tanner's notes. She'd taken the scene in a completely different direction. While Tanner had silently questioned it, he'd understood the choices she'd made and thought them smart ones. He had gone on after that one take, not following up on how he had wanted her to play the scene and not requesting they go again, this time filming the scene with his direction in mind.

"She ignored everything you told her to do," Paige continued. "Do you know why this film isn't clicking? It's because of Chloe Turner. You're not directing her, Tanner. You're indulging her."

A thought occurred to him. "You're jealous. Of her."

"Who wouldn't be jealous of a woman like Chloe?" she countered. "Perfect face. Perfect body. Perfect acting pedigree. Celebrated by all. But I could have told you that she wasn't right for this role, Tanner. I guess I'm more than a little hurt that I wasn't even consulted on your choice. You've asked my opinion on so many things, but you didn't ask it on the most important choice of all."

Paige picked up her purse and slung the strap over her shoulder. "You're wondering why things are a little off. A little hollow. It's because Chloe isn't right for Gwen. Yes, technically she's doing everything she's supposed to do. She knows her lines. She's giving you emotion when you ask for it. But she's holding back on you, Tanner. You just can't see it. Chloe is too brittle to be effective as Gwen. I've stressed to you that Gwen is vulnerable. She's just lost her husband. She's doubting the relationship they had because of the things she's found out about him since his death. Gwen is bruised —but *not* broken. She's looking for a lifeline and thinks she's found one with Peter reentering her life. She's guarded but still hopes she can trust him at the same time. They have a history, a sweetness between them. First love is powerful."

She hesitated and then added, "Vulnerable to Chloe means something different. She's portraying Gwen as too weak. Too helpless. Yes, she's a bit fragile. But Gwen isn't powerless. She's sensitive. Not prone to stupidity. That's where Chloe misses the mark. What you're going to get from her is a technically correct performance but one without heart."

Paige shook her head. "You need to do some soul searching right now, Hollywood. You can make the film with a big star's name and make a mess of it. The look and feel of it already is great. That comes through the raw footage every time we view the dailies. But it's going to be style over substance. Audiences aren't going to like this Gwen, the one Chloe has created. If you don't have an audience rooting for your heroine, you've lost them—and control of the entire movie."

She went to the door. "I'm going to walk over and have dinner with Sarah. You have a lot to consider, and I don't want to get in your way."

She left. Tanner stood, stunned by what she'd said.

Was Paige right? Did Chloe miss the essence of what he was going for? Were the slight changes the actress made in the direction he gave her meant to make her look good and not capture the character?

He made himself a sandwich and sat at the kitchen table to watch the dailies from start to finish, day one until now. He finished viewing the first day with a sinking feeling, watching the footage with new eyes. He moved to the second day of filming, the feeling only growing stronger.

Paige was right. There was a strength beneath Gwen's fragility. She had an innocence about her. Hope in her fellow man, especially Peter Willoughby, her first love. Chloe Turner's performance hit most of the marks, but it was missing that intangible which would be the difference in making *Shadows of the Past* good instead of great.

He cursed aloud, knowing he had made a huge mistake in casting Chloe. He had run every important decision by Paige except this one. The most important one. He supposed he'd been blinded by Chloe's beauty and resumé, only thinking of how his first film would star an Academy Award-winning actress. Objectively, he could see that he and Chloe had chemistry together. If it would have been any other film, that would have been enough. But Chloe was missing the key component of Gwen. Gwen had a likability about her, one that audiences would empathize with and relate to. Even with Chloe's talent and the makeup department toning down her looks, audiences would still see Chloe Turner trying a little too hard to be the small-town girl caught up in something almost beyond her.

Tanner needed those filmgoers to root for Gwen from the beginning. She was one of them. Chloe could never be that.

How was he going to go about firing her?

He needed to act immediately. Only a few parts of what they'd filmed this week would be able to be salvaged because Gwen Foster had already been in so many scenes. But Paige was right. He had known in his gut things weren't ringing true. On paper, everything worked, but in the movies? The screen revealed all. Chloe Turner wasn't meant to play Gwen Foster. He had been too dazzled to see that. He didn't know if the leaders on his film crew knew this and were too afraid to speak up, or if they had been like him, compromised in their opinions because of the stature of Chloe's reputation.

Tanner called his assistant director first.

"What's up, Tanner? Do we need to work tomorrow? I'd be happy to do so."

"Objective answer needed. Don't take time to think. Is Chloe Turner right for the role of Gwen Foster?"

A brief pause and then, "No."

"Then why didn't you tell me?" he asked angrily.

"Because . . .I hadn't really thought about it. She's a big name. She brings a lot of cachet to the project. She's done an excellent job so far. Knows her lines. Has shown a side of herself that most audiences haven't seen." The AD paused. "And yet it took you saying this now for me to put my finger on it. Chloe is . . .I don't know, maybe a little too . . .savvy to be Gwen. A little *too* world-weary?"

"Thanks for confirming. Talk soon."

Tanner hung up and dialed his cinematographer, who answered on the first ring. "Watching the dailies again, Tanner?"

"What's it like photographing Chloe Turner?" he asked.

"She is a dream, Tanner. The woman has no bad angles. She is almost . . .too perfect."

"That's not Gwen," Tanner said flatly. "Gwen is

pretty. But Gwen has flaws. She is a female Everyman. I think there's a disconnect on this film. Between the material and Chloe. Paige said that Chloe's performance is technically correct. But I think what she was getting at is that it lacks heart. The emotion I'm looking for."

"I think Paige is a very wise woman," the cinematographer said carefully. "She may not be experienced in the filmmaking business, but Paige has good instincts. You should have cast someone such as Paige to play Gwen. She has a fragility—and yet possesses an inner strength and resolve."

"That is genius," he said. "I'll be making some changes. I'll let you know."

He hung up, excited about the idea of Paige playing Gwen.

But would she do it?

It meant turning Chloe loose. He needed to inform the actress tonight of his decision. Dreading the thought, Tanner texted her.

Are you free tonight? We need to talk.

His cell rang almost immediately, and he saw from the Caller ID that it was Chloe. What he had to say couldn't be done over the phone. He owed it to the actress to let her go in person.

"Tanner, it's so good to hear from you. Would you like to get together now?"

"Yes. Can—"

"I can come right over," Chloe told him. "See you soon."

He worried about how she would take being let go from the production. He wouldn't want it known that she was fired from the project. That was too harsh. He could get Martha Young to delicately word a press release, something about a mutual decision to part ways. It was done all the time in the business, usually citing artistic differences. He could say he had a different vision of the character and while Chloe had embodied many of the characteristics of Gwen Foster, after filming began, he decided to go in a different direction. Yes, that's what he'd tell Chloe.

Because it was true.

Tanner wished Paige could be here with him when he gave Chloe the news. He hoped his fiancée would be proud of him for realizing he had made a casting mistake and quickly rectifying it. At least he had discovered it early in filming. True, they would lose several days and have to revamp the production's schedule, but better now than being in the editing room, stuck with a film he didn't want to cut because he saw it wasn't working.

He called Paige, hoping she might cut her evening short with Sarah and come home. His call went to voicemail, however. He decided to leave a message but not refer to what he was about to do.

"Hi, babe. Just wondering if you and Sarah were having a good time. I hope you hurry home. I miss you."

Tanner paced the room, wondering how Chloe would respond to her abrupt dismissal from the project. He decided to have wine poured when she arrived. Chloe was known for enjoying a glass or two. Maybe that might soften the blow. He opened a cabernet and let it breathe, putting it on the coffee table and retrieving two wine glasses.

Then the doorbell rang. He went to answer it and saw Chloe, looking radiant—and nothing like Gwen Foster. He didn't expect his leading lady to resemble the character in real life, but Tanner saw now he'd been awed by Chloe's looks and tremendous talent. In the future, if this film were well received and made a profit and he had a chance to direct again, he would be certain to include Paige in every decision he made. Even if she agreed with him, that confirmation would give him the confidence he needed to move forward.

Chloe smiled seductively, and for the first time, Tanner realized the actress had been flirting with him during the production. He'd been so caught up in being her director that he hadn't realized it. He was sure Paige had noticed, though. There had been a coolness between the two women, and he worried that Chloe had said something to Paige. If she had, he would learn about it now and make certain he apologized profusely to his fiancée for being so thick.

"Come on in, Chloe," he said, giving her a friendly smile.

"I was so pleased to hear from you, Tanner," the actress said, stepping inside and looking around. "Is Paige not here?" she asked innocently.

"No, she's having dinner with Sarah Meinholdt."

"Good."

That one word—and the way Chloe said it—put Tanner on high alert. Part of him thought he should just spit it out and tell the actress she'd no longer be required on set, but another part of him said he better handle her with kid gloves, else she might spread falsehoods about the production and him through social media, where she had one of the biggest followings of anyone in Hollywood.

"I was about to pour some wine if you'd like a glass," he told her.

"You can offer me wine anytime, Tanner Haddock," she said, her voice low.

They moved to the sofa, and Tanner poured each of them a glass of the cab, handing Chloe hers. She lifted it and tapped it against his.

"Here's to a wonderful collaboration. One I hope will go beyond this film."

Tanner set his wineglass on the coffee table and stood abruptly, seeing the confusion on her face as he said, "We might make a film together in the future, Chloe. You're talented as hell, and our chemistry rings true."

She set down her glass and stood too close to him. He took a step back.

"The dailies are showing me that it isn't working, though. It's almost as if you're too big a star to be playing Gwen Foster."

She placed a palm on his chest. "You mean you need someone a little bit plainer. Pretty but wholesome."

"Yes. I didn't know it. You're a terrific actress, but what's coming across on screen isn't what I need to capture for my first effort as a director." He paused. "I'm sorry, Chloe. I'm going to have to replace you. You'll receive your full salary, per the contract, but it's just not working."

Her palm still rested against his chest, and her free hand latched onto his forearm. "But you do see how *we* work, Tanner, don't you? I've felt it from the moment we met. We're good together. Our chemistry is undeniable."

"We may be able to find a project to do together

down the road," he said, trying to pull away. "But this one isn't it."

Her arms suddenly went about his neck, her hands locked behind his nape. "I can give up Gwen Foster—but I refuse to give you up."

She yanked hard. His mouth crashed down on hers. Tanner tried to pull away, but Chloe was having none of that. He tightened his mouth, preventing her from deepening the kiss, and quickly turned his head.

And heard the gasp.

He looked up and saw Paige standing in the doorway, her face shocked at the betrayal she thought she saw.

"Paige, this isn't—"

She turned and fled.

Tanner tried to pry Chloe from him. She made it difficult by shifting, pushing him back so that they landed on the sofa. His back hit the cushions, her atop him. She looked down, satisfaction on her face.

"I told her you'd get tired of her. I don't care if I'm in your silly little film, Tanner. I just want to be with you. We will be the next Hollywood power couple. Unstoppable."

He forced her off him, scrambling off the couch. "I never want to see you again, Chloe. I won't say a word against you, but I will never work with you again."

Disbelief filled her eyes. "You're choosing *her*? Over *me*? She's nothing, Tanner."

He glared at the woman who had just imploded his life. "Paige Laramie is my everything."

Tanner grabbed his keys and ran out the door.

21

Paige ran blindly from her house, no destination in mind. She ran for several blocks, gripping her keys until the pain of the pressure caused her to come to a halt. Nausea filled her, the image of Tanner and Chloe locked together all she could see. She turned and vomited in the street, her body shuddering violently as she stumbled away and continued moving unsteadily down the sidewalk.

She had known this would happen. Her gut had always told her she wasn't good enough for Tanner. That someone with his looks, intelligence, and charm wouldn't waste his time on someone as average—and messed up—as her. Yet she had made the decision to commit to Tanner. To open her mind, her heart, and her soul to him. For three months, they had lived in a blissful bubble, growing close and loving one another. The past week of filming had begun to put distance between them, though. Yes, they'd been on the set together and came home to the same house, but he had been wrapped up in his directorial duties. She had understood that. It wouldn't have been fair or possible to have his undivided attention. He had a film to helm.

But she had also seen how Chloe Turner flirted

with him. Tanner hadn't really responded to it. At least, not in front of Paige. She hadn't wanted to question the choice he'd made for the leading role in his film. After all, it was *his* film. His fingerprints needed to be all over this production. She gave him her opinion when he asked, but he was free to do as he pleased.

Paige began sobbing, her stomach aching, thinking of all she had lost tonight. Her newly-gained confidence in herself was shot to hell. Her heart had been trampled. Her trust in Tanner broken beyond repair. Yet rationally, she understood. Oh, they'd made a deep connection because of their past encounter and their small-town, common roots. But she wasn't of the world he'd chosen to live in. Filming around the globe. Attending premieres. Every public outing fodder for the tabloids.

Angrily, she wiped away her tears, knowing she had done this to herself. She had opened her heart willingly when she should have shut the door in Tanner's face that first day and kept it closed.

But would she really give up the past months with him?

No...

In all honesty, Tanner Haddock had done her a tremendous favor. He had pulled her from her shell and pushed her out into the world. Shielded her from it and walked beside her as she ventured beyond the confines of Sugar Springs. Never again would Paige be tethered to this place or any other. Tanner had shown her that she was resilient. She had overcome horrible events in her past, things she had let define her for far too long. But she was done with that. Tanner had actually done her a favor. He had let her see just how strong she was. How capable she was of standing on her own, tall and proud, brave beyond words.

And he had introduced her to love. Physical love. Emotional love. While she couldn't picture herself giving her heart to any man in the future, she wouldn't trade the time she'd spent in his company. Tanner had helped her learn some life lessons. She would never again doubt herself. She was who she was *because* of what she had survived—and she would survive this betrayal.

Paige only wished it could have been anyone but Chloe Turner.

She started jogging again. She didn't want to see Tanner. If she went to Nana's house, that would be the first place he looked. If he didn't find her there, he would go to Sarah's. She wondered if she could make the drive to Dallas and take refuge with Vivi. Her friend would probably shoot Tanner on sight if he tracked Paige there.

No, she needed time away. To heal. To put aside her hurt. And then she decided she would go where Tanner would never expect her to turn.

Owens.

It would be the last place he would look for her. She knew he would seek her out. Apologize. In the big picture, Tanner was a good guy, that same small-town boy he'd been all his life. He would tell her how sorry he was. Paige wasn't ready to hear any of that just yet. She didn't know if she would even return to the set. They didn't need her. Tanner had hired an excellent crew. She'd already booked places to film and gotten the necessary permits. Prepared the shoot's schedule. She wasn't really needed beyond that. Any directorial decisions Tanner needed to make would be ones he could decide on his own or with the advice of his AD.

In the meantime, she wanted time away.

Paige turned the corner and saw a black truck coming her way. Not knowing if it might be Tanner's, she raced into the closest front yard and hugged the large oak, allowing the tree's trunk to block her from the road. Slowly, the truck drove by. She held her breath, moving gradually around the tree so that she still couldn't be seen. Taking a chance, she leaned out and saw it was Tanner's truck, but he was already at the corner, turning right.

Since he was looking for her, now was her chance to go home and get her car. She raced there, seeing the garage door wide open. He'd been in a hurry not to close it. Paige moved inside and to her closet, throwing a few changes of clothes into a suitcase and grabbing her laptop and chargers. She tossed her things into the trunk and then left, praying she wouldn't cross paths with Tanner on her way out of Sugar Springs.

She reached the town limits and increased her speed. Looking at the gas gauge, she would need to stop for gas in the next half-hour. She did so and then drove straight through to Owens. On the way there, she decided to take a huge risk and didn't stop until she reached the Haddock ranch.

When she pulled up in front of the house Tanner grew up in, doubt filled her. Was she crazy to seek help from Jeff and Helen? Maybe so. Still, they had been there for her long ago. A bond existed between them, and her heart told her she could count on them.

She went to the front door and glanced at her watch, seeing it was just after ten. No porch light burned. In fact, no lights were on that she could see. They had probably gone to bed already. Helen was an early bird, at the stables with the horses by five every morning. Paige didn't know exactly what time Jeff went into the station, but he might go to bed when his wife did.

Paige paced outside, wondering if she should simply drive to Tanner's place. It was never locked. She could simply spend the night there.

Someone switched a lamp on inside, then the porch light came on. Her mouth grew dry. Suddenly, coming to her ex-fiancé's parents for support seemed like an idiotic decision.

The door opened. Jeff stepped out onto the porch. Paige hurried up to greet him.

"I'm sorry if I woke you," she apologized.

"Not me," he said. "I don't sleep much. I was reading in the den and thought I heard someone pull up. When no one knocked, I went back to reading. Then my spidey sense told me someone was here."

"I shouldn't have come," she said, taking a few steps back.

His steady gaze pinned her into place. "But you did. I'm sure you had a good reason, Paige, especially since I don't see Tanner with you."

"No, you won't be seeing us together anymore." Tears welled in her eyes. "I'm sorry I came, Jeff. It was a mistake. I can't ask you to take sides." Paige turned.

"Wait." He strode toward her, reaching her in a few strides. "At least let me give you a hug. You look as if you could use one pretty badly."

He opened his arms, and Paige walked into them. She began sobbing as he enveloped her, his warmth comforting her. Yet he looked so much like his son, it made it hard for her.

"Come inside," he urged. "You're too upset to drive anywhere. We'll have a cup of tea. Everything always seems better once you have a cup of tea in you."

Paige let him lead her into the house. They went to the kitchen, and he pulled out a chair from the table.

"Sit. I won't bother putting the kettle on. That takes too long. I'll just nuke the water."

She sat as he bustled about the kitchen, filling two large mugs with water and placing them in the microwave. He retrieved a tea caddy and set it on the table. They had bonded during her visit to the ranch, both of them enjoying herbal teas over coffee.

The microwave beeped, and he returned with the mugs, setting them on the table. She had selected peach and opened the packet, dunking the teabag several times.

"Talk to me," he urged. "What happened between you and Tanner to make you think things are over?"

Fresh tears flooded her eyes, and Paige brushed away the ones which fell.

"I don't think we were ever meant to last," she said softly. "I do think Tanner coming into my life again was fate. He's done a lot for me. Boosted my confidence. Made me believe in myself. Encouraged me to try writing full-time."

She dunked the bag again several times and then let go. "But he's out of my league in every way possible, Jeff. Surely, you can see that."

He gazed at her steadily. "My son is a remarkable man, but don't sell yourself short, Paige. What I see before me is a resilient young woman. You've overcome so much in your life. After you left Owens and returned to Sugar Springs, you became a top student. You've had a successful career in teaching and now you're beginning another one as a screenwriter. You are a focused, very determined woman. I believe you can do pretty much anything you choose."

She took a soothing sip of the tea, letting its

warmth wash over her. "I have a confidence now which I lacked, probably ever since my parents divorced. Tanner has helped me see my worth. For that, I will be forever grateful to him. But the worlds we inhabit are too different, Jeff."

"I know he has to be a part of something very different when he leaves Owens. He's said so himself. But I believe my boy stays true to his roots even when he's gone from here. If there's been trouble between the two of you, I believe you can work it out."

"What if I don't want to be a part of who he is when he returns to California? Or go on locations with him for weeks at a time?" She swallowed painfully. "I think he's been able to adapt to the different worlds he inhabits. I'm not really willing to do that. I appreciate what he's taught me. What I've learned by being with him. But not every relationship is meant to last. You and Helen are simply two of the lucky ones."

The police chief smiled. "We are. But I think you and Tanner could be, too. Every marriage consists of compromise, Paige. It all depends upon how much you love the other person and how much you're willing to move the needle to meet them. Sometimes, it's halfway. Honestly, most of the time you can't compromise fifty-fifty. You might have to give ninety to his ten one time, and the next time it's a thirty to seventy split."

Jeff paused. "How much you love him—and want to be with him—will dictate how much you're willing to compromise."

Paige couldn't tell this kind man that his son had cheated on her. Even though she loved Tanner more than she could have thought possible, she wasn't willing to compromise by sharing him with another woman, especially one as superficial and manipulative as Chloe Turner.

"I think Tanner came into my life for a reason, Jeff, and it's time for both of us to move on now. He helped me blossom into a person I really like being. I've helped him in his quest to become a good director. But we have different things we want out of life. I'll never forget him."

She took another sip of her tea and then placed the mug on the table. Standing, she said, "Thank you for being a part of my life. For what you did to save me. For being here now, with your calming presence and steady advice. But I think I'll go now."

"It's late, Paige. Stay the night. If not here, go to Tanner's place."

The thought of not having to drive this late at night and find somewhere to stay helped her to make up her mind.

"I'll go to his place."

"Does Tanner know you're here?"

"No. I doubt he'll call you looking for me, but don't lie to him if he asks if you've seen me. I'll spend the night and then be gone tomorrow morning." Resolve filled her. "I have things to do in Sugar Springs."

She would speak calmly and rationally with Tanner when she returned tomorrow. Tell him it was over. Offer for him to continue staying at her house for the remainder of the summer while he shot *Shadows of the Past*. Sarah wouldn't mind if Paige moved in with her for a few weeks. But she would no longer go to the set, for this movie or any other one. From now on, she would sell her screenplay and move on to the next one. Whoever bought it could interpret it however he or she wished. She would remain on the periphery of the movie business.

Jeff bent and brushed a kiss on her cheek. "Call me if you need anything."

"I will," she promised, knowing what she needed to fill the hole in her heart would take time and distance. Maybe she would find a cabin to rent for the rest of the summer instead of staying in Sugar Springs. She owed it to Tanner to speak to him in person and formally end things between them. But she liked this area. Broken Bow was beautiful. If she could find a cabin to rent, she might spend the rest of the summer here. Writing. Walking.

Healing.

Jeff walked her to the car, and Paige drove to Tanner's house. The one she had thought they would share, making trips back to Oklahoma after he'd finished filming his latest project.

She got a glass of water and took it to the bedroom with her. Brushed her teeth and washed her face. Peeled away her clothes and took a long, hot shower, trying to banish the images flitting through her mind of showering with Tanner. Of making love with him in the shower. In this bed.

Fortunately, the sheets were clean and carried none of his scent. Paige fell into a dreamless sleep, not even aware of the tears she shed for all that she had lost.

22

———

Tanner immediately drove to Nana's, leaving his engine running as he bailed out of the truck and raced up the porch steps. He pounded on the door relentlessly until Nana answered, wearing pink sponge curlers in her abundant gray hair.

"Tanner Haddock, are you trying to rouse the dead?" she accused.

It was obvious Paige wasn't here but he had to ask anyway. "Have you seen Paige?"

Nana's lips pursed. "You've had your first fight. No, she didn't come here."

"It wasn't a fight. She saw something that she thinks she saw, but she didn't," he said, not bothering to explain the situation or his irrational statement. "If she comes here, please tell her to call me. And then *you* call me. I'm afraid she'll leave. Call me and don't tell her you've called me," he pleaded.

"I won't take sides, young man," she warned. "If you've messed up—or if Paige has—then you'll have to work it out between you." Nana paused. "But I will let you know if she stops by."

He hugged her. "Thank you."

Quickly, Tanner returned to his truck, trying to think where Paige might go. He thought he would try Sarah Meinholdt next. Unfortunately, Sarah hadn't talked to Paige since they'd finished their pizza from Romano's and Paige had walked home.

"There's been a huge misunderstanding," he told the drama teacher. "If you see her, let me know."

"If either of you has screwed up, Tanner, it can be fixed," Sarah said. "No one is perfect. You've really made a difference in Paige's life."

"She's changed my entire world," he said fervently. "I'm no longer me without her."

"I'll keep this quiet," Sarah told him. "I hope you find her soon."

Grimly, he nodded and returned to his truck, aimlessly driving around Sugar Springs. Paige had been on foot when she left. Her car was still in the garage when he rushed out the door to find her. Of course, she was a runner with immense stamina. She could have run all the way to Sugar Lake in the amount of time she'd been gone. Hell, she might even try to run all the way to Dallas to Vivi.

He'd talked with Paige's best friend a few times when the two women had FaceTimed together, and Vivi had even come to Sugar Springs for a few days in May to meet him. Viviana Romano was a spitfire and extremely loyal to Paige. He wondered if he should call Vivi and decided to wait. Tanner didn't want the world knowing of the trouble between him and his fiancée.

If she still even was his fiancée.

He'd told Sarah Meinholdt the truth. Without Paige, he couldn't see a life for himself. Everything he pictured included Paige. Every goal he had. Every idea he thought about. Every wish for the future, she was a part of it. He had to find her and straighten out the horrible misunderstanding.

While Tanner had done everything he could to encourage Paige and assure her of his steadfastness and love for her, she had always seemed to have doubts about the two of them being together. She had vocalized a few times how she was surprised someone of his stature would want to be with a no one like her. He had done what he could to assuage her fears. He knew she didn't trust men. Not after what her father had put her through. But he truly thought things were fine between them.

She hadn't liked Chloe Turner, though. He had been dead wrong about the actress being right for Gwen. Tanner had been so enthusiastic about an Oscar winner coming onboard that he hadn't realized he'd never asked Paige for her opinion about the actress. And from what Paige had said, Chloe had no doubt fed into Paige's fears of Tanner straying, especially with someone like Chloe.

Paige had hit the nail solidly on the head. It was Chloe's performance which was lacking, ruining the movie he was trying to make. He didn't believe now that the actress was capable of giving him what he required for the role of Gwen. Maybe that's why she veered from the direction he gave her for various scenes. He'd merely racked it up to Chloe making choices as an actor, ones that he had tried to respect. Tanner could see now how Chloe was delicately manipulating him, though. As a director, he had the final say. He should have asked for another few takes of scenes when she altered his direction and ignored his notes. He would have been able to see right away that she wasn't able to perform as he'd asked. He wondered what poison the actress had spewed at Paige, who had stoically taken whatever had been doled out, never speaking an ill word about Chloe to him.

Well, Chloe was out.

And he held out a sliver of hope that Paige was still in.

Though she had never acted before, she knew Gwen better than anyone. Tanner believed that Paige could capture Gwen's essence. Her hope. Her fragility. Her strength.

All he had to do was find her now. Convince her he loved her. That he'd dropped Chloe from the production. And that he wanted his fiancée to take Chloe Turner's place.

Piece of cake.

He drove the streets of Sugar Springs for a few minutes, knowing finding Paige might be compared to looking for a needle in a haystack. He would head home. Surely, she would show up there at some point.

When he returned, the garage door was still open. He had left so quickly, he hadn't bothered taking time to close the door.

And Paige's car was gone.

She must have returned while he was out searching for her. Quickly, he went inside. One drawer in her bedroom was still open. A few hangers were on the floor in her closet. An empty space where her small suitcase usually stood let him know she'd come home and packed a few things before taking off. Tanner was certain Paige was headed for Dallas and Vivi. With it being Saturday night, Vivi would still be at her restaurant, though. Paige wouldn't be in Dallas for a couple of hours.

He decided to call Reg. His security head had come to Sugar Springs a couple of weeks ago and assessed things. Brought a couple of security guards who patrolled the shoot. As Nana had promised, though, the citizens of Sugar Springs had closed ranks, especially when they found out Tanner and Paige were engaged. No paparazzi had made it onto set, and he had sent Reg home, keeping the guards for insurance.

"What's up, mate?"

"I need your mad hacking skills, Reg."

"Let me crack my knuckles, and we'll get started."

Tanner heard the loud crunch over the phone.

"Booting up. What do you need? Someone bothering you or Paige? Or Chloe Turner? How about Nana? Now, that one's a live wire. If she were a bit younger, I'd take a run at Nana myself."

Quickly, he explained how he'd let Chloe go from the production. How she'd come onto him. And how Paige had walked in on them, Chloe pressed against him.

"Misinterpreted the whole thing," Reg said drily.

"You could say that. She's been gone about forty-five minutes now. I checked a few places in town, and she wasn't at any of them. Came home and found her car gone. I know you did your usual, thorough work-up when you were here."

"Of course, I did so. I have everything from her grade school transcripts to her credit cards and driving license information. I also have her car's license plates and VIN," Reg said crisply. "I know I didn't ask her permission or yours, but I put a tracker on her automobile. I also installed the same software on her mobile that I've placed on yours, again, unfortunately, without her permission. I didn't want to worry her about things such as stalkers."

Reg paused. "I looked well into her past and know how you first met, Tanner. Paige has gone through a lot in her life. I thought I was making things easier on her by not alerting her to some of the dangers in your life. I figured we'd have a sit down soon enough and have a full-blown conversation, most likely when you left the bubble in Texas and came back to California to edit your film."

"I could kiss you, Reg," he said. "Please, just tell me where she is."

"While we've been talking, I've activated the software to track her car and mobile, as well as any credit card use. Hmm."

Tanner's impatience grew. "Tell me where she is. My best guess is that she's heading to see her friend Vivi Romano in Dallas."

"Well, she did leave Sugar Springs and filled her car's tank not too long ago." Reg named the town, which Tanner knew wasn't along the interstate to Dallas. "This is interesting."

"What?" he demanded.

"I think Paige might be on her way to Owens."

"Owens? Why the hell would she go there?"

Because it was the last place he might search for her.

"Never mind. I'll head that way now."

"I could be wrong," Reg said. "I'll keep monitoring her progress and let you know when and where she stops."

"Thanks, Reg."

"Not a problem, Tanner. I hope you are able to resolve things. Paige is simply a lovely woman."

He hung up, wondering about the choice she had made if she truly did head to Owens now. The place held such bad memories for her.

Then he recalled their time together there in March. How being in Owens had been the beginning of Paige's healing. How his parents had embraced her with open arms. She was choosing to go to them now. To family. Maybe not blood relatives—but those who had looked after her in a time of crisis and need. She needed them again now.

Tanner didn't even bother packing a bag. He had clothes at the ranch he could wear if he needed a change of clothing. What was most important was to get to Paige and make certain she understood the truth.

That he couldn't live without her.

On his way out the door, he called his AD, telling him that Chloe Turner would no longer be welcomed on the set and would be replaced as soon as Tanner could find a suitable actress to take the role.

"Please let the security team know about this. I doubt Chloe will come around, but I don't want her anywhere near filming. Can you look over the schedule and see if there's anything we can shoot on Monday and Tuesday not involving Peter and Gwen?"

"Hmm. A few crowd shots. Several exteriors of various buildings around town which the characters go into. I could have the stunt doubles do those. I can probably make enough work for those two days. After that, Tanner? We need you and definitely need Chloe's replacement for filming, else we'll fall behind schedule."

He slid behind the wheel and started up the truck. "We might have to shut production down briefly," he said. "I don't want to do it, but I'd rather have the right actress in the role than waste more time with the wrong one."

"Agreed. Okay, I'll fiddle with things. Keep me posted."

"You're in charge Monday in case I can't get back.

Paige and I have to make a quick out of town trip. Run with what you see fit."

"Will do," the AD agreed cheerfully.

He made his way through Sugar Springs and hit the highway which would take him first to Paris, Texas, and then toward Broken Bow. At first, he thought he might call his parents and give them a heads up that Paige might stop by. Of course, she could go straight to his house instead and try to see them in the morning. He went back and forth and then decided not to call and alert them to the problems between Paige and him. Tanner hoped they could work everything out, with no one other than the handful of people he'd spoken to being wiser.

After an hour on the road, his cell rang. His heart quickened when he saw who was calling. "Reg, any news?"

"Paige is definitely in Owens, Tanner. Her car stopped a few minutes ago at your parents' house. I've got the exact coordinates."

"Thanks for letting me know. Call me back in case the car moves an inch."

Though he wanted to call her, he had kept from doing so, not wanting to cause her to flee, which she might do if she knew he was on his way to her. He also itched to call his dad, knowing Jeff Haddock was the night owl in the family and that Paige must be with him right now. Hopefully, his dad's easygoing, steadfast nature would soothe Paige and convince her to stay.

After several minutes passed, his phone rang again. His heart sank when he saw Reg's name on the Caller ID.

"Is she on the move again?" he asked, worry filling him.

"Yes. She left a few minutes ago but stayed on the property. Wait. She's stopping again. She's at your house now, Tanner."

"I'll bet Dad persuaded her to stay the night since it's getting late." He glanced at the dashboard clock. "It's almost ten-thirty now. I'll be there in another hour if you'll simply keep monitoring her whereabouts. After that, you can go off the clock, Reg. Thanks for giving up your Saturday night. I owe you."

"A healthy bonus at Christmas is always appreciated," quipped Reg.

"You got it," Tanner promised, ending the call.

He sped through the dark, hoping he was right and that Paige was settling in for the night. Deciding to take a chance, he called his dad, who didn't even bother with saying hello.

"Yes, Paige was here. She left and went to stay the night at your house. I won't ask what happened between you because it's none of my business. My best advice is get your ass up here and straighten things out. You don't want to lose this one, Tanner. Paige is special."

"I'm already on my way. How is she?"

"Shaken. Whatever happened, that girl loves you. Do whatever it takes to hold onto her."

"I plan to, Dad." He paused. "I'm glad Paige turned to you."

"I think she knew she could trust me. I was here for her once before. I'll always be here for her. For you, too, Tanner. I hope you know that. How much I love you and how proud I am of you."

"I know that, Dad. I love you, too. Thanks for taking care of her."

Knowing Paige had stopped for the night and he'd be with her soon helped free the tension which had filled his body. Still, he knew hard work lay ahead of him. His fiancée was not one to fold easily. She had been wronged, and he had some groveling to do, especially where it concerned hiring Chloe Turner.

Tanner arrived at the ranch and headed straight for his place. Sure enough, Paige's vehicle sat outside. He moved up the sidewalk, his heart racing, wondering if she'd listen to reason or if he might be able to kiss her first. He decided kissing was the way to go. His kiss would tell Paige everything she needed to know.

The house was dark as he entered. He slipped off his shoes and used his cell's flashlight to make his way through the house and to his bedroom. The door was closed. Taking a deep breath, he turned the knob and entered, moving to the bed.

Paige was curled on her side, facing away from him. Setting his phone to silent and placing it on the nightstand, Tanner stripped off his clothes and climbed into bed next to her, gathering her into his arms. She mumbled something but didn't awaken. Knowing she'd had a long, hard day and needed sleep, he decided not to wake her. Instead, Tanner wrapped himself around her. If she tried to leave the bed, he would know.

He inhaled her vanilla perfume, a calm settling over him. He would make things right.

And then never let this woman go. Ever again.

23

When Paige awoke, she was surrounded by the delicious warmth of Tanner. Something tugged at the back of her mind, and she remembered the horrible nightmare she had had. It must have gone on and on throughout the night because the details seemed so clear and real to her. It had involved her confronting Tanner about casting Chloe Turner without even giving her the consideration of voicing her opinion. Leaving the house, only to return and find her fiancé and Chloe in a lip lock, Chloe wrapped around Tanner. Then the long drive to Owens, where she had sought refuge and advice from Jeff Haddock.

No, something was wrong. She didn't remember her dreams most of the time, much less in such incredible detail. Her throat was still tight from all the tears she had shed.

Opening her eyes, Paige saw she wasn't at home. She was at Tanner's house on the ranch in Owens.

And Tanner was in bed with her. As if nothing had happened.

Immediately, Paige began scrambling, trying to get away. Out of his arms and this bed. But her movement only awakened him. His arms locked around her like a steel vise. He wasn't hurting her. He just wasn't letting her go anywhere.

Fresh tears sprang to her eyes, but she told herself she was through wasting tears on this man, one who had betrayed her in the most hurtful way possible. She had spent years not crying, not even with her mama's illness and death. She clenched her jaw tightly and stilled, hoping he would release his hold on her.

He didn't.

"Paige, I know you're upset with me, but we need to talk. We have a lot to say to each other. At least I have a lot to say to you—and I beg that you listen. Hear me out."

"I will," she said, her voice shaking. "If you let go of me."

"Babe, I feel like you're the proverbial deer in the headlights right now. If I do, you'll fly out of this bed and into the bathroom and lock the door. I'll never get a chance to explain things."

Anger rose within her. "Why should I give you a chance?" she demanded. "What is there to explain? You betrayed me, Tanner." Her voice broke, saying his name. More quietly, she added, "I don't blame you, actually. You're meant to be with someone like Chloe. None of this was ever real."

Suddenly, he flipped her so that they faced one another. Before she could bolt from the bed, his arms went around her once again.

"That's where you're wrong. I know you think you saw something that made you run. That made you think I had been unfaithful. That is as far from the truth as possible, Paige. I love you."

She winced, hearing those words. Words he had

said to her and she had echoed to him during these past few months.

"Those are just words, Tanner. You don't mean them. Or maybe you think you do. Maybe you fancy yourself in love with two different women."

She saw the hurt flash in his eyes. For a moment, Paige doubted herself. What she'd seen. Once more, she struggled to free herself.

Tanner looked at her sternly. "I will let go—if you promise not to run. I want to have a conversation with you. Two adults, trying to keep the lines of communication open between us."

She didn't say anything, locking her jaw and blinking a few times, gazing at him stoically.

"All right," he said softly, his grasp on her easing.

The minute it did, Paige flew off the bed, aiming for the bathroom. The door had a lock on it, and she wanted to be safely on the other side of that door. She needed a barrier between them, afraid his sweet words would sway her, and she would forgive him.

Tanner had anticipated her move, however, and reached the bathroom door just before she did. He locked his fingers around both her wrists and looked at her, disappointment in his eyes.

"I thought I could trust you."

"I thought I could trust *you!*" she fired back, miserable because she still loved him so much, despite everything.

"Fair enough. But I'm still going to talk. You're going to listen. When I'm done, you can ask me any question you'd like."

"I would prefer you put on some clothes," she said primly, glancing away from his magnificent, naked physique.

He had the decency to blush. "Sorry about that. I

got in late and was tired. I just threw off my clothes and fell into bed." His gaze met hers. "I'll get dressed and give you time to do the same. Will you promise to meet me in the kitchen?"

She looked at him a long moment and knew she needed to hear him out. It didn't matter what he said. Her mind was already made up. She knew she'd needed to formally end their engagement face-to-face. Not over the phone or via a text message. This would save her all the worrying she would have done if she'd driven home and confronted him in Sugar Springs.

"All right, I promise."

He released her, and she went into the bathroom, closing the door behind her. Paige didn't lock it, wanting him to see that as a sign of good faith. She went to the toilet, not sure if she needed to sit on it or throw up in it.

She got ready, brushing her teeth and hair, which made her feel more human. She didn't hear anything on the other side of the door and opened it slowly. Tanner was nowhere in sight. His heap of clothes she had seen on the floor was now gone. The door to the bedroom was also closed. She went to her suitcase and pulled out fresh underwear, along with a new pair of jeans, shirt, and bra. Dressing quickly, Paige put the T-shirt she'd worn to bed back inside the suitcase and closed and locked it.

Going to the kitchen, she heard noises coming from it. She saw the tea kettle had been on to boil, and Tanner stirred something in a bowl.

"Pancake batter," he told her. "I used a powdered egg. It won't taste as fresh. The batter's just a mix, but it'll do."

"I'll see to the tea," she said, opening packets of cinnamon apple for them and taking the kettle off the stove, pouring the hot water over the teabags. She dunked both teabags, watching Tanner as he poured the batter onto the hot griddle, flipping the pancakes and then stacking and bringing them to the table. He'd already set out a tub of butter and a bottle of syrup.

They ate in silence. She was determined not to be the first to speak. When he finished and she had, as well, he took their plates and rinsed them, leaving them in the sink.

Tanner returned to the table. "I screwed up, Paige. I know that now. The last few days, I knew the movie wasn't working. I know it did on the page, but there was something lost in translation from page to the actual filming. At first, I thought it was me, trying to helm the production and act in it. But I didn't see that in the rushes. I've actually been pleased with my performance so far. You've given me a terrific understanding of Peter Willoughby, and I'm using all I know, pouring my heart into my performance.

"The disconnect was with Chloe Turner. You were exactly right about everything you said. I cannot believe I've run literally every other decision by you, eager for your opinions, and yet I hired Chloe without even asking what you thought of her. I was blinded by the fact that she was a name actress. That she came with a prestigious pedigree and that shiny, new Oscar. I had seen her in a few other productions, and I thought with the right direction, she would easily grasp what I needed for Gwen Foster."

He raked his fingers through his abundant hair, a sign that he was thinking, trying to work out everything. Paige had seen the gesture many times as they worked. Still, she kept silent.

"Chloe doesn't have what it takes to be Gwen. The

moment you said it aloud, it was so glaringly obvious to me. I immediately called a few of the top crew and asked them about it. They also thought something wasn't quite working and couldn't put their fingers on the problem—until I mentioned that you thought the problem was with Chloe and her performance. It was like a light bulb going off in every single one of them."

He reached and took her hand. Paige let him do so, mostly because she knew it would be the last time he did so. Even though he now understood that Chloe had been miscast, Paige wasn't ever going to forgive him for the scene she had seen between them.

"I made another mistake in calling Chloe and not having you there," Tanner continued. "I didn't think it would be fair to give her the news that she would be replaced over the phone. I owed it to her to explain why I had to move in another direction and would be letting her go from the production."

Hesitating, he added, "Chloe has a huge following on social media. I'll admit that I was afraid if I didn't finesse things the right way, she would blow up, via social media. When I told her I needed to see her in person, she immediately offered to come over. I guess I've been pretty thick because I had no idea she was interested in me."

Tanner halted, meeting her gaze. Paige didn't say anything, so he continued.

"I let her know that I would be replacing her immediately. I never used the word fired with her. I told Chloe I would pay her the entire salary promised in her contract. Not that it was that much. She was working for peanuts, compared to what she usually earns. What I didn't know is that in her head and heart, she had never committed to this movie. To her character. She only took the role because she wanted to get close to me. She started spinning some crazy tale about how we were meant to be together and conquer Hollywood. I stood and told her that wasn't going to happen," he said flatly. "That I wanted her to leave."

He swallowed, and she saw the pain in his eyes.

"She latched onto me. She kissed me. Frankly, I was so stunned, I didn't move for a moment. And when I grasped her shoulders and pushed her away, that's when I saw you."

Tanner's eyes welled with tears, and Paige knew he wasn't acting.

"I love you, Paige. I've told you I've never loved another woman—and I never will. If you can't find it in your heart to forgive me, I'll move on if that's what you truly want. But I'm telling you now that I'll spend the rest of my life alone, missing you."

Her throat grew thick with unshed tears. She had misread the situation entirely. Jumped to a false conclusion because of her own insecurities. Tanner hadn't deceived her. He hadn't cheated on her. He was a good man, a much better one than she deserved.

Both his hands now gripped her hand. "I'm telling you the God's honest truth, Paige. I made a huge mistake not consulting you in this casting decision. I made an even bigger one not realizing that Chloe was flirting with me and trying to come between us. And I sure as hell never would've been alone with her in a room and allowed that kiss to happen."

He looked at her, his eyes pleading with her as much as his words. "You're the only woman I want to love, Paige. You're the only woman I want to be with. I love you in so many ways. I love the crazy way you leave half-empty glasses of water everywhere. How you line your shoes up by the door and tap your fingers when you're thinking. You're the best kisser I've ever had the privilege locking lips with. When I touch you—when I come inside you—I'm complete. And completely me. I'm only half a person without you, babe. I want you in my life forever. I need you more than words can ever express. I want to grow old with you, rocking on that porch outside, having made movies with you. Babies with you. A life with you that we can both be proud of. I can't change what's happened up until now, but I can change as a person. This whole incident has made me realize that perhaps I am still that naïve kid from Owens."

Tears spilled down Tanner's cheeks. "Please, tell me you'll forgive me. That we have a chance to be together. That we will always complete one another and make our dreams come true."

He looked at her, his eyes so hopeful, and yet his body incredibly tense.

"I've never thought I was good enough," she began. "I always thought I lacked something. When I met you again—when everything clicked between us so quickly—I thought it was like some incredible fairy tale. Yet something inside me always told me we weren't going to last. That you would do your movie and move on. I told myself I could live with that. That I would be happy to have what I could of you for as long as I could, and that when you left, I would keep a piece of you with me forever in my heart."

Paige swallowed. "What I found is that I didn't want to give you up, especially to a conniving witch like Chloe Turner."

The corners of Tanner's mouth turned up in a smile. "Yeah?"

"I was ready to drive home to Sugar Springs today and tell you it was over between us. That you knew enough about the script to film on your own without any more help from me. I was even going to let you stay in my house while you filmed."

"Where were you going to be?"

She shrugged. "I didn't know. I thought I would figure it out."

Tanner spoke from his heart. "I've made mistakes, Paige. I'll make more in the future. I'm a flawed man. Hopefully, those future mistakes won't be as terrible as the ones I'm asking forgiveness for now. I don't expect you or me to be perfect. I just want us to be together."

"I'm sorry I didn't believe in us enough," she apologized. "I still lack confidence, especially where you're concerned, but I hope you'll be patient and work with me on that. I have issues, lingering feelings from my parents' divorce and my dad kidnapping me. I want to seek professional help. I believe a therapist can help me get over some of my issues."

She paused and then vocalized what would always be in her heart. "The most important thing I need to tell you is that I love you, Tanner. I can't imagine being apart from you. Ever."

Suddenly, she was in his arms, and he was kissing her senseless. Paige reveled in his taste. His touch. His very nearness. Tanner swept her off her feet and took her to the bedroom, where he made love to her twice. The first time was fast and furious, full of exploding passion and heat. They lay in bed, their fingers laced together, talking for a long time about what they wanted in life, personally and professionally, both as individuals and as a married couple.

Then Tanner made love to her with such utter tenderness that Paige felt secure even as she shattered in his arms. He held her close, and they both wept tears of joy. Tears that spoke of how they had almost lost what they had together. How they had almost walked away from a love that was meant to be.

They showered together, lathering and stroking one another's bodies, lost in the wonder of physical love. They dressed and Tanner said, "We need to get back to Sugar Springs. We have a lot of decisions to make, starting with one I haven't run by you yet." Mischief glinted in his eyes.

"What are you up to, Hollywood?"

"Well, I had a scathingly brilliant idea, Laramie. One I naturally want to run by you, but I think you'll agree and see the brilliance of. Who knows this script better than anyone?" he asked.

"Me," she responded without hesitation.

"Who gets Gwen Foster more than anyone on the planet?"

"That would be me again," she joked. "What are you getting at?"

"This." He took her hands in his and cleared his throat. "Paige Laramie, I think *you* would be the perfect person to play Gwen Foster in our movie."

24

P aige was stunned, gawking at Tanner.

"Say something, babe," he encouraged, squeezing her fingers. "What do you think? You know Gwen like no one else. I have faith in you that you could *be* Gwen."

Slowly shaking her head, she said, "I'm not meant to play this role, Tanner. Or any role. I'm not an actress."

"Sure, you haven't been trained, but has that stopped Nana? Look at what a natural she's been in the part of Gloria." He smiled encouragingly. "Maybe acting runs in the Fisher family genes."

"No, it's not what I want to do. Yes, I understand Gwen Foster because I created her, but I could never play her." Her gaze met his. "But I know exactly who could. Sarah. Sarah Meinholdt."

She watched Tanner absorb her words, mulling over it. They had spent a few dinners in Sarah's company, and Paige knew Tanner liked her friend quite a bit.

"She's been invaluable on set in organizing things," he said slowly, and she knew he was trying to wrap his head around her idea. "Have you ever seen

Sarah act before? I know she's a drama teacher, but I know nothing about the experience she might bring to the table."

"I only saw her in high school productions here, but it was obvious how talented she was. She won a drama scholarship to college. Did regional theatre summers during her college years, and she had the lead in numerous productions while she attended TCU. Sarah left Texas for New York and was in several Off-Broadway and Broadway productions. Never the lead, but I know she has the acting chops to play Gwen."

Paige saw lingering doubt in his eyes as he said, "Then how did she wind up in Sugar Springs? If she were meeting with success in New York, why would come back home and teach?"

"Her dad developed Parkinson's and needed care. Her mom and brother died in a car accident when Sarah was in high school. Her dad was all she had left of her family. You understand small towns, Tanner. You would've come home if your mom or dad needed you."

Her fiancé nodded thoughtfully. "You're right. Family trumps ambition. At least with someone raised with those small-town, core values. How is her dad doing now? I haven't ever heard her mention him."

"He passed away just before Christmas this past year."

"I'm surprised she hasn't left teaching and tried to return to the stage."

"We actually talked about it," Paige told him. "She went up at spring break to visit some of her actor friends and take in a few productions. When she came home, she said while she'd missed the theatre world, she knew she was doing good things for students right here in Sugar Springs and felt a commitment to them. Our production schedule would have us finishing the shoot before school started. Yes, it would be close, but Sarah could still do this film and go back to teaching another year.

"I'm asking you to trust me on this, Tanner. I know Sarah can do this. That she can transform into Gwen."

"I do trust you," he said. "I will always trust you and your instincts. If this is the case, we need to get back to Sugar Springs ASAP and convince Sarah to take on this role. I've worked it out so that we would have Monday and Tuesday to prep her, but we would really need her to start filming on Wednesday. If Sarah turns us down, I'll have to halt production so we can find our new Gwen."

"Then let's head out. Should we stop by your parents' house on our way out of town?"

"No, I don't think so. They would want us to stay and visit a while. We've got too much to do. I'll text Dad and let him know we're leaving."

Tanner retrieved Paige's suitcase and placed it in the car for her. He texted his dad and told her, "Dad knows things are fine between us. He said he hadn't even mentioned to Mom that we were here. Let's keep this little blip under the radar if that's okay with you."

"I agree. We understand now that we always need to communicate. I'm not saying we won't ever fight, just that we know now to always talk things out."

He cupped her cheek. "I wish we were riding back together, but I know we both need our vehicles." He looked at her hopefully. "We could talk the entire way, though. Would that be okay?"

Paige smiled. "I'd like that."

He opened her car door for her, and she got in. Tanner leaned down and kissed her. "There's more of that waiting for you when we get home," he promised, causing desire to flicker through her.

This time Paige understood he really meant it. Tanner was a man who knew his own mind. He was sure of what he wanted in life, both professionally and personally. *She* was who he wanted. It might seem odd to others—including herself—but she had no doubts now that he truly loved her and that they had a long future together. Paige didn't know what that future held. Maybe collaborations. Hopefully, children. But they would be together and grow in love as the years rolled by.

She waited until he was in his truck before starting her car. Seconds later, her cell rang, and she answered it. They talked the entire way back to Sugar Springs, making no stops. When they arrived, they went straight to Sarah's house, her father's former house, a small, two-bedroom frame close to the high school.

Walking up the sidewalk, their hands joined, the door opened before they reached the porch. Sarah looked at them warily.

"Things are fine between us, Sarah," Tanner said. "The misunderstanding's been cleared up."

Relief filled her friend's face. "I'm glad to hear that. I've been worried."

"Can we come in?" Paige asked. "Tanner and I have something to talk over with you."

"Of course."

Sarah ushered them inside and asked if they wanted coffee or tea.

"Some iced tea would be great," Tanner said.

They talked a bit about the production and Sarah's students who were volunteering on set.

"Getting this kind of practical experience at their age is almost unheard of," Sarah said. "Especially since they aren't even having to leave home to get it. It's rare when a film production comes to a town such as Sugar Springs. My students are soaking up everything."

"I really appreciate Freddie Otts," Tanner said. "I needed a personal assistant, and Freddie seems to anticipate what I needed before I even know I need it."

Sarah laughed. "Freddie can be an overachiever. He's the upcoming senior class president and also captain of the basketball team. He gets good grades, too. Freddie has a love for acting but isn't very good at it. He knows it. That's why he likes to head up the crew instead. He's organized and has a nice way with others."

Sarah paused. "But you haven't come here to talk about Freddie Otts. Why are you really here, Tanner?"

They had decided not to sugarcoat anything, and so Tanner said, "I've let Chloe Turner go from the production. Paige helped me figure out that Chloe was wrong for Gwen Foster. We'd like for you to take over the role."

Sarah blew out a long breath. "I already knew about Chloe's firing. Or rather the delicately-worded decision that you're going your separate ways. It was on a few sites last night and has gained more steam today on social media."

"She's covering her ass," Tanner said. "I hadn't even contacted my publicist to draft an announcement. I was afraid Chloe might go nuclear on us."

"No, I don't think she'd do that," Sarah said. "Chloe is savvy as far as this business goes. She may have an Oscar win under her belt, but she doesn't want to gain a reputation of being difficult. You might be a first-time director, Tanner, but you're still golden in Hollywood. If others suspected bad blood between you, they would immediately take your side over Chloe's. She's playing it smart and using the creative difference standard line."

Sarah paused. "As far as me taking on Gwen's role? I'm not sure about that. I haven't done any acting for a few years now, and I've never been in a movie. All my experience was on stage."

"Stage actors have the best training. They're the most prepared," Tanner assured Sarah. "Paige and I believe you're right for Gwen. I can understand where you might have doubts."

Sarah laughed. "You think? You're asking me to step in for an Academy Award-winning actress and pick up as if nothing was out of whack. I haven't rehearsed. I don't know the lines."

Paige spoke up. "We have faith in you. We know you can do this. At least, would you try? If you don't think you're right—if we don't think you're right—we can all agree and move on. Just give the role a chance."

Sarah mulled over it. "Then let's have a little test right now. Let me get my copy of the script."

She had given Sarah a copy so that the drama teacher would be familiar with all the scenes and be able to use her student volunteers in the best ways possible. Paige turned to Tanner.

"I knew she would be reluctant. You can't blame her. It's a lot of pressure to put on her."

"I think Sarah is a resilient person," he said. "I believe she'll thrive under pressure. If she can capture the attention of teenagers and hold it as she has in teaching, becoming Gwen will seem like playtime in the sandbox for her."

Sarah rejoined them at the kitchen table. "Where would you like to start, Tanner?"

He gazed at Sarah steadily. "No softballs." He told

her what scene he wanted to use, and Sarah visibly swallowed.

"All right," she agreed. "Nothing like putting everything on the line."

Sarah found the spot in the script, and Tanner said, "This is where Gwen is at her most vulnerable. She has let down her guard and allowed Peter in, but doubts about him are creeping to the surface. Gwen is sounding him out now, without trying to seem as if she's doing so. She has control of the situation, but only by a thread. Gwen will fight to keep the upper hand."

Sarah nodded thoughtfully, absorbing his director notes. "Got it."

She closed her eyes, and Paige knew her friend was slipping into the role, sinking deeply into Gwen's roots. When Sarah opened her eyes again, Paige saw the vulnerability and also Gwen's budding resolve to get to the truth. Sarah glanced at the page and then back to Tanner, speaking her first line.

The scene unfolded for the next few minutes. By the time it finished, Paige had goosebumps all over her.

While she was ready to jump up and cheer and hug her friend, Tanner was taking a far different approach.

Quietly, he said, "Did you feel it? The tension? The discovery?"

Sarah said, "Yes. You pushed me near the end."

He sat back, crossing his arms, a satisfied smile on his face. "I did. And you responded beautifully."

"I'd like to try it one more time if we could," Sarah said. "This time, I want to go at it from a slightly different angle."

Paige worried a moment, knowing how Chloe

Turner had insisted on trying scenes her way, ignoring Tanner's notes. She said nothing, though, wanting to see how this played out between director and actress.

"I'll follow your lead," Tanner said and gave his opening line.

The changes Sarah made to the scene were subtle, but they rang true to Gwen's character and enhanced the dialogue. When they finished this second time, Paige began applauding. So did Tanner, a huge grin on his face.

"You have great instincts, Sarah," he praised. "I knew you would understand Gwen. I like what you did. I want to see more of that. I hope you didn't have plans for the rest of today because we have a lot of work ahead of us."

"I have the part?" Sarah asked, looking hopeful and yet fearful at the same time.

"You definitely have the part," Tanner assured her.

They spent the rest of the day going through the entire script with Sarah, discussing Gwen's goals and what motivated her. Tanner gave clear direction of what he wanted in each scene from Sarah, his notes concise and thoughtful. In turn, Sarah had some excellent questions and contributed small, subtle ideas that would add a rich layer to a scene. By the end of a very long day, Paige knew this decision to cast Sarah Meinholdt as Gwen Foster would guarantee *Shadows of the Past* would be a critical—and hopefully commercial—success.

"I think we'll leave you alone tomorrow," Tanner told their new lead. "You can work on learning your lines. Hell, you already seem to know a lot of them anyway from rehearsing today."

"I've always had a gift in that regard," Sarah told them. "I can learn lines more quickly than most actors. If you'll let me know the updated schedule, I can make certain I work on learning the lines in those scenes first."

They talked over the adjustments they could make, Paige noting them on her laptop.

"I'll send this revised copy of the schedule out to everyone," she said. "The exteriors and a few of the small scenes can still be shot tomorrow, Sarah. That'll give you all day to work on those scenes."

"The lines will come fairly easily," her friend said. "Tanner, are you needed on set tomorrow, or can your AD handle those shots?"

"I can work with you all day, Sarah, if that's what you'd like. You're saving my ass by agreeing to take on this role."

"You're giving me an opportunity to test myself. To see if I want to play it safe and remain in teaching or if I'm ready to jump again into the acting game."

"Then I'll be back tomorrow morning. Whenever you're ready to rehearse," he said. "Just text me."

Paige and Tanner went home, and she called Nana, assuring her grandmother all was well. When she got off the phone, Tanner enfolded her in his arms.

"You did it, babe. You've saved the production."

"It's a first step," she said. "Yes, I believe Sarah is right for the role. But you've got the majority of the film to shoot. It's going to be several long weeks of hard work, then you'll be in the editing booth for weeks after that."

He kissed her. "Take some credit. I would never have thought to use Sarah, but you suggested her right off the bat. I knew from that first scene we read together that she would be the only choice. And I can feel the chemistry between us. That's the magic you cannot create. It's either there or it isn't. Of course, good writing is always key," he said, nuzzling her neck.

"Flattery may get you somewhere, Hollywood. In my bed, to start."

He kissed her softly. "There's no place I'd rather be, Laramie."

Taking her hand, Tanner led her into the bedroom —and they found a piece of paradise on earth.

25

———

If Tanner pulled this off today, it would be a miracle. The amount of planning which had gone into today had been at a level he likened to a spy movie or some elaborate sting operation. Of course, he had Freddie Otts at the heart of things. That boy knew how to get things done.

He waited until Paige awoke on her own, tamping down his nerves. He was happy to see she was the one who initiated sex. Although she would be the first to admit that she still didn't quite think of herself as the kind of woman a Hollywood superstar fell in love with, his fiancée was growing in confidence. They had agreed when the film's shoot ended and she returned with him to California, she would find a therapist and begin sessions with him or her, trying to make sense of her complicated childhood and deal with the shadows in her own past.

Paige gave him a delicious kiss, one which heated his entire body. It was nice to be in love. To have a partner he trusted implicitly. And a woman who was everything to him.

Soon, Paige straddled him, starting at his mouth and kissing the entire length of his body. She reached his cock, which had sprung to life, eager for attention, and made certain she made love to it with her fingers and mouth. He had to ease her off him so that he wouldn't come. Quickly, he returned the favor, kissing her everywhere. That place behind her ear which was so sensitive. The slope of her shoulder. The curve of her hip. By the time he slipped on a condom, he was ready to explode.

With it being the Fourth of July and no filming occurring today, they were able to lie together in one another's arms and talk for an hour after they'd made love.

"How are we going to celebrate your birthday?" he asked, knowing he had most of the times during the day already planned and coordinated with others.

"Oh, I really don't do much."

Tanner knew from talking with Nana that Paige never acknowledged her birthday because it was the day her mom had passed away. He wanted the memories of that terrible day to recede for her and hoped today would be the start of that process.

"Well, that's going to change today. Our new policy is to celebrate birthdays with enthusiasm. You know mine is the first of October, so that will give you plenty of time to plan a fabulous day for me," he teased.

"It is nice to have the day free," she said. "It was sweet of you to give the crew yesterday afternoon off, as well."

Tanner had done so in order to give the people involved some time to handle arrangements, but he had chalked it up to the next day being a holiday.

"I do have one idea," he told her. "I think we need to be in downtown Sugar Springs for the parade today."

"You want to go to the parade?" She chuckled. "It's

nothing like the Rose Bowl Parade, that's for sure. You should know that. The high school band will march. There will be kids who've decorated their tricycles and bicycles riding in it. Most people would think it's pretty tame entertainment."

He kissed her. "Most people don't come from a small town like I do. Actually, I'm the one who's from a small town. Compared to Owens, Sugar Springs is a thriving metropolis. Besides, I have intel that says the town is honoring Sarah today. That she'll be riding in a convertible and kick off the parade as its grand marshal. Come on, Laramie. Let's grab some breakfast and head downtown."

He talked her into a light breakfast, saying that he definitely wanted to investigate the food booths after the parade ended.

"I haven't eaten kettle corn or had a funnel cake in ages," Tanner said.

They both dressed casually in shorts and T-shirts, at least for now. He had their marriage license in his navy blazer's inside pocket. They had finished filming last Wednesday around three in the afternoon, and he had dismissed the crew, telling Paige since they had some extra time, they should go to the county courthouse and apply for the marriage license. Tanner told her he'd already looked into it, and the license would be good for ninety days. The film's shoot would be done by then, and they could go to the courthouse and get married the day after filming ended. Tanner explained there was a three-day wait once you received the marriage license. This way, they wouldn't have to wait. They could just get married when filming wrapped.

Paige had agreed, not suspecting what he had planned for the July Fourth holiday.

Tanner kept his cell's ringer turned off but had set it to vibrate. Several times while Paige was occupied, he checked his texts, seeing that Operation Surprise Wedding was moving forward at full steam.

They left the house and walked to the center of town. The parade would enter the square and go completely around it before ending at the high school. It started soon after they arrived, and he saw how happy Paige was, her cheeks flushed as she smiled and waved to various students and other participants in the parade. When the convertible carrying Mayor Tommy Milton drove by, the mayor winked at Tanner and then gave him a thumbs up. It had been Mayor Milton's job to see that the county judge would be at the high school at three o'clock this afternoon for the wedding.

After the parade, they wandered over to the adjacent park. Nana had been right when she told Tanner that Sugar Springs would close ranks and protect not only his production but him as a person. While he noticed a few people snapped their picture, he wasn't asked to pose for selfies or stop for autographs. He had taken time at the end of filming each day to do selfies on the set with various cast members and volunteers, about a dozen a day. He wanted to give everyone a chance to get a picture taken with him, especially those high school students who were volunteering their summer to work on his production. The amazing Freddie Otts had even put together a spreadsheet, listing cast, crew, and volunteers and noting who was to have a photo opp with Tanner after the conclusion of filming each day. The teenager continued to impress Tanner with his organizational and people skills, and he thought Freddie might want to consider a career in the film business.

Tanner looked about and felt that Sugar Springs would always be a home to Paige and him.

"Let's get you a funnel cake," his fiancée said, directing him to a food booth where the sweet smell of cinnamon drifted through the air.

"They call them elephant ears other places," he told her as they sat in the grass and pulled bits of the fried dough, sprinkled with powdered sugar, into their mouths. "I learned that on a movie I did in Idaho one summer."

As they ate, they did a little people watching, and Paige told him about some of the people they saw and their stories. When they finished eating their funnel cake, he leaned over and licked the corner of her mouth, where a smudge of powdered sugar remained.

Laughing, she said, "I hope there's more of that to come in my birthday celebration."

"Later."

Helping Paige to her feet, they strolled through the park, taking time to ride the carousel and Ferris wheel which had been set up.

"You had a lot of students in the parade. Do you think you will you miss teaching?" he asked.

"I certainly won't miss grading papers," she said matter-of-factly. "Or faculty meetings. No, while I did enjoy being in the classroom with my kids, I like what I do now even more."

He threaded his fingers through hers as the Ferris wheel stopped. They were at the very top of it and had a wonderful view of the town and could even glimpse Sugar Lake in the distance.

"Would you like to work together again?" he asked. "I think we've done a good job of it this time around."

"I've never tailored a script to someone in particular," she mused. "It would be interesting to have you in mind as I wrote. Yes, I would like to work together again. Maybe I could write something you wouldn't star in. A piece you might simply direct."

"You could always serve as a producer again. You've whipped all of us into shape during this production."

"And take Freddie Ott's place?" Paige joked. "I'm afraid that teenager has been bitten by the film bug. I thought Freddie would go to college and major in business because he's so savvy and knows how to put people at ease. Now, I'm thinking after graduation that he'll show up at our door in California, looking for a job."

"Not everyone is meant for college," Tanner said. "Look at me. I've done okay with just a high school diploma under my belt. If Freddie truly is interested in the film business, I'll be happy to take him under my wing and make sure he learns what he needs to in order to be successful."

"He's gotten a ton of experience being your PA. Let's make sure he graduates and then see where his interests lie."

The Ferris wheel started up again and they made another few complete circles before the ride's operator let them off. They found a booth and each ate a corny dog as they walked the grounds. Tanner knew it was now time to get Paige home.

"Why don't we head back and shower?" he suggested. "This has been a hot day, and I would love to freshen up before I take you out. Maybe we could go into Tyler and catch a movie before we have a celebratory dinner. Do you have anywhere in mind you'd like to eat?"

"You grill a mean steak, but there is a steakhouse in Tyler that everyone raves about. I've never tried it, but it would be a nice place to have a quiet dinner." She paused. "Thank you for this day, Hollywood. I've spent too many years ignoring my birthday."

He cupped her cheek. "I hope you realize I celebrate you every day of the year, Laramie."

Leaning in, he kissed her softly.

"Let's head home," she said. "I may need shower sex as part of my celebration."

When they went inside, she saw a dress lying on their bed.

"What on earth?" Paige asked, going over and picking it up, holding it against her and turning to face the mirror. "Did you have something to do with this?"

"A little bit," he admitted. "I knew I wanted to take you out for your birthday. I also wanted you to have something nice to wear, so I called Vivi and had her find something in Dallas."

"How did it get here?" she asked, puzzled.

Lying smoothly, Tanner said, "I had Vivi mail it to Nana and told Nana to bring it over after the parade ended so I could surprise you."

Paige looked at herself in the mirror. "I love it." She turned and set the dress on the bed again. "I should text Vivi and thank her."

Knowing Vivi Romano was bursting at the seams, having kept his secrets for the last couple of weeks, Tanner quickly intervened, saying, "You know it's a holiday, Paige. The restaurants in Dallas will be packed. Even if you only texted Vivi, she probably won't even have time to look at her phone today.

"Besides," he said, grinning at her, "the two of you will need more than a text. It'll be a long conversation tomorrow about things."

"You're right. Want to hit the shower with me now?" she asked, a come hither look in her eyes.

"Actually, you go ahead. I thought I'd call Mom and Dad and wish them a Happy Fourth. Alana and Karl, too."

"Okay," Paige agreed. "Maybe evening shower sex can be in the cards."

The moment she left the bedroom, Tanner began texting furiously, making certain everything was in place. He touched base with Vivi, Sarah, Nana, his mom, Ron Jackson, and Freddie Otts. All was under control. Once he knew everything was running smoothly, he went and laid out his own clothes on the bed, checking again to see the marriage license was still in his inner coat pocket.

Paige came into the bedroom, one towel wound about her head and another around her body. He gave her a slow kiss and then broke it, heading for the shower himself. By the time he got out, she had finished with her makeup and was dressed.

"You look fantastic," he said, coming behind her and wrapping his arms around her waist, nuzzling her neck.

"I'll go dry my hair in the bathroom while you're getting dressed," she said.

"Why don't you put it up in that twisty thing you do sometimes?"

"A chignon? Sure, I can do that. As hot as it is, it'll be nice to have my hair off my nape."

Tanner dressed quickly and continued his texting, finishing by writing out a text to Joe Bob Milton. The principal was supposed to call him just before they left the house. Tanner would send the text right before they walked out the door.

Paige entered the bedroom, and he gave a low whistle. "You look amazing."

"You clean up pretty well yourself, Hollywood,"

she said, clasping his lapels and pulling him down for a sweet kiss.

"I looked at movie times while you were finishing up. We've got our choice of two. A romantic comedy or a superhero extravaganza. Depends upon what time we reach Tyler and what the lines are like at the box office."

"I'll be happy no matter what we go to see. Let me grab my purse, and we can head out."

Paige left the bedroom, and Tanner hit send on his message to Joe Bob, remembering to turn on his ringer. He joined her in the kitchen and claimed his keys from the rack hanging by the kitchen door as his phone rang.

"I hope this isn't Sarah calling to tell me she has laryngitis and can't film tomorrow," he teased. Pausing a moment, he added, "Hmm. It's Joe Bob."

She looked puzzled. "What on earth is he doing calling you?"

"Maybe Joy wants another line in the movie. Here, I'll put it on speaker. "Hey, Joe Bob, what can I do for you?"

"We've got a problem, Tanner. I know you were set to film at school the next couple of days. I'm not sure that's going to happen. A pipe burst. I'm up here now, and it's a genteel mess. You might want to stop by and see. You might have to juggle your schedule a bit. I'm trying to get plumbers here now, but with it being a holiday, I'm having trouble finding someone."

"We'll come right over, Joe Bob," Tanner promised, ending the call.

He slipped his phone into his jacket pocket. "Do you mind if we stop by the high school? We may miss the start of the movie if we do."

"I don't mind. We need to see what the damage is,"

Paige said worriedly. "We're filming in a few spots. Hallways. The auditorium. The gym. If the water damage is in the gym, that will definitely disrupt our schedule. If the gym floor is flooded, they'll have to rip it up. That will be a huge headache for them and us. I might have to call a nearby town and see if we can arrange to film in their gym instead. It's too big a scene to try and shoot it somewhere else. That empty, dark gym adds to the ambience of the scene."

"Don't borrow trouble yet," he said. "Let's go assess the damage, and then we can go to Plan B if needed."

They went to his truck and drove to the high school. Tanner pulled up into the small parking lot in front of the high school, where teachers and visitors parked. The lone vehicle sitting in it was Joe Bob's truck. Tanner had arranged for everyone else to park their cars on the opposite side of the building, in student parking, where the gym was located.

The principal stood in front of the school and moved toward them as they got out of the truck. Worry filled his face. Tanner kept a straight face, wondering if he had cast the wrong Milton in his film because Joe Bob certainly played the part of a fretting administrator well.

"It's bad," the principal said, shaking his head. "Thank goodness I found someone in Tyler who's driving over to assess the damage. Come on in. I know Joy said something about shooting in the gym tomorrow. I'll let you look at that first and see what you think."

Tanner slipped his hand around Paige's. She looked sick to her stomach. He hated putting her through this and almost brought the entire farce to a halt. But he wanted her to be surprised and didn't want to let down everyone who had helped him put everything together.

Silently, they followed Joe Bob down the deserted hallways of the school. When they reached the gymnasium's doors, he stopped.

"I've got the lights on so you can see everything clearly." Opening the door, the principal said, "Go ahead."

They entered the lit gym and close to one hundred people shouted, "Surprise!"

26

Paige's eyes roamed the gymnasium, taking in so many people she knew and loved. There were people from the film's cast and crew present. Fellow teachers. Townspeople, such as Ida Lou and Brynn Mattson.

Turning to Tanner, she said, "You certainly know how to celebrate a girl's birthday."

He pulled something from his pocket and handed it to her. Curious, she opened it, seeing it was the marriage license they had purchased last week. Understanding dawned within her, causing her heart to race.

"This can be more than a birthday celebration," Tanner told her. "If you're ready to marry me, Mayor Milton has provided a county judge to do the honors."

Tears sprang to her eyes, and she grabbed him, pouring all the love she had for this man into a kiss. Vaguely, she could hear the cheers coming from the crowd gathered.

She broke the kiss. "You went to a lot of trouble, Hollywood," she said, smiling.

He returned her smile. "I had a legion of help, Laramie. You're a pretty beloved person around Sugar

Springs. That—and Freddie Otts working his usual magic."

"Oh, whatever would we do without Freddie Otts." Paige paused, gazing into the eyes of the man she loved. "I lost Mama on his day. That's why I never celebrated it after her death. It didn't seem right. She would approve of you, Tanner, because she would see how much we love one another and what a good man you are."

With tears swimming in her eyes, she added, "Yes, I will marry you today. I feel Mama's presence with us. This day will move from a day of mourning to one of joy."

Tanner kissed her softly and then pulled away. He turned to those gathered and shouted, "It's on! We're having a wedding!"

New cheers rose, and suddenly Vivi was by her side. Paige threw herself into her best friend's arms.

"I hope you like the dress," Vivi said.

"It's spot on, Bestie," Paige declared. "I would like for you to stand up with me. You and Sarah."

Paige began looking around and found Sarah, motioning her over.

"Tanner wouldn't even let me text you," she told Vivi. "He said you would be too busy at the restaurant to talk on a holiday."

Vivi laughed. "He probably thought I would fold and spill everything. I probably would have." She smiled. "He's definitely a keeper, Paige."

"I think so, too," she said softly, hugging Sarah. "I suppose you were in on this, too."

Sarah laughed. "Half the town was in on this, Paige. You don't know how many times Tanner sent you off to do something away from the set so we could organize today and finalize the details."

Freddie Otts appeared. "Paige, we need to go ahead and get started. Let me show you where you're going to go."

He led her and her two friends to where Nana stood, and he said, "Nana is going to walk you down the so-called aisle."

Tears welled in Paige's eyes, and she hugged her grandmother.

Quickly, Freddie got everyone settled down and had people move to sit in the bleachers. Paige saw Tanner go and join a man who she assumed was the county judge. Ron Jackson, Tanner's stand-in and close friend, went to stand beside him as did another man. She guessed he must be Billy Stewart, her groom's longtime friend from Owens.

The place quieted, and she heard the strains of a violin begin, seeing it was one of her favorite students she had taught two years in a row who now played. A woman came and handed bouquets to her and her two bridesmaids, and Freddie gave a nod. Sarah began walking toward the center of the gym, and Vivi fell into step a few paces behind her. Freddie held up a hand, making sure Paige and Nana stood in place until the bridesmaids reached the middle of the gym's floor.

Then he nodded to the violinist, who broke out in Mendelssohn's *Wedding March*.

Paige turned to Nana, who said, "Let's do this."

As they moved toward the rest of the wedding party, she only had eyes for her bridegroom. Not only was Tanner breathtakingly handsome, but he was the best man she would ever know. His heart was pure gold, and he was right—he would always be that small-town boy from Owens, Oklahoma. The one who had captured her heart. Her soul. The man who would forever be her everything.

She and Nana reached the others, and Tanner leaned down and kissed Nana's cheek. He then escorted her to a spot on the front row of the bleachers, next to where Jeff and Helen Haddock sat, and then returned, taking Paige's hand in his.

They faced the judge, who said, "I'm Judge Johnson, Paige. It is a pleasure to preside over your wedding."

With that, the judge began the ceremony. She listened to him talk about how marriage was a life event, a journey in which two individuals who loved one another came together and walked through life as one. The judge cautioned them never to lose their individual identities but added they would always be better and stronger because they were united by love and would stand together to meet the challenges life threw their way.

When it came time to speak their vows, Paige handed her bouquet of dahlias and sunflowers to Vivi and turned to face Tanner, who captured her hands in his. She had been to weddings before, but the words she now spoke to the man she loved held a deeper meaning.

Tanner turned and held out his hand, and Ron passed Tanner a ring. Although they were engaged, they had been so busy that they had never chosen an engagement ring for her, much less discussed wedding bands. Now, Tanner slipped a ring onto her finger, a gold band soldered together with an engagement ring, a diamond solitaire of generous size but not one too ostentatious.

When it came time for her turn, Vivi handed Paige a wedding band, whispering, "I hope you approve of my choice."

She did—and spoke of the promises she would keep as she placed the ring on Tanner's finger.

Judge Johnson pronounced them husband and wife, and Tanner took Paige into his arms for a long, loving kiss. He broke it, and Vivi handed Paige her bridal bouquet.

Tanner looked at her and beamed. "We did it." He turned to those seated in the bleachers and threw his arms high as he called out, "We did it!"

Their guests gave them a standing ovation as Tanner led her toward the bleachers. He twirled Paige, and she spontaneously threw her bouquet over her shoulder. Mrs. Dunaway, her seventy-five-year-old neighbor, caught it, waving it high over her head as she played to the crowd.

Freddie Otts appeared and had a photographer in hand. He instructed the guests to head to the cafeteria, where the reception would be held, and asked the wedding party and relatives to stay behind for pictures. It didn't take long for that, and then she escorted her new husband to the cafeteria. A line formed as they arrived, and so many people came through it to wish them well. Miss Biggs, the elementary school teacher who had worked with Paige so closely, the inspiration for Paige wanting to become a teacher. Hailey Bennett, Laramie Fisher's agent, and her husband George, frequent director to Tanner. Mayor Tommy Milton and his wife. Campbell Cox, her attorney, and his wife Betty, who had taught across the hall from Paige and was her good friend. Campbell told her that he was retiring soon, and Laramie Fisher would need to find another lawyer.

"Hopefully, you can make that my son," the attorney said. "I'm trying to talk Walker into coming back to Sugar Springs."

Knowing Walker Campbell was now a hotshot attorney in Dallas, Paige doubted that would happen, but she merely smiled at the Coxes and thanked them for coming.

She finally got to speak to Alana and Karl. Her new sister-in-law was visibly pregnant now and absolutely beautiful. She hugged Paige and told her how happy she was to have her in the family, saying she was ready for a sister.

Ida Lou from the diner came through the line. Marge Echols, who had taken over Paige's classes in the spring did, as well, along with Joe Bob and Joy Milton. Police Chief Roscoe Hamilton, whom she had heard was considering retirement, congratulated them, telling Tanner he would be happy to organize the security in case they wanted their film to premiere here in Sugar Springs. So many present—and Paige felt their love, knowing Sugar Springs would always be home to her, no matter where she and Tanner went.

They finally sat, and Ida Lou changed from wedding guest to caterer. Along with Freddie's help, stations had been set up through the cafeteria, with many of the bride and groom's favorite foods. They ate and then went from table to table, visiting with their guests. Mr. Romano, Vivi's father, cried as he hugged her, telling Paige how she had been like a daughter to him, and he was glad she had found her true love.

They ended up once again at their original table, where Tanner's parents and Nana chatted up a storm. Paige sat next to Helen Haddock, who took Paige's hands in hers.

"I knew you were special when we first met, Paige. You have lived up to your potential and beyond.

Thank you for loving our boy. Welcome to the family." Helen embraced her.

Freddie touched her shoulder. "It's time for the dancing," he announced. "I have some of your band students in the gym who'll play for you and Tanner."

Her husband said, "This wedding wouldn't have happened as smoothly as it did without your efforts, Freddie. If you can pull off something like this and keep it a secret, I don't think there's anything you can't do. When you're ready, come see me about a job. I don't care if it's after you graduate from high school or college. Even after you've worked as an adult for a while. I can find a place for you."

Freddie beamed. "I'll take you up on that, Tanner."

Tanner led her back to the gym, with their guests following. The lights now were dimmed. Paige went to the dozen musicians to thank them for playing at their wedding.

As Tanner led her to the center of the gym, the crowd lined the floor around them to watch their first dance as a married couple.

"I picked a song I hope you'll enjoy," her groom told her.

He glanced to the band and nodded. The music began. Paige smiled.

It was Roy Orbison's *Oh, Pretty Woman.*

She and Tanner danced as if there were no tomorrow. He twirled her about, and she felt like Julia Roberts. No, better than Julia Roberts—because she had Tanner Haddock as her husband.

The song ended, and Tanner asked everyone to join in the dancing. He handed her off to his dad, while he danced with his mom during the second dance.

Two hours later, Paige was exhausted from all the

dancing, but it looked as if this party might continue for hours. They had taken a brief break to cut the three-tiered wedding cake, which Ida Lou had rolled down from the cafeteria, but she was ready to slip away and spend time alone with her new husband.

Freddie joined them and said, "This might be a good time for the two of you to leave. After all, you've got to be back on set early tomorrow morning."

"Have you planned out our honeymoon for after we finish shooting?" Paige teased.

Grinning shameless, Freddie said, "No—but I can arrange things if you'd like."

Tanner clapped the teenager on the back. "I proclaim Operation Surprise Wedding a rousing success."

He shook hands with Freddie, and Paige hugged Freddie.

With the music still playing, they eased out a side door and left the school, strolling slowly to the other side of the building until they reached his truck. Tanner helped her inside and then took his place behind the wheel.

Turning to him, Paige said, "This day was perfect, Tanner. The most magical one of my life. I always secretly wanted the *Pretty Woman* fairy tale. The entire kit and caboodle. You've given me that—and so much more. I love you so very much."

They leaned close and kissed.

Tanner broke the kiss. In his best imitation of the last line of the movie *Pretty Woman*, he asked Paige, "What's your dream?"

She cradled his face in her hands. "This. Here. Now. You and me. Forever."

Paige kissed her new husband, eager to see what life would bring their way.

EPILOGUE

MALIBU—LATE JANUARY

P aige awoke, the last bits of her dream dissipating.

Tanner stroked her arm and asked, "Were you dreaming of Greece again?"

"Mmm-hmm," she murmured, reaching for him.

Her husband made slow, tender love to her and when they finished, they spooned together, her back pressed to his front, his arm about her, his palm cradling the bulge of her belly.

They had left Sugar Springs at the beginning of August once filming had been completed on *Shadows of the Past*, traveling to Greece for a delayed honeymoon. Though Paige thought they should first travel to California so Tanner could work on editing the film, he told her the break would be good. That it would give him a fresh perspective once he returned to the project.

They spent three, idyllic weeks in Greece, and she came to love it as much as he did. The house they rented was on the water, and they basked in the sun, sitting at the water's edge as the waves rolled in and out. Occasionally, they would stand and run into the surf, playfully splashing.

It was there they made the baby she now carried. Paige was five months along and just beginning to feel the baby kick inside her. Due in May, they had recently learned it would be a girl. Tanner was over the moon and had been combing books and Internet sites, trying to hit on the perfect name.

She felt the flutter of a kick and moved Tanner's hand to the spot, resting her hand atop his as he brushed his lips against her nape.

"Let's go to the beach before the announcement drops," Paige suggested.

Tanner rose from the bed and helped her to her feet. They dressed warmly since Malibu mornings this time of year were in the upper forties. Leaving the house, they walked down the stairs leading to the beach. It was almost six o'clock by the time they got there, and they had the sand to themselves.

Paige had given up running last week. Her obstetrician had told her walking would be better for her and the baby, as well as other forms of exercise.

Tanner kissed her and left for his morning run, while she began a series of yoga moves. She had never practiced yoga before her marriage, but Tanner had for years and had introduced her to his favorite poses. Paige got online and watched a few videos which illustrated the best poses for pregnant women. She now ran though the series, which was quickly becoming her routine, and completed it as Tanner jogged into view.

She handed him his bottle of water, and he guzzled the entire contents. They sat in the sand together and watched the sunrise, a ritual they had grown to enjoy in contented silence, holding hands, the waves rolling in and out in front of them.

"I suppose we should go home and see about the noms," Tanner finally said.

This morning, the Academy Award nominations were being announced. *Shadows of the Past* would qualify since it had been scheduled for a limited release run between Christmas and New Year's in New York and Los Angeles. After the new year began, it opened nationwide to strong reviews a few weeks ago. Critics raved about Tanner's transformation from his usual hero to fiendish sociopath. They had also been generous in their praise of Sarah's performance, calling her a fresh new face on the Hollywood landscape. Her friend had returned to teaching speech and drama at Sugar Springs High School after filming ended on *Shadows of the Past*, but Sarah was already receiving a multitude of scripts and had told Joe Bob Milton that while she would finish out the academic year, she would resign afterward to pursue new opportunities.

The surprise had been the accolades which Nana had received for her supporting role as Gloria. Many critics singled out Nana as the glue which held the film together. While Nana had been thrilled to receive such recognition, she had told Paige and Tanner that she would not be entering the movie business. Nana had shared this at Christmas, which they had spent in Owens with Tanner's family. Nana had driven up to the ranch, joining them for the holiday celebration. The entire holidays had centered around the newest addition to the family, Alana's baby boy, which had been born at the beginning of October.

Tanner stood and took Paige's hands, pulling her to her feet. Hand in hand, they climbed the steps to their house. When they reached the top, she looked over her shoulder, thinking this view would never grow old. While they would always keep the Malibu property, wanting a place in California because of movies being shot in the vicinity, they had made the decision to make their home base Owens once their children reached school age. They wanted to raise their family in a small town, giving them that experience and cementing those core values important to both of them.

For now, though, they would remain in California for a majority of the time during the next few years. They had also kept her small house in Sugar Springs, though for the time being, Paige had rented it to Rory Addison, the teacher who had been hired to take her place in the Social Studies Department at the high school.

They entered the house, and Tanner said, "Let's get breakfast in us first."

He made breakfast for them, serving hot oatmeal with a sprinkling of brown sugar and a bowl of fresh blueberries and sliced strawberries on the side. Besides their hot herbal tea, she drank a tall glass of milk to get in extra calcium, while he opted for orange juice.

Once they finished the meal and cleaned the kitchen, Tanner claimed their phones from where they charged, and they went to sit in the den.

"Will you be disappointed if you don't earn a nomination?" she asked.

They had never talked about this, but Paige knew how important this film was to her husband, both as a director and an actor.

"I've tried not to think about it," he admitted. "I know how fickle this town can be. I really don't care about awards, other than the fact they bring recognition and attention to a film."

He cupped her cheek, stroking it with his thumb. "I would like to see you be nominated, though."

"Then I guess we need to check and see if that's happened," she said, turning on her phone at the same time he did.

Numerous text messages lit up the screen. Instead of reading them, she said, "Why don't we watch our recording first?"

"Agreed," Tanner said, setting his phone on the coffee table and grabbing the remote.

He turned on the TV and pulled up the DVR's queue of recordings. Slipping his arm around her, he pushed play. They both burst out laughing when they saw one of the two actors who would be announcing the nominations this morning was none other than Chloe Turner. Chloe had kept silent about her firing and had signed a contract to be in a new franchise based on a popular book series. The only time they had seen her in a restaurant, she had offered a cool smile and then turned her head as she passed them, no words passing between them.

The announcements began and she found her heart beating quickly in anticipation.

She was thrilled to discover that Sarah had earned a nomination for Best Actress. To their delight, Nana had also been recognized in the Best Supporting Actress category.

Tanner did not receive a Best Actor nod, which disappointed her, especially since he had already received one from the Screen Actors Guild and Golden Globes. Still, the nominees in that category had given some of the best performances in the last decade, and she could understand why each of the actors had earned his nomination.

When Chloe mentioned there were only two categories left, Tanner stopped the tape. "We'll need to get online to look for screenplays. Even though you and I know writing is the key to everything, those won't be a part of this big reveal."

"Wait. Let's finish watching. Then we can see about me. After all, the two biggest categories haven't been announced yet."

Chloe smiled brightly as she announced Tanner's name, along with four others in the Best Director category, Paige whooped with joy, throwing her arms around her husband, kissing him over and over.

"I knew you would earn a nom," she said, happiness filling her. "You worked so hard on this film. You deserve the recognition."

The final category was Best Picture. *Shadows of the Past* did receive a Best Picture nod, but it would be up against stiff competition.

"I don't expect the picture—or me—to win," he admitted. "It's been a big year in film. I'll play the standard card that it's an honor to be nominated—because it truly is."

They turned off the TV, and Tanner began typing on his phone. "Here we go. This year's full list of nominees." He scrolled down and then said, "Yes! Laramie Fisher. Best Screenplay." He paused. "But not for *Shadows of the Past*. The recognition is for the previous script you sold."

Tanner put his arms around her. "Congratulations, babe," her husband said, kissing her thoroughly. "It's a pretty big day in the Haddock household."

Paige called Nana first and put her on speakerphone. They both congratulated her grandmother, who said she might get used to this idea of being a celebrity in her seventies.

"Hailey Madison has already called me this morning," Nana said, referring to their agent. "She's trying to convince me to unretire and try another acting role. I don't think I will, though," Nana continued. "I was meant to play Gloria. I did a fine job of it, and I'd like to go out on top. Congratulations to the both of you, though. I'm only sorry you weren't nominated for the *Shadows* screenplay, Paige."

"It's probably a good thing she wasn't," Tanner said. "It's rare for anyone to be double-nominated in a category. I think it splits the vote. Paige will have a better chance of winning if she's not competing against herself."

They said goodbye and called Sarah Meinholdt next. She answered on the first ring.

"Can you believe it? I can't believe it. Who would've thought this?"

"You're talented, Sarah," Tanner told the teacher. "This is only the beginning for you."

Paige heard a sound in the background, and Sarah said, "That's the bell. I've got to go. Conference period is over. Time to go back to the real world for a bit."

"Call me after you leave school," Paige urged. "We can talk more then."

They spent the next hour responding to texts and listening to voicemails congratulating them. Hailey wanted them to go out for a celebratory dinner at Spago this evening, saying she'd already made reservations. They agreed to meet George and her at the restaurant.

Caught up now, Paige and Tanner turned off their phones again and placed them on the coffee table in front of them, where they propped up their feet. Tanner slipped an arm around her shoulders, and Paige rested her head against his chest.

"This is only the beginning, Laramie. I foresee

many more Oscar-nominated screenplays in your future." He rested a hand against her belly, and the baby kicked in response. "Right now, though, I want to concentrate on this upcoming production."

Tanner kissed her—and Paige knew this baby would be loved and cherished. That her life with Tanner would be full and complete.

And even better than any fairy tale she might ever imagine.

ALSO BY ALEXA ASTON

<u>SUGAR SPRINGS</u>

Shadows of the Past

Learning to Trust Again

A Perfect Match

A Fresh Start

Recipe for Love

<u>MAPLE COVE</u>

<u>Another Chance at Love</u>

<u>A New Beginning</u>

<u>Coming Home</u>

<u>The Lyrics of Love</u>

<u>Finding Home</u>

<u>HOLLYWOOD NAME GAME</u>

Hollywood Heartbreaker

Hollywood Flirt

Hollywood Player

Hollywood Double

Hollywood Enigma

<u>LAWMEN OF THE WEST</u>

Runaway Hearts

Blind Faith

Love and the Lawman

Ballad Beauty

<u>SAGEBRUSH BRIDES</u>

A Game of Chance

Written in the Cards

Outlaw Muse

<u>KNIGHTS OF REDEMPTION</u>

A Bit of Heaven on Earth

A Knight for Kallen

<u>SECOND SONS OF LONDON</u>

Educated by the Earl

Debating with the Duke

<u>DUKES DONE WRONG</u>

Discouraging the Duke

Deflecting the Duke

Disrupting the Duke

Delighting the Duke

Destiny with a Duke

<u>DUKES OF DISTINCTION</u>

Duke of Renown

Duke of Charm

Duke of Disrepute

Duke of Arrogance

Duke of Honor

<u>MEDIEVAL RUNAWAY WIVES</u>

Song of the Heart

A Promise of Tomorrow

Destined for Love

SOLDIERS AND SOULMATES

To Heal an Earl

To Tame a Rogue

To Trust a Duke

To Save a Love

To Win a Widow

THE ST. CLAIRS

Devoted to the Duke

Midnight with the Marquess

Embracing the Earl

Defending the Duke

Suddenly a St. Clair

THE KING'S COUSINS

God of the Seas

The Pawn

The Heir

The Bastard

THE KNIGHTS OF HONOR

Rise of de Wolfe

Word of Honor

Marked by Honor

Code of Honor

Journey to Honor

Heart of Honor

Bold in Honor

Love and Honor

Gift of Honor

ABOUT THE AUTHOR

A native Texan and former history teacher, award-winning and internationally bestselling author Alexa Aston lives with her husband in a Dallas suburb, where she eats her fair share of dark chocolate and plots out stories while she walks every morning. She enjoys travel, sports, and binge-watching—and never misses an episode of *Survivor*.

Alexa brings her characters to life in steamy historicals, contemporary romances, and romantic suspense novels that resonate with passion, intensity, and heart.

Keep up with Alexa
Visit her website
Newsletter Sign-Up

More ways to connect with Alexa